Dreams of Chaos

By Allen Stroud

Book One of the Death of Gods Trilogy

ISBN: 978-1-910987-08-7

Other Death of Gods Books:

The War of Orders
The Fractured Sky
The Magic of Wisimir

It is the 14th century. Since time began, wizards have walked amongst us. They wield magic and live across the centuries, seeking to transcend mortality by acquiring our faith and devotion. Their manipulations lie at the heart of our religions, they promise heaven so that they might become eternal gods and rule over us forever.

Dreams of Chaos, book one of *The Death of Gods* trilogy, is an epic fantasy story of alternative history that tells how the world was broken and made anew. It is the official fiction of the computer game *Chaos Reborn* by *Snapshot Games*.

Dreams of Chaos copyright © 2016 by Allen Stroud.
Cover Art by Svetoslav Petrov.
ISBN: - 978-1-910987-08-7

Contents

Foreword

There is something intrinsically intimate about writing.

The book you are reading is a complete work. You will likely never know all the places in which I wrote it. No doubt the locations, situations and circumstances occurring as I did, were wide in variety. Some might be quiet evenings sat on a couch, others a snatched minute on a train, or just before sleep whilst camping in a field.

I cannot know in what circumstances you will elect to read my book. I've spoken to many people about where they like to read. Most say they read in bed with a light on just before they go to sleep.

We are sharing this text, me as the writer and you the reader, as a truly intimate experience. You have given me your undivided attention. I must respect that and give you the best possible story. This is what makes books a unique medium. The story is something we can share, but your experience of it is unique.

The fantasy books that meant most to me when growing up are still associated with the memories I have of first reading them, the escape into a world unburdened by my every day concerns. Looking back now, some of them were awful, but at the time when I read them they were just what I needed. That's why books, good or bad, can mean so much to people, they are part of their formative years.

I want this to be a good book. Julian Gollop's games were a formative part of my childhood. I played *Laser Squad* and *Lords of Chaos* constantly, so the opportunity to work on *Chaos Reborn* and to write the official fiction of the game was one I jumped on. I've tremendous respect for all the work being done at Snapshot Games and want to make sure my contribution lives up to that, but also, I want these stories to stand up on their own.

Dreams of Chaos is the first book I have attempted to write that incorporates real world mythology on a broad scale. There is a deliberate attempt to engage with legends that are beyond my cultural comfort zone. Researching a multitude of history, faith and religion across the world has been a fun experience and hopefully circumvents some of the ruts that my fantasy writing might get stuck in. It means this book and its sequels will have a different flavour, particularly to my other fantasy work, something which I think will be very important.

That said, there's common themes and connections, which I hope readers will enjoy.

I'm sure plenty of people reading *Dreams of Chaos* will be more knowledgeable than I am on some of the real events woven into the story. For that I apologise. I've done as much research on these ideas as I could. I want things to be right and for this fiction to build on history, taking us in a new direction. Hopefully what you have is right enough to let you imagine and dream. I am sure your pictures of the scenes I describe will be different and likely far better than the ones I see in my head. But that is part of writing's magic, its ability to conjure characters, places and situations that intrigue and interest us.

A book will always be imperfect to the writer, but this one is ready to let go. I hope you enjoy it.

Allen Stroud

Prologue

I remember when you were both born. That evening, just as the sun slipped below the hills, we took your mother to the circle in the woods. She was barely able to walk, so my brothers and I fashioned a chair we could carry her in. I expected no-one to be there. Those that still clung to our ways held little hope. They believed the old blood would prove too thin as it had for my parents and all those from before. But as we arrived, I could hear the singing in celebration - thirty or more people from the village, all those who secretly share the faith. Each of them came to us and gave your mother a gift then whirled away into the throng. Flushed faces, already caught up in the beginning of our ecstatic dance.

We carried her into the centre and gradually the ritual took up its purpose, the cleansing of your souls as you passed from the divine to our corrupted world. Our hope was to re-invoke the old times and that you be delivered pure, like the ancient ones.

The music swelled and everything became a riot of colour around me. I held on to your mother's hand and reached out to the swirling crowd. Hands touched mine as they went by, a thrill of energy and purpose in each celebrating soul, willing fortune and favour on you and your sister.

I remember the pain on her face, the blood on her lip where she'd bitten it. A dual birth, arduous and exhausting, five years before a woman named Anya had the same and she had been young and healthy.

The first time you both cried it was together, a strange united moment and then it passed and you were both handed to my sisters to be anointed and washed; our mortal hands imperfect to the task, but our purpose joyous and clear. My eyes never left your mother's, but I heard you and welcomed you into my heart and when the time came held you both, praying to the sacred lady that we had brought you to this blighted world as whole and blessed angels.

I could not know then how we had failed.

Timeline of Significance

1300: Pope Boniface VIII declares a Jubilee or Holy Year, with plenary indulgences for pilgrims who make their way to Rome. The formal ritual of the tea service begins to become popular in Japan.

1301: Edward I, conqueror of Wales, bestows the cherished title 'Prince of Wales' on his own heir, the future Edward II. Andrew III of Hungary dies without an heir, bringing to an end four centuries of rule by the descendants of Arpad. In Bengal, King Ruknuddin Kaikaus, dies and is succeeded by his brother Shamsuddin Firuz.

1302: In Granada, Muhammad II dies and is succeeded by his son Muhammad III. The estates-general of France gather for the first time, in Notre Dame, to consider the king's relationship with the pope. Dante Alighieri, a member of the White faction in Florence, is sentenced to death by the Blacks. He flees the city, never to return.

1303: Church power is in decline. Concerned about kings taxing church property, Pope Boniface VIII issues a papal decree, *Unam Sanctam*, to maintain Church authority over kings. King Philip IV of France sends men to seize Boniface from one of his palaces. Boniface is rescued but shaken by the experience and he dies soon afterward. Edward I of England invades Scotland, aiming to subjugate it.

1304: A new pope, Benedict X, has enemies in Rome, the result of conflict over who should be pope. Benedict dies, supposedly after eating poisoned figs.

1305: French influence in the College of Cardinals results in the selection of the Bishop of Bordeaux, who becomes Pope Clement V. People in Rome, opposed to a Frenchman as pope, riot. William Wallace of Scotland is captured, taken to London, convicted of treason, hanged and his corpse drawn and quartered.

1306: King Philip IV of France expels Jews from his realm.

1307: Muslims drive Crusaders from the Middle East, including the order called 'The Knights of the Temple of Solomon' or the Knights Templar. The Templars arrive in France…

AD 1303

A forest of torchlight in the darkest of nights, the land seething with bodies, soldiers and their attendants, standing outside Chittor, awaiting the will of their master, Alauddin Khiliji.

Rani Padmini gazed down on the gathered army from her window. The walls of Chittor were strong and had resisted for many weeks, but in that time the bellies of the people became weak. Hunger, always a stronger weapon than swords, and brought with it despair.

"The end draws near, my love."

She turned. In the doorway lit by candles stood her husband, Rawal Ratan Singh, forty-second ruler of Mewar. He wore armour and a helm of burnished bronze under his *kesari* robe, a curved sword at his side, draped with a sash on his belt.

"You ride out then?"

"Within the hour," he said. "The bells will announce us and we will finish in a storm of steel."

She felt tears. They said their goodbyes days ago and knew what must be. Rawal had the old blood in his veins, but not enough to master the magic.

"I would go with you."

"You know that cannot be."

The truth pained them both. Her command of magic had always been strong and the adulation of her people empowered her. Khiliji's sorcerer, Chetan would want her. He would sample her flesh and learn the secret of her gift. There had to be no chance of her being taken – alive or dead.

"The *jauhar* is ready?"

"Yes," she replied, smiling at him through wet eyes. Her heart lurched. "The ritual chamber is prepared."

"Then you must go."

"And you – to your men."

They stood in silence, staring. Rani tried to picture his face, to commit each and every line to memory; the thick moustache and strong brown eyes, the scar on his nose from childhood; the strong stance and thick fingers that could be gentle when he wished. Many more things about him would remain with her and each she would cherish.

When she was done, she nodded to him. He bowed in return and left.

After that nothing mattered. She drew the *mehndi* symbols onto her palms and magic stirred in response. The oldest dye held the most potency and burned, starting a fire in her flesh as it should.

Barefoot and holding a candle, she went down the stone stairs to the lowest floor. The women of Chittor had gathered as she requested and took their places at the edge of the ritual chamber. She went to the centre and the vast pile of oil-soaked wood. At the touch of her candle, a strong flame sprang forth. Her magic fed it, gave it shape and purpose.

All around her, the women sang. The room became warm then hot, all moisture drawn from the air. She cast aside clothes, watching them burn. Then, naked but for her woven paint, she stepped into the fire.

The pain made Rani flinch and scream. Every instinct told her to step back, to run from the scarring heat. But her purpose was greater than such concerns.

In her life she had been beautiful, admired and coveted as a possession. Few saw past the visage into her mind and soul. Fewer still could appreciate those alone. With each moment in the flames, the mortal form died and what it contained leapt free.

She became spirit and flew from the room to the sky. Below, she saw the battle and in a last thought of joyful grief, watched her husband's end.

It began to rain.

AD 1307 – The First God Dies

Chapter 1: The Old Blood

Looking back many times over the years, Piers Gaveston wasn't sure what woke him that night; a quiet footstep on the staircase perhaps? The inhalation of breath as the figure raised the knife? A flash of moonlight upon the blade?

He opened his eyes, reached up with both hands and caught the wrist of his would-be assassin, halting the point of the knife an inch from his ribs. The man's arm in his grip and purposeful stare held him in the moment. Complete silence between them as they struggled, neither wishing to wake the other inhabitants of the house, but for very different reasons.

Two hands on the hilt of the weapon. Strength and weight told. The knife descended, its point pricking the skin of Piers' chest.

Desperately, he changed tactics, shifting his legs and kicking out, turning in the small bed, rolling the man towards the floor. The assailant gave a grunt of surprise and lost his balance, falling with a muffled thump. The blade clattered away.

"My lord, are you all right?"

A concerned voice from outside, Piers ignored it and leapt from the bed, driving a fist into his opponent's face and bare foot into his gut. The man grunted again and made a grab for his ankle, but too late. Piers snatched up the pillow from the bed and dived at the window, head first.

The wooden frame and glass shattered. For a moment he was flying in darkness. Then cold water assaulted him from all sides. Piers let go of the pillow and kicked out, holding his breath, staying underwater swimming as fast as possible. His lungs burned, but such pain must be endured. He was of the old blood. He could withstand a mortal's needs for a long time.

A very long time.

He thought of his wife and children still in the lodgings. They would be safe so long as he didn't go back. That meant leaving Sandwich – the small English coastal port town and finding help.

An hour after the attack he swam up and raised his head from the water. He'd moved to a dark spot under a pier. He could see a gathering of shadows around the Inn he'd fled from. Some would be genuinely concerned, others would be looking to find him and finish him.

Quietly, he swam in the opposite direction.

Katya stared down at her brother.

He was sat in his usual place at the table, but today held his head in his hands, weeping. She knew why – *Father.*

The news wouldn't be good, so she hesitated before asking. Her gaze strayed from him, taking in their home and memorising details, as if she might never return. The gaps in the walls, where the straw thatch peaked through, the black cauldron cook pot that steamed throughout the day and the pile of blankets beneath where she slept with her sister. It was a hot spring afternoon and flies intruded on their private moment. She turned, staring at the dividing wall. She could hear her mother murmuring in a gentle tone, accompanying her father's weakened breaths – *won't be long.*

She looked at Andrei, her brother, again, sat amidst the empty chairs, his shoulders quivering. She wanted to reach out and take him in her arms, but he would reject her touch, they all would, believing themselves sullied and unclean to her and her sister.

She stared at her father's chair, remembering him there. The laughter and smiles were gone now, it would remain empty, a hole in their lives that would never be filled.

Finally she summoned her courage and asked the question.

"How… long?"

Andrei glanced at her, as if she were a stranger. "Hours maybe," he said. "The apothecary says the pain is gone, but he won't last the night."

Katya bit her lip. "If I tried—"

"No. He would hate you."

They fell to silence, listening to the weak noises from the other room. Eventually, the emotion around Katya became more than she could stand and she left quietly, leaving her brother to his grief.

She walked down the thin road from the village towards the woods, keeping her eyes upon her feet as people passed. They moved aside, giving her room, even those who did not believe were wary enough to respect the superstition. Those who did knew better.

They were not allowed to touch her.

Eventually she found herself by the river at a familiar spot and approaching the person she'd been subconsciously seeking – her sister, Galina, sat as always, with a pile of washed clothes beside her, staring into the water. Katya walked up quietly. No need to announce her presence. Galina always knew where she was.

"How is Andrei?" she asked, without turning from the water.

"I thought you'd want to learn about father."

"I know about father," Galina said.

Katya nodded and sat down. Galina always knew. She picked up a smooth stone and threw it into the water, disturbing it for an instant. "Andrei is in pieces. He wouldn't let me help."

"He was right to stop you," Galina spoke softly, as if to someone else then turned toward Katya. Hers was a heart-shaped face with thin lips, a mirror to Katya's, apart from the dark blue eyes and a tiny scar on her cheek from their first fight in the womb, mother said. Galina brushed back her brown blonde hair. "Father would never forgive you."

Katya frowned. She picked up another stone between a finger and thumb and concentrated. The magic came to life, a shivering thrill that ran down her arm. Gradually, her hand closed and her fingers came together, forcing a hole right through the middle of the rock. When she was done, she held it out. "What's the point in this if I can't help the people I care about?"

Galina's gaze didn't waver from hers. "Perhaps the power you have would aid him, but could you control it?" she made a face, "if he died at your hands, what then?"

"At least I'd know I'd tried."

"And the village would too. We have enemies, those who do not believe as we do. You have heard their names for us, *witches* they say. If you give them an excuse, they will take us both far from here." She plucked the stone from Katya's hands and dropped it into the water. "We must give them no reasons and do as father wished until the time is right."

"But when will the time come?"

"Trust me, I will tell you."

They sat in silence together for a while, both staring into the water, Katya trying to glimpse something of what Galina saw. She asked her about it before, but never understood the answer. *I see what passes,* Galina always said.

It was a strange bond they shared, each with a power incomprehensible to outsiders and each other. But the village elders claimed them as gifts from heaven, which frightened Katya even more.

She'd been told the stories of course. How the old blood guided them and gave them a shepherd to bring them to the creator. The villagers believed the world to be made by evil, and death to be a final act; a return to paradise, casting off the corrupt form of the flesh.

Katya and Galina were supposed to be the shepherds, the purest of those born with the old blood. The village watched them closely when they were young and saw the signs. The elders wanted them married off at fourteen summers, but so far their ailing father had persuaded them to wait for another two seasons.

"We need to leave Bregovo," Galina said, voicing Katya's thoughts for her and making her smile. It was a habit from childhood, as they grew older, the bond between them had changed and become less distinct, but she still felt it.

"Where could we go?" she asked. "We have family and friends here, without them—"

"We will be fine," Galina said. "Mother and Andrei will be better without us." She stood up from the river and began gathering the bundle of clothes into two piles which she put into two large sacks. "I brought everything we'll need – food enough for a few days. We'll take the road south to Vidin. No-one will notice us gone until nightfall."

Katya watched her. "Don't you want to see Father?" she asked, "to make your peace?"

"I did that weeks ago," Galina held out one of the sacks. "I'm sorry you didn't get the chance."

Katya's hands curled into fists. "You never told me you knew!"

Galina didn't reply, just held out the bag. With no fuel, Katya's anger ran out of her as quickly as it came. She took the sack, wrapping the strap around her shoulders. "You didn't tell me because you knew I'd try to help him," she muttered.

Galina nodded and smiled sadly. "There is nothing for us here. Time to go."

Without another word, both sisters turned and fell into step towards the road.

"Through here, my lord."

Avignon. Far beneath the bishop's palace, keys rattled in the lock of a large wooden door at the behest of an old priest bent double with age. In front of him, Piers Gaveston, now exiled advisor to Prince Edward II of England, waited alone with customary impatience. The ceremonial robes of the Temple of Solomon were itching his shoulders, but he held his tongue. It was never wise to irritate a priest in his own home, no matter how feeble the man seemed.

The door opened into a dark void. Piers gritted his teeth and strode forwards. Light sprang from old candles either side of him as he walked into the gloom, banishing the black. The spell was a simple one, reminding the wicks of their purpose and revealing a vast chamber, built for grand design and fallen into neglect.

The sound of Piers' hard boots echoed across the flagstones. It smelled damp down here, the air close and oppressive in the summer heat. "We are far from heaven in this ungodly place," he muttered.

The priest chuckled. "The bounty of our maker lies but two steps from his dungeon, my lord." His words in Latin were little more than a rattling whisper in the gloom as he limped forwards. "This way."

Piers followed him to a second door. Once again, the priest produced a key and unlocked it, ushering him through. The corridor beyond was well lit, so Piers let the spell upon the candles lapse. The murmuring of voices confirmed he had reached his destination.

"Welcome brother," a woman's voice, speaking French. She was waiting by the door, older than him, but still beautiful with the ageless quality possessed by all those with the gift. He smiled, recognising the family traits of her Plantagenet heritage – a calculating stare, strong brow and nose. "Lady Eleanor," he said and bowed.

"We were expecting you yesterday," she remarked, holding out her arm, he took it and walked with her into the room. She wore a similar temple order vestment, but cut favourably for a woman, colours befitting her rank that could never be worn in public. "How fare my scions?"

"There is some disagreement," Piers replied. "Father and son are very different people."

"*La jambe longs!*" Eleanor said her lips quirking into a smile. "Ah Edward, so like my Richard, he is, but no lion. A mind of cold steel – dull, yet strong."

"I am banished from court," Piers confessed. "I had hoped to ask aid of the Temple to restore me."

"We are aware," Eleanor said. "The matter is in hand."

The corridor opened outward into a wide circular chamber, like an underground amphitheatre with concentric circles of steps acting as seating. A solitary stone chair was the only exception, occupying a space facing them. Piers gazed up and around in wonder. He could not see the chamber's source of light, but it was as bright as the noon day sun.

"Is this your first visit?" Eleanor inquired.

"It is," Piers said.

"You will get used to it."

On the benches sat an assortment of priests in the same sackcloth as the one who had guided him and amongst them, others wearing the robes of the temple. He counted perhaps thirty of each, engaged in hushed discussions. Some faces he recognised from different royal courts. One man glanced their direction and smiled at Eleanor, she inclined her head in return.

"A friend?"

"Once he was," she said and turned in the other direction to a vacant section of the steps. "We should sit there."

Piers guided her to the chosen place. He noted etched runes covering the slabs and the detail of crisscrossed scratches. "Has this chamber always been here?"

"No, it was constructed shortly after His Eminence came," Eleanor said. "The stones are from the first Lycaeum in Greece, moved here at great expense. More renovation is planned. Avignon will be the new Rome."

"I've never been to Rome."

"These days, the journey is worth more than the destination." Eleanor ran her fingers along the hem of her temple vestment. "Rome is not what it was. Too many of the elders have grown weary of this world and lie in slumber, dreaming grand dreams. Avignon is the future, we have seen it."

Piers frowned and leaned towards her, lowering his voice. "Seen my lady? You mean a vision?"

"Yes."

"I thought they were just rumours."

"The word of God is no rumour brother, your gift is part of his truth and there are others who can deliver his mysteries to us." She looked up from the vestment, her eyes circling the room. "You will glimpse his truth in this chamber tonight."

Piers nodded. His gaze strayed from his companion to something beside the doors. At first he thought it to be a soldier on guard, but it remained stone still. He realised he was staring at a strange suit of armour. The outlandish attributes that sprang from a box on its back fascinated him. He could see no purpose whatsoever in the ropes that ran from there to its thighs and neck.

"What is that?" he asked Lady Eleanor and pointed.

"The Empyrean engine," she replied. "You will learn its purpose soon enough."

Purposeful footsteps echoed on the stone and the conversations quieted. A man strode into the room, his long grey beard and bald head setting him apart from the tonsured priests and the groomed temple members. But the two armed knights at his side and a long cloak of white with a red cross emblazoned on each shoulder made him instantly recogniseable.

The Grandmaster, Jacques de Molay.

18

Instinctively Piers was on his feet, Eleanor beside him, the whole room half a beat behind. De Molay paused, looked left and right at each face, then continued to the stone chair. When he was seated, the gathered audience returned to their places.

De Molay had led the Templars for fifteen years since the death of the previous leader, Thibaud Gaudin. The circumstances around Gaudin's death were still unclear; he had apparently been 'exhausted'.

"Bring in the seer," de Molay ordered.

The scraping sound of metal against stone came first before two more knights emerged from the corridor dragging an old woman between them. She wore rags, the blood and grime of a captive life staining her arms, legs and face.

"Begin!"

It took all four of the knights to wrestle the woman to the centre of the chamber. Her struggle was pathetic, but desperate and extravagant. She knew her fate and fought for each extra moment of life.

But it was no good, and slowly they overpowered her, forcing her into the correct position, kneeling before the Grandmaster.

When she was in place, de Molay stood and walked down the steps to her.

"For those of you joining us for the first time, this woman is a *sibyl*, captured from her Grotta in the Umbrian mountains. She is a witch and relic of ancient heathen times, but though she has abused her gifts, her blood retains the power it was given. We will redeem her soul by putting it to proper use, using the spell we were taught."

The Grandmaster drew a curved knife from his belt and grabbed the woman's arm, slashing open her flesh. She screamed and blood dripped onto the stone. Piers saw channels cut into the floor and watched the red rivulets run into a runic pattern in front of the stone chair. De Molay's lips moved soundlessly as he held the woman's arm over the stone symbol. The old priest with the keys appeared by his side. "Petitioners, step forward!" he announced.

Eleanor nudged Piers' arm. He got up hesitantly, reviled by the scene. He had seen the atrocities of war, where men lingered for days with the worst wounds, their suffering did not compare to the feeble torture of this woman, but if he turned away, his commitment to the temple would be questioned.

He stepped forward, taking his place in the line of eager penitents.

"What crop should be sown in the fields of Garonne?"

"Shall we gather another crusade against the devil king of Trinacria?"

"Does my father rest with the Angels?"

19

The answers from the women were inaudible, but each petitioner left the line promptly. Piers reached the front and spoke his question.

"How can I regain the favour of the English king?"

Bloodshot eyes held his. He saw resignation on the woman's face. She knew she was dying, bleeding onto the floor for a faith she did not share, but de Molay's spell held her and compelled her reply.

"The King will love you best after the hill and the sands. Aballava's curse returns. In fall, be aboard ship to return to his shoulder."

Hands pushed Piers roughly to one side, the old priest from before knelt in front of the woman, the stained knife in his hands. One swift motion and the blade went into her ribs, she gasped as blood drenched the floor and the man's sackcloth robes. He leaned forwards, whispering a question in her ear. She shuddered and shook her head. Then he grabbed her throat, insisting. Finally she nodded and he released her to collapse in agony upon the stones.

De Molay stood over her. "End it," he said to one of the knights. The man nodded, drew his sword and drove it through the woman's chest, killing her instantly.

The chamber was silent. The knight wiped his sword on the dead woman's rags.

"The *sibyl* has spoken to me!" the old priest announced. "Our faith is strong; we may open a path to heaven, as it was in the first days!"

"Then you all know what you must do," de Molay's words washed over the room. "Gather the brethren. In two days we will return to this place and make the attempt."

When Eochaid Ollathair left the land of Ériu, he did so in sorrow. Cethlenn of the Crooked Teeth had wounded him, breaking the mortal binds on his soul at last.

He stumbled from the field of Maige Tuired, dragging with him his great club and stirring pot. He came to the passageway at Brú na Bóinne and laid down his burdens. He bled life into the last magic brew he would make and thrust his great club into the earth that it might grow again into a tree.

He ventured into the passageway alone and to the room where life meets death. As the sun shone into the heart of Brú na Bóinne, so Eochaid Ollathair wove his last spell, opening the door to the underworld then he transformed and took his true place as guardian and watcher of our lands.

The Tuath Dé that lived came after the Dagda with the last of the beaten Fomori and pitched them into the dark, far beneath the earth. There they joined the last Fir Bolg and would dwell until the end of days.

Afterwards, the Tuath Dé went their own way. Some drank of Ollathair's brew and took Milesian form. Others made new legends of themselves before finding new passage to the world of the Gods.

Chapter 2: The First Horseman

It was long after sundown. Firelight cast strange shadows in the dark. Wrapped in a blanket, Katya prodded the burning wood, making sparks fly and imagining the shapes as flickering forms of men, women and children, leaping and dancing in celebration; a memory of the old rituals and the stories her father once told her.

She'd never been this far from Bregovo. The elders forbade her to go more than a mile from the outlying farms, but it no longer mattered what they thought.

Beside her, Galina lay sound asleep, her breathing even and relaxed. Not for the first time, Katya envied her certainty and confidence. They were two sides of a coin. The old blood gave her sister glimpses of the future and a sensitivity to the nature of things. In Katya it manifested physically. She'd been an angry child, spontaneous magic erupting whenever she'd lost her temper, until she learned to control her gifts.

The flames were hypnotic, gradually soothing her. The sadness she felt at not saying goodbye to her father wouldn't go away, but there was nothing she could do. He would die in the darkness, with his wife and son holding his hands. Even if she and Galina had been present, they would not have been allowed to touch him, for fear they might become corrupted and lose their gifts. *No more of that now,* she realised. *We are strangers to all those we meet.* The prospect excited and scared her at the same time, banishing any hope of rest.

Galina dreamed.

She knew it was a dream. The illusions of her mind held more colour than the real world. Since childhood her sleep had been an adventure in itself. At times she wandered out of her body as it rested, but tonight she stayed where she slept.

The woodland remained the same as the camp she remembered, but the hues of green, brown and red were vibrant and fascinating. The small fire her sister crouched over became a rainbow of colour, leaping and whirling against the black sky.

There were waving lines of light between Katya and the flames. Galina had seen this before when her sister was concentrating on something, small tendrils connected her to the object of her attention. Galina knew what they were – strands of magic emanating from her sister and reacting with the fire.

Then something drew her attention, a movement just outside the light. A pair of eyes stared out of the darkness, watching Katya. Cautiously, Galina moved towards them and, when she was close enough, she woke up and her hand shot out...

A howl of pain, humanlike, but not human. Katya's head snapped around, to see her sister holding the spindly wrist of something in the darkness and dragging it out.

"Hold still!" Galina shouted. "I'm not letting you go!"

The small creature that emerged was no more than two foot tall, with mottled red skin covered in hair. Bulging eyes flicked between both sisters, plainly terrified. "*Orisnizi!*" it cried out. "Please! No eat, no eat!"

Galina grabbed his other arm and pulled him towards her. "We're not going to eat you," she said. "But why were you spying on us?"

"*Orisnizi!*" the creature repeated, pointing at Katya. "Eat for magic!"

Katya found herself smiling at the idea. "I'm not going to eat you," she said. "Answer my sister's question."

Their captive stopped struggling. "Not spying – brought here," he nodded at Katya. "Called me."

"No I didn't I—" Katya stopped herself and turned to Galina. "Could I have?"

"I'm never sure with you," Galina replied. She let go of one of the creature's arms and shuffled round to sit in front of the fire. "Who are you?"

"I am *juje*," the creature replied.

"Is that your name?"

"No! Power in names, not to be given! Once told, never taken back. I am *juje* as you *orisinizi*."

Katya frowned. Both words were unfamiliar, but the creature seemed insistent. "How long have you been here?" she asked.

"Always. Always been here."

"Are there more of you?"

"Many! But not here, away. Gone." The creature looked sad and waved its free arm. "*Juje* alone now."

23

Galina let go of his other arm. The *juje* didn't try to run. "You aren't alone now," she said.

The creature shrugged and also sat down. "Make no difference, *orisinizi* not *juje*. You leave when sun come."

"That is our intention."

"I no leave, not till…" the creature hesitated as if unable to choose the right word. "End?"

Katya flinched as she thought about her father again. "I think I'll sleep now," she said to Galina.

"Let you both sleep, yes?" The creature's expression became earnest. "I guard for *orisinizi*, make sure slumber peaceful." An infectious gap-toothed smile framed the end of the sentence, making Katya smile in return.

"I'd like that," she said.

"Then sleep. *Juje* watch."

Katya glanced at the creature then at Galina who nodded. "Very well," she said. "We will trust you."

"I understand, honoured by *orisinizi* trust."

Katya lay down. After that no-one spoken, she thought about staying awake to keep an eye on the creature, but her eyes wouldn't let her and she soon drifted off into a restful and dreamless sleep.

The next thing she knew was the light touch of her sister's hand on her shoulder.

"Time to wake up."

Katya looked around. The fire had long since died out and there was no sign of the *juje*.

"What happened?"

"We both slept," Galina replied. "But if you mean, what happened to the little man we saw, well… if he was real, he's not here now."

Katya sat up. It was well after dawn and her sister had cleared and packed their belongings. She peered at the ground near the fire, but there were no footprints or any other clues. "Perhaps we did dream it?"

"It wouldn't be the first time we've shared a dream," Galina said. She stood up and shouldered her carry sack. "I let you sleep as long as I could, but we must be off now."

Katya nodded, quickly stowed her blanket and put on her boots. In moments, they were back on the road and walking south. Galina passed her two flatbread biscuits. Katya recognised them as Mother's from the day before. She ate one and put the other in her sack. "What's happening to me?" she asked.

"What do you mean?"

"I mean what happened last night? The *juje*. If he was real, he said I called him."

Galina shrugged. "You've always had gifts. We never explored them because father told us not to."

"Was it a dream or not?"

"What is a dream anyway? Things I see have been real when I woke up, or come to pass a time after. Other folk talk of silly sleep stories, I don't remember one that hasn't happened or happened a few days later."

"Is that how you learned about father?"

"It was."

Galina didn't elaborate and they walked on in silence for a time. Katya fell into staring at her feet again. Step after step after step on the dirt track, wide enough for carts, but not important enough for stones to be laid. They were fortunate, if they had left in the wet season, the road would leave its stain on them. As it was, dust made the air rough and her throat raw.

"There's a rider on the hill."

Katya glanced up and saw the figure in the distance straight ahead. The rider sat motionless, the horse side on to them. It was a man, painfully thin and wearing strange clothes, with cloth wrapped around his face. His horse seemed emaciated too, the bones of its legs jutting out prominently through its white skin. When they started up the hill, he dismounted and began to walk down, towards them.

Galina hissed a warning and stopped. Katya halted too, a couple of steps ahead. The man didn't stop until he was ten strides away. He walked with a long thin staff, a foot taller than he was. Up close his skin was darker than any she'd seen; his eyes, bloodshot and his expression, oddly hungry. "What brings two girls to the road this fine day?" he asked, his voice soft, but carrying without effort. "How might a stranger help you on your walk to Vidin?"

"How do you know where—" Katya began, but Galina silenced her with a wave of her hand.

"Strangers have to earn the trust of those they speak to," she said cautiously. "All manner of folk travel these roads, good and bad."

The man seemed to find this amusing, biting back a chuckle and wiping a line of drool from his lips with the back of his hand. "Well said for one so young," he replied. "How might a gentleman prove his worth?"

"By leaving us be," Galina said.

The amusement in the man's face faded, but the air of hunger did not. "If that is your wish, it can be respected," he said, "for a time."

"You'll let us pass. Then, if we meet again, we'll look upon you with more favour," Galina answered. Katya glanced at her. She had a fixed expression on her face and her right hand was hooked into her belt. She kept a skinning knife there, a poor match to the man's walking stave, although his gaunt appearance suggested she might have a chance.

"Agreed," the man said. He spat on his hand and extended it to Galina, who hesitated. "If you don't take it, there is no bargain, just words," the man warned.

"Here," Katya reached into her carry sack and pulled out the flatbread biscuit she'd saved. "This will be our token, better than any handfast."

The man stared at the biscuit and licked his lips. Once again, drool escaped onto his chin, but he seemed oblivious this time. "A dangerous gift for one such as me," he said.

"You look hungry," Katya replied. "This will help."

"Perhaps not in the way you think," The man glanced at his horse then stepped forward and plucked the biscuit from her hands. "I accept. When we meet again I will gaze favourably on *you* as well." The emphasis plainly excluded Galina. He bowed and drew his mount to one side, holding the biscuit in his palm under its nose. The creature attacked it feverishly. "We will detain you no longer," he said. "I give you the road."

Wordlessly, Katya and Galina resumed walking. After a few minutes, Katya glanced back over her shoulder, but the horseman was nowhere to be seen. "We didn't dream that," she said.

"No," Galina replied, "and we've not heard the last of him, I'm certain."

The antechamber of Pope Clement V's Avignon residency was light, airy and cool, but it did not banish the memory of what Piers had witnessed the night before.

He sat on a cushioned bench, waiting with three other supplicants, each with queries for the pontiff. He'd been there an hour and was growing restive, his gaze raking over his rivals as they attempted to busy themselves ignoring him and each other. Surely, the pope would know his request was far more urgent than any of these concerns?

26

Piers had been a church sanctioned wizard for many years. Aged five, he had been taken by his father to the Cathedral of Saint-André in Bordeaux and trained in the use of his gifts. The eight years he spent in a special wing amongst senior monks and specialist teachers. In 1297, aged thirteen, he had been branded with the *caduceus* serpent and staff, and permitted to accompany his father to England to complete his training and take up service with the English king. Five years later, he'd been given the opportunity to join the Temple.

Surprisingly he'd never met Raymond Bertrand de Got, Archbishop of Bordeaux, who became Clement V on his ascension to the papacy in 1305. After his inauguration, Clement's expected move to Rome had not occurred for a variety of reasons, and now might never happen. To the congregations of faithful across Europe, little ever changed, but in the upper echelons of the Church, a game of politics was being played and above that, another game of real power.

A priest in a plain black vestment appeared at the chamber door and beckoned to one of the petitioners, who strode forward for his appointment. Gaveston gnashed his teeth in frustration. He stood up and walked over to a painting on the wall. The frame and canvas were ornate and expensive, but the brushwork crude and ill conceived. He hunted for the painter's name and found an illegible scrawl. The Avignon palace was not the Vatican, it had a rustic charm, but would never compare in grandeur.

The priest returned and ushered out another of the petitioners. Piers gave him a hard stare, but he didn't appear to notice and walked away with his charge, the soft click of the doors as they closed was the perfect rebuttal. All things would happen in an order determined by the pontiff and his administrators.

Piers glanced around again. He picked up a discarded book from one of the tables. It was roughly made, the pages held together with twine, and covered in spidery writing. Here and there a drawing appeared; concentric circles, in which he read the word – *Inferno*.

"Do you like my work?"

Piers turned. The last of the petitioners was looking at him and gestured to the book. "Incomplete as yet – my research is unfinished," he said in Italian accented French. "I hope to conclude by the end of the year; a fitting scholastic work for His Eminence to bring to Rome."

"Is this what you want to meet with him about?"

"I am not waiting to meet with him. I was waiting to see you."

Piers frowned. "I'm sorry, but my audience must be with—"

"His Eminence has no interest in your report on de Molay's intentions, or his plan," the man waved his hands. "Leave a shepherd to attend to his flock, we are not sheep." He took the book from Piers' hands. "Anything you say to His Eminence would disturb a mind already clear in its task."

"Its task?"

"To herald the new direction of our church, to bring heaven's word directly to the faithful."

Piers tried to hold the man's stare, but found he couldn't, such was the strength and passion in those clear blue eyes. "You cannot claim to know such things."

The man smiled and held up the book. "With the aid of magic, I interrogated the three hundred and twenty four cadavers, the rotting minds of the dead, disturbed from eternal sleep. Their collated confessions allowed me to shape this work and create a map of the world beyond. I have learned all I can of their resting places, but this book? It is nothing. It will be chopped up and censored into a version suitable for the masses then distributed to all with interest. Those that can read Latin will feast on its pages and ruminate to its application. By comparison, the diligent work of the Temple will ensure that in three days, the first living souls will touch heaven. That is true progress."

Piers frowned, recalled what he saw in the chamber. "The armour in the corner of the room, was it yours?"

The man's smile widened. "Yes indeed! The latest iteration of our work. A knight must be correctly attired to brave a new world. The lore of our forefathers informs our ritual, their faith shows us the way. Our paladins will be clear of purpose and heart, through the purity of our ceremony."

"The woman sacrificed last night was no believer."

"Indeed she was not, but she carried the gift, as do you and I. It manifests differently in us, depending on our nature. Some, like yourself, may invoke power, others like me, examine and understand it." The man sat down on the bench where Piers had been sat before. "You undertook the position of watcher to the English king with a clear understanding of what it meant, did you not?"

"I accepted my gifts were part of my faith, agreed to be trained and put to use," Piers replied. "I was one of many."

"But you rose to prominence at the English court. You gained access to your charges, proving yourself a worthy successor to Lady Eleanor and have been rewarded with entry to the Temple. Now you are seeking a way to restore your position and come here for assistance," the man laughed. "But, you did not expect to be given prophecy, you expected someone to accompany you to London to lean on King Edward."

Piers shrugged. "The Temple chooses to aid me as it wishes."

"However, it means you do not know what to do with yourself," the man said. "You expected to be trading favours for assistance, instead, you have been given time, a space from your vocation. It would be best that you use it, learn to understand the Temple's mission here in Avignon, question and ask things of us; ask of your predecessors." He laughed again. "The good lady of Aquitaine is always keen to educate those who attend to the interests of her family."

Piers felt his face colour. "You suggest I keep my own counsel then? Look to my own affairs?"

"I suggest that if you wish to learn, you learn, rather than condemn when you know so little of which you speak."

"Is that a threat?"

"Does it need to be?"

I write to warn you Your Holiness, of the consequences of your actions.

Rome is the centre of our faith and has been since the earliest days of anarchy. The work of our ancestors to create an organisation lasting more than a thousand years is being undermined by your intransigence.

For centuries, the empire of our faith relied on its beating heart. In Rome you are but a step from sage council and ancient wisdom. Your continued prevarication in Avignon places you in a vulnerable position and threatens the purpose of our work – to bring our faith to the world.

The individuals you surround yourself with are not appropriate to your status. The work of troubadours and devouts is indeed part of understanding the word, but it is but a part, and the mysteries should be discussed and debated with those who are correctly ordained to speak of them.

I am concerned that your absence from our church's heart and the removal of the Curia to Poitiers will fatally undermine the structure of our faith. I ask that you consider the matter urgently and reconvene your court in the Basilica of St Peter as it should be.

Nicholas de Balmyle – Canon of Dunblane.

Chapter 3: A Question of Honour

In the early evening, the tea house was quiet. A cold breeze blew from the ocean to the east, a message perhaps, from the edge of the world.

The garden was carefully kept. The stones washed, brushed and neatly arranged in lines. Flat slates formed wave like patterns at regular intervals; nothing out of place – a testimony to accuracy and effort.

Teru walked up the seventeen steps to the pavilion table carrying the cups, pots and herbs he would need. A large iron flask steamed over hot coals. He drew water, taking care to fill the metal spoon with only as much as was required for each cup. The painted patterns lining the receptacles were incredibly intricate, each one different from the other and partnered to the intended guest.

The *cha-no-yu* tea ritual was new to the islands and not widely practiced, but to the Tengu it was a tradition that came before negotiation and diplomacy. The distraction of ceremony prevented thoughts of violence and harm.

Teru looked up as the air tightened; the prelude to a storm perhaps? More likely the arrival of a guest before time. "You are early," he said without looking up.

"For a ritual to have power, it must be respected and adhered to," a woman's spoke in stiff Japanese. "You should understand my nature."

He turned in the direction of the voice. She stood at the bottom of the steps, a foreigner with dark eyes and long black hair tied with a simple grip. She wore thin trousers and a shirt, her arms exposed, showing the intricate lacing of scars that covered her skin. He knew the rest of her body would be the same, a testimony to her victories in battle. Only her face remained unadorned. No enemy had touched it. In her right hand she held a bloody knife. He smiled.

"Is that to be your means?"

"It needs to appear crude, like a violation."

Teru nodded. "I had hoped for more honour in my death," he said.

The woman frowned. "There is a great deal of honour in this. I have not surprised you to slip a knife in your ribs or poisoned your food. Instead I confront you openly."

"I am not prepared."

"Which is understandable."

Teru moved quickly. A hand snatched the scalding tea cup and flicked it at the woman. She didn't move. The cup hit her shoulder, the liquid staining her shirt and spilling onto her scarred skin, but she didn't flinch. Another scar. "Thank you," she said, "you will be remembered."

She advanced up the steps, slowly, purposefully. Teru threw a second cup, but this time she dodged easily. He backed away, noticing her lips moving and feeling the air change as before when she'd appeared. The table was between them and the large metal spoon in his hands. He swung it at her, but again, she moved aside, diving across the table and slamming into him.

He fell backwards into a sitting position, a sharp pain in his stomach. He glanced down and saw the hilt of the knife sticking out of his thin robes, a red stain, spreading across the fabric.

"It is done," the woman said standing over him.

Teru glanced up at her and tasted blood. The world began to darken like an eclipse. He focused on her sad smile and tried to get up.

He couldn't.

Galina was right. As the sun went down and they stopped to camp for the night, the sisters found the strange horseman sat under a tree tending a small fire. He still wore his long coat and hat.

"You followed us," Katya said.

"That would require me to be behind you," the man replied with a toothy smile. "Instead, I anticipated you would stop here and waited."

"What do you want?"

"Come now, we agreed our second meeting would be favourable," the man said, prodding the flames with his staff. "I have done all you asked. We are no longer strangers."

Galina sighed. She walked forward, put her carry sack down and seated herself. Katya did the same. They kept the fire between them and the man. Something about it made her shiver rather than get warm.

"What is your name?" Galina asked.

"There are many," the man replied. "Faim, is a name others use for me. You need not tell me your names, I already know them."

"How?"

"Because before we met, I visited your village looking for you. I learned your names from the people there."

Katya stared at him open mouthed. "How is my—"

"Your father is well. Once you both left, he recovered," Faim stared directly at her, ignoring Galina. "He was holding you back."

"Do you mean I made him sick?"

"Your magic did. He was trying to protect you and keep you from the world. When you left, his health improved."

"You're lying," Galina said.

Faim smiled, but didn't look at her. "Am I lying, Katya?" he asked.

"No he's not." She knew instinctively. Her gaze strayed to the fire. "This is magic isn't it?"

"Yes, I cast the spell just before you arrived."

"You're like me then?"

"Yes."

"But not like her?" she pointed at Galina.

"No," Faim leaned forward. "The gift is not as strong with her."

"Are we *orisnizi*?"

Faim laughed. "An old name, no doubt dreamt up by your villagers. Didn't they tell you what it means?"

"They never mentioned it," Katya said. "We heard it from someone else."

Faim shrugged. He put down the staff and took off his hat. Unkempt straggles of dark hair spilled out. The centre of his head was bald, plainly not by choice. "I came to these lands to find you. There are less and less people born with the gift outside the established orders. I had to reach you first, before they did, to give you a choice."

"There is always a choice," Galina said. "We choose to sit and listen to you, or not."

"The day someone takes all choices from you is the day you learn the value of free will," Faim replied. "The people of your village are good people, honest folk. They tried to protect you and keep you safe in ignorance – a different kind of prison. They denied you things, but never used force, which is why, eventually, you decided to leave." He was addressing them both now, his gaze flicking from one to the other. "You are of the old blood, gifted with the magic and the long life. If you stay, you would watch everyone grown old and die. Even if you learned to control your power, you'd still outlive them all." The last of the humour faded from his voice. "If you stay free, eventually you'll be separated too. Galina has the blood, but not in the way you do."

They sat in silence for a long time after that. The words were like stones in Katya's stomach. She wiped away tears, cursing herself crying for people who weren't even dead. Faim's explanation unlocked feelings and awoke questions. She could sense the people of the village and knew her father was alive. Something of them reached out to her, sustained her in a way she couldn't define.

"What should we do?" Galina asked.

"Do?" Faim turned away, picking up his hat and examining the brim. "Live and find your way. I am no teacher or sage. My purpose is to make you aware of what you are. The exploration of it is yours to share as you will. All things are hungry for knowledge and power, how you find these things is for you to determine."

"So you won't teach me then?" Katya said.

"No, I will not," Faim said. His red eyes narrowed into slits. "Unless you wish to strike another bargain?"

Katya frowned. "We have nothing to give you."

"You have more than you realise."

"You followed us and talk to us, merely to let us go?" Galina said. "What is it that you really want?"

"You are both powerful," Faim said. "I wish to release that power and make it accessible for you. I want everyone like you may find their own path, unrestricted by the requirements of others. I will need your help in this."

"How?"

"I'm not sure yet."

"You ask for a future favour then? What do we get in return?"

"I will show you enough to protect yourselves against those who will seek you out, a few simple rotes that you can use and learn more from later."

"But who would come after us?" Katya asked.

"You were protected and kept secret from those who do not believe as your people do," Faim explained. "The priests of the churches and cities will come. Only they will not offer you a choice."

"They would kill us?"

Faim shook his head. "Not if they can help it. Many of them are gifted as you are and came from similar stock. No, they will take you to their secret places, purge you of your past and make stone of your minds, turning you into their enforcers. If you refuse, they kill you, so as you see, another prison and not really a choice."

After dark, Avignon was a quiet place. Piers Gaveston sat in a tavern on Rue Limas. Wine, bread and cheese improved his mood a little, but not much.

As the common room filled, he wandered out, leaving an assortment of provincial conversations. Out here in the portside establishments, the presence of the Church and its pontiff seemed less obvious, but it was a thin façade. Scratch under the surface and the growing influence of the papacy revealed itself. Pardoners harangued people on street corners and the bells of service rang out regularly in each church.

Piers found himself walking towards the multi arched Pont Saint-Bénézet that spanned the twin forks of Le Rhone. It was a clear night and stars filled the sky. He reached the gate tower on the riverside and stopped, leaning out over the water, watching it slip by in the dark.

His thoughts went back to what he'd seen and been told, trying to reconcile it with his faith. The Church's edict of magic did not permit what was being planned. Things were often done that broke those laws, but never beneath the house of the Pope himself. *At least not that I know of.*

De Molay and the Italian's words of a portal to heaven, of travelling to the blessed realm troubled him greatly.

Piers' fingers rubbed idly at the marked symbol on his wrist, the *caduceus* brand he'd been given when he'd been sanctioned as a wizard. Arrogance was a perennial flaw amongst those with the gift, but he knew his place and the correct limitation. The priests had schooled him well. The magic came from a blessing passed to the first men. It was the duty of those with the gift to shepherd those without. Those who did not accept the path became its enemies.

Which side does de Molay belong to?

Piers heard a noise from above, the sound of wings – *large wings.* Instinctively he ducked as something swooped overhead. The faint trace of a spell in the air and the shadow of a bird above, larger than anything he'd ever seen. It wheeled quickly, screamed and dived at him again. The snap of claws and beak, close to his ear and then the creature was on him, its weight and strength pinning him to the ground. He screamed and raised his hands to protect his face. Lines of pain erupted along his arms. He screamed again, but this time coherently, invoking the words he'd been taught as a child and felt the power well up and burst forth in response. The bird cried out.

And then he was alone again, lying on his back, bleeding on the cobblestone street.

Since the times of antiquity and before, the gifted asked questions of their bestowed abilities. They appealed to the heavens for answers, seeking out responses in the stars, interpreting signs and fate to arrive at a multiplicity of answers.

It fell to a lesser creature to develop a response we could understand and make use of – one of the first whose blood did not prove strong enough to wield the magic, but who demonstrated an unprecedented understanding of its workings. **The Philosopher** *founded his Lycaeum on a reasoned answer determined by evidence. If creators exist, we have been chosen by them to be empowered. The purest of blood live lives that span centuries and some find a means of transformation that renders them eternal.*

All around us, there is humanity, a finite people, blind to power and purpose. They are our chorus and our measurement, weaker in all respects to us, but above the animal with their inquiring minds, use of language and strength of will. They are related to us, loved by us, loyal to us and clearly kindred. We live amongst them as heroes, leaders and wise counsel. But we share the same light, the same soul. If there is a purpose for us, there must also be a purpose for them.

The Philosopher determined these purposes to be one and the same. His work, the **Manual Alchemical** *is our guide. If the most powerful of us can transcend the mortal shell, becoming eternal, it follows that all lesser brethren are on a similar path toward transformation.*

The Philosopher claims mortal existence is a trial and preparation for the path chosen for us. Each of us is capable of transcending this form. For some, this transcendence comes through living a life in balance of the humours, of dying and being reborn to a new life, closer to the eternal state.

The days of heathen antiquity are long past. We have learned much more. We know the truth of heaven and our Lord as imparted to us by his raised servants. We see transcendence and watched the most chosen join the eternal choir. Their guidance shapes our future that we might bring all humanity into the grace of the divine.

Thomas Aquinas – Summa Magiolaie.

Chapter 4: The Arrival of Death

"I fear her Highness's condition worsens, my lord."

Sir Ralph de Monthermer nodded absently, whilst sat staring out into the fields through the open door of the stables. It was a cold morning, the pre-dawn air, misty and quiet. The words of Benetto, the Augustinian monk who had come to find him were not news, they were expected.

He looked up, meeting the man's eye. "She has taken confession?"

"Yes."

"And been given the rites?"

"Indeed, as she requested."

The sound of hooves echoed out of the mist. In the yard, a horse and cart drew up, an old man crouched over the reins. Sir Ralph did not recognise him, but guessed his purpose. "The corpseman is here. Prepare the child and instruct him my wife is to follow. They shall go together."

"As you wish, my lord."

A rustle of robes and the monk walked out towards the cart. The corpseman drew back his hood revealing an old shrunken face and bald head. Sir Ralph watched the two men converse. Agreement came with a swift nod. Benetto returned to the house through another door. The horse stirred, no doubt sensing others in the warmth of the stables, but settled quickly with a quiet word from its master.

Sir Ralph shivered and drew his cloak in about himself. His tears were shed long ago when Joan first took with child, their fifth – a chancy proposition – but she had been fit and strong still, and they took the sign as providence, a blessing of their union. Each of their previous children failed the sanction, but that was a blessing too, meaning the Church would not take them.

His gaze went back to the corpseman, catching the man's eye. He read power in that stare and something rebellious. The man nodded and touched his hood, but there was no deference in the gesture.

"My lord, you should come."

Benetto again at the door, his words soft but insistent. Sir Ralph nodded and stood up. "Who is that man, Benetto?" he asked.

Benetto glanced out of the door at the corpseman. "His name is Obidiyah, my lord."

"I've never seen him before."

"He is new to Clare and taken work before he travels to the next town."

Sir Ralph nodded. The explanation was not unusual and there were more important matters to attend to. He sighed and waved Benetto on, following him into the house.

"That was foolish."

A cool spring morning in Avignon and Piers lounged on a cushioned chair listening to Lady Eleanor. Her bedchamber in the Tour St Laurent was elegantly furnished, but reflected the past she belonged to.

The lady herself sat on the bed, a brush discarded beside her. Despite her years, she remained a beautiful and vibrant woman; a streak of silver, the only mark of time in her hair, the lines of her face, regal rather than aged.

"I have legitimate concerns over what de Molay is planning," Piers said carefully. He had not told her about last night's altercation on the bridge. "I wished to speak to his holiness about them."

"It will be perceived as an attempt to betray the Temple."

"I cannot stop people from thinking. If this whole business were more open and honest—"

Eleanor held up a hand. "Piers, please, you are young and like so many, full of opinion without the wisdom years bring. The faith needs your energy and strength, but you must learn the way of things here."

"The man I met said much the same," Piers sighed. "What would you suggest I do?"

"Ask me your questions first then see what issues remain in your heart."

"Very well, can you promise to be truthful with me?"

Eleanor arched a brow. "Would you bind me with oaths?"

"No, I suppose not."

"Indeed."

For a moment he struggled to order his thoughts then selected a starting point. "Why does his holiness not go to Rome?"

Eleanor smiled. "You read the *Summa Magiolaie* and the *Manual Alchemical*? The Vatican is a source of wisdom to the world, the basilica home to many generations of our kind whose days have passed. In the vaults beneath St Peter's halls, there are catacombs, where generations of faithful servants lie in reverie. Occasionally, they stir and awaken, returning to bring their truth to our church. Sometimes these visions are helpful, sometimes they are not."

Piers frowned "So, his holiness did not like the advice he received?"

Eleanor's smile slipped for a moment. "It is a little more complicated than that. Benedetto Caetani tried to restore the primacy of the Church as instructed by representatives of the eternal choir. You recall his fate?"

Piers nodded. "If you mean Boniface VIII, I remember. He was kidnapped from his house in Anagni and tortured. He died soon after his release."

"Indeed. The Church sought a means to mediate in this new reality. The power of kings becomes a challenge to the clarity of our vision. It is difficult to reconcile this with those who have slept with Angels for a long time and are unaccustomed to change."

"So… the Pope is here for his protection?"

"Yes. The Curia is in Poitiers for the same reason. Cardinals attend to the catacombs and the reverie. In time, His holiness may return to Rome, but only when new auguries awaken."

Piers thought about this carefully. "So, what is de Molay's part in this?" he asked. "Why the ritual and the sacrifice of pagan witches?"

"This is not the first time the eternal choir has caused problems," Eleanor explained. "Whilst we are afforded the luxury of being outside Rome, the Temple can offer an alternative. The grandmaster is an ambitious man. He wants to provide Clement with a means of intercession. If we could speak to heaven directly, we gain a means of surety."

"*Migdal Bavel* is the story of an arrogant people who built a tower to heaven." Piers said. "Are we not doing the same?"

Eleanor stood up from the bed and walked towards him, barefoot on the stone floor. "The stories of Babel were contrived by our peers, they were never meant as cautionary tales for us. The use of the *sibyl* woman was a practical choice. The removal of unbelievers is part of the Temple's mandate from the Church. She would have been executed by other means. This way, her gift is put to a righteous end."

"You accept this then?" Piers said. "You agree with what the grandmaster is doing?"

"I accept it," Eleanor replied carefully. "And so should you."

The road to Vidin widened as they journeyed south. Faim led his horse between the two sisters, instructing them in a low voice.

"The magic manifests in many ways. The Church recruits those with the gift and sends them to asylums where they are branded. Priests indoctrinate them in a set of rituals, allowing them to use their power in authorised ways. There are spells they can cast, ones that don't disrupt the natural order of things."

"But you don't follow that?" Katya asked.

"No, I don't." Faim chuckled. "Church wizards like to think of themselves as intelligent and responsible wielders of power. In reality they are slaves to a system."

"We were taught about God," Galina said. "We are all on a path to his glory. This world is corrupt. When we leave it, we become pure again."

"The only evidence of a creator exists in his creation – the world," Faim replied. "Something made this, something made us. The Church likes to think people get to meet him through their priests and reading their good book."

"Most folk in the village cannot read. Does that mean they cannot get to heaven?"

"According to the Church it would."

"The elders taught us to sing and pray outside," Katya said. "How can we be heard indoors?"

Faim shrugged. "People believe many different things. I choose to accept that. You must find your own way to your magic. The Church will try to force you to their path and if you refuse, they will kill you."

"Why don't they kill you?"

"Because I don't let them."

The open fields became woodland. Around noon, they passed through a small hamlet; four buildings next to the road with a small bridge over a river. Faim called a halt and Galina sat on the stones next to the bank. Katya went to join her, but Faim's hand touched her shoulder. "Do you sense something?" he said.

"No I… What do you mean?"

"Up ahead. Do you sense anything unusual?"

Katya frowned gazing in the direction he'd mentioned. Three horses were tied to a fence post next to the largest of the four buildings. The faint sound of voices came from inside. "No, nothing," She replied. "My sister might—"

"I didn't ask her, I asked you."

"Then no."

Faim scowled, handed her the reins of his horse, straightened his hat and began to walk across the bridge. Katya hesitated. She glanced at Galina, who busied herself collecting a pile of sticks from the stream.

39

She walked over to her. Without looking up, Galina took the reins of the horse. "Go," she said.

Katya turned away and hurried after Faim. He was a little way ahead. She caught up on the other side of the bridge and fell into step behind him. The voices from inside the building were louder now, one of them high pitched and pleading. She couldn't make out the words.

"Stay behind me," Faim said, "and whatever you do, don't run away." He broke into a loping jog, his long coat dancing around him. She followed, slowing as he did by the tethered horses. He undid their reins and prodded them, speaking harsh, sibilant words. The ears of the first pricked up immediately and all three bolted, making for the open road to the south.

The commotion silenced the voices from inside the largest of the buildings. The door opened and a greasy haired man in chainmail, lacing up his breeches, stepped out. He squinted at Faim. "What do you want grandfather?" He glanced at Katya and leered. "You brought us another gift did you?"

She'd seen men stare at women like that before when soldiers came to the village. She guessed what it meant; to them, she was an object to be used. She remembered Faim's words about freedom again. *I don't want to be used.*

Without warning, the soldier caught fire.

She tasted magic; it was her spell, a more powerful version of what Faim showed her the night before. The flames were dark red and hungry. The man shouted, screamed and then stumbled back into the house. More shouting followed. She glanced around to find Faim staring at her.

"There is an innocent in there," he said calmly.

All the power collapsed, rolling out of her like a wave. She fell to her knees, suddenly exhausted. But the shouts didn't stop and she still smelt burning. "I didn't mean…"

He was already moving, the long coat snapping as he leapt through the door. More shouting and then he emerged dragging another person with him – the woman they'd heard from before. He threw her to the ground then turned back to the doorway. He spoke three words she didn't recognise and the air thrummed with power. The roof caught light; even the stone seemed to be burning. Katya pressed her hands to her face, trying to shield herself from the intense heat. Beside her the woman curled herself into a ball and whimpered.

40

Galina watched the house burn.

She sensed her sister's anger and her magic, but this wasn't her power, it was the man Faim's doing. She sighed. Her sister wasn't in danger, but she didn't trust him.

She stared down at the twigs and small broken branches she'd gathered from the river. To anyone else, they would be nothing; dead cast offs left to return to the earth. She rummaged in her carry sack and drew out more discards from the lake near the village and their camp on the road. Gathered together it became a substantial pile.

As a child, the gift came easily to Galina. She'd always known she didn't have the power of her sister, but she sensed magic wherever it was, feeling the potential of living things and glimpsing the future in her dreams. Now she stared at the bits of wood, closed her eyes and let herself be guided. A curved stick in her left hand pressed together with a forked branch in her right, a twig slotting into a hole between them, a curled branch next, a straight stick into its centre, another twig and another. She felt the wood merging, the last energies of former lives converging and finding new purpose in her hands. She knew she could never unlock the magic in what she was making, but Katya... she opened her eyes and looked up, seeing the unnatural fire take hold of the building.

Katya might.

The fire was out, disappearing as quickly as it came. Katya raised her head and saw Faim stood as before in front of the building. He glanced down at her and offered a hand. She took it and stood up.

"Not quite as I intended, but no doubt they deserved their fate," he remarked. "You are impulsive, I like that."

He walked over to the woman. She remained curled up, her shoulders shaking. Faim crouched down, touching her gently, but she didn't calm.

Katya glanced at the house. The thatched roof had fallen inwards, the wooden beams burned through in seconds. No normal fire would have done this. The flames she and Faim had raised had been far hotter and hungrier; sealing the fate of the three men inside.

She walked towards the door and stepped into the charred ruin; once a farmhouse of sorts, a family had lived here, not unlike her family. Now their life was gone, burned beyond recovery. *Where did they go? Why was the woman alone with the men?* The answers weren't likely to be pleasant.

She backed out of the house and walked to one of the other buildings – a small store. Inside she found the body of a boy lying face down in his own blood, a wooden post driven through his chest. He couldn't have been more than eight years old.

The tears came then, remembering children in her village playing in the summer sun. They'd been cautious of her and kept their distance, but she'd watched them from the doorway, seen them smile and laugh.

"Who would do this?" she said, hardly realising she'd spoken aloud.

"The Church," Faim replied. He dropped a white piece of cloth into her hands. She turned it over to see a neatly stitched black diagonal cross with a shaped 'P' running vertically through it. She looked up at him. "Now you understand?" he asked.

"Yes," she replied. "I do."

The gift is not inherited by all of us. Since the earliest days when the watcher lay with his charge, the blessing became imperfect. Some amongst the older councils believe this was when we lost our way and became deaf to the voice of our creator, but others point to the work of the half breeds. Their blended minds understand the processes of the gift far better than those who wield it. They are the smiths, the artisans and crafters to our purpose. The crafting of totems, portals, staffs and other enchantments would not be possible without them.

It is therefore fitting that they, the weakest, but most insightful, should lead us. They are closely connected to the mortals who we were given to protect and though they live long lives, cannot transcend as we do. It is for them, our fathers, mothers, brothers and sisters we must labour to bring about Heaven on Earth, so that they may know the heart-filled joy they work with us to create.

Over time we divided. The coming of the son brought division with the Hebrew and later the Muslim, the schemes of Cerularius brought division with the East and the heresies of other wayward cults. These squabbles must end. Our purpose is the same, enlightenment and transcendence for all. We seek a return to the divine the gifts our Lord granted us and it must be a return for all.

Father Bartolo of Sassoferrato.

Chapter 5: Portals

Back and forth went the knife, shaving away the layers of wood.

Tuia felt at peace as he worked. The blade stripped away years of growth, revealing history in the flesh. Trees told their story in their trunk and limbs. The circles and the imperfections spoke of stormy seasons, adversity, injury and growth. Suffering was easy to find, but the smoothness of happy times spoke to him as well. Sometimes when he touched the finish, those days spoke to him. He saw rich sunlight and good, regular rain. Glimpsing these memories made him glad, privileged and proud to witness what was – a window into the old days.

He looked up from where he sat on a rock at all the glistening trees around him. *Si*, the moon, had not risen yet, leaving her flaming offspring to light the world. The end of the rain season approached. The waters would recede, but the jungle would go on. Life thrived here, the multitude of creatures and plants crammed into the land were a testimony and celebration of the way things had always been, back through more time than the wood in his hands would know.

Amidst the living, one thing stood out. A huge arch, carved from a single slab of stone. It had existed for longer than the tree remembered. Vines embraced the massive structure, obscuring much of the scratched writing on its surface. It had been perfectly aligned by its maker. In the early mornings, Tuia saw the sun rise through the gap between the two supporting slabs. A huge carving decorated the lintel – the image of a woman holding a staff in each hand – the gatekeeper, who abandoned her charge long ago.

Only Tuia remained in her place.

As he stared, the space between the pillars rippled and a man appeared, a man he recognised. The strange long cloth he wore, the staff and beard set him apart from anyone else in Tuia's life. He was tall and pale, unlike anyone on the Piura river.

Tuia leapt down from the rock, leaving his knife and carved wood. He walked barefoot to the gateway, right up to the man, who bent at the waist in greeting as he always did. Tuia smiled, showing all of his teeth and returned the gesture. "Od-or-ic," he said, pronouncing the man's name carefully in the strange tongue as he'd been taught. "You here for trade?" he asked.

"Trade, yes Tuia," Odoric replied. He reached beneath his clothes and pulled out a short wooden object – two sticks, one shorter than the other joined as an imbalanced cross. Tuia took the item, examined it closely and frowned. The finish was good, but the maker had shaped the tree flesh against its nature, compelling the parts into union with treated twine.

"Trade this?" he asked.

"Give you this and many more," Odoric replied. He touched the cross with a slim finger. "Sacred symbol."

Tuia pointed to the sky. "Symbol of maker?"

"Symbol of world maker, yes."

Tuia frowned. Si would not have made this. She would understand the tree and shape it according to its nature. Odoric or one of his people had crafted it. He studied Odoric's hands, they were soft. *Not him then.*

Tuia put down the cross and opened a cloth pouch, shaking the contents into an open palm. Three tiny stones glittered in the sun, the clear stones he knew Odoric liked. The tall man smiled and plucked them up, stowing them in a pouch of his own. "My thanks," he said.

"Welcome," Tuia replied. He had hundreds of glitter stones. Three were a good trade for the wood. He would take it apart, study the finish and improve his own craft.

Odoric bent down and laid out another six crosses, each identical in shape to the first. "Give these to others," he said, "world maker wishes it."

Tuia shrugged and nodded. He would do as the tall man asked after he learned the maker secrets of each. If they were too good to give away, he would make new crosses and give them to the strange fisherman of Huanchaco. He glanced up at the sky. Si would be watching so he would make better crosses than Odoric's. "What else you want?" he asked.

"To visit the city," Odoric said. "Will you guide me?"

"Chimor long days' walk from here," Tuia replied. He pointed to himself and shook his head. "Tuia not leave gateway."

"Then find some other to help," Odoric said.

Tuia stared at him. The man's voice sounded like a town elder. As watcher of the gateway, Tuia did not listen to them. He shook his head again. "You find a guide." He pointed to into the trees, at the path to the nearest village. "That way you find people."

Odoric's gaze strayed in that direction. He chewed his bearded lip then stepped forward. "Very well," he said, "my thanks."

"Welcome," said Tuia and bowed again. He watched the tall man disappear into the trees. When he could no longer hear him, Tuia scooped up the crosses and returned to his rock.

In mid-afternoon, Piers left the bishop's palace to return to his lodgings in the city.

The talk with Lady Eleanor gave him a sense of perspective. The temple's work on intercession might resolve a problem stretching back hundreds of years or it might make it worse. The risk was being taken by others, not by him. The reason he'd come to Avignon had been satisfied. He was better off staying away and waiting out the time as the dying witch had suggested. *If I believe her words*, he thought, but questioning that involved more questioning of the Temple's faith and purpose.

He was close to his lodgings on the Rue Limas and near to the place where he'd been attacked. He gazed up into a cloudless sky, turning around and spotted a tiny speck far up in the distance, moving slowly, wheeling and circling, like a bird of prey. Could it be the same creature? He judged himself safe in the daylight, but made a decision not to venture out that night.

He reached his destination and headed straight upstairs to his room without a glance into the commons. He unlocked the door and went straight inside…

…to find a man sat in a chair next to his bed.

"Master Gaveston!" A gnarled hand grabbed his in a fast handshake. "My name is Elbo Smogg. I hoped the lady would let you go tonight, so we could talk."

"You let yourself into my room?" Piers said.

"Just so, and would have slept in your bed too if you hadn't returned, shame to see it go to waste."

Piers' guest was quite a sight. A stained tabard, mismatched hose – the sort a jester might wear – unkempt reddy brown beard to his waist and strange bulging eyes. The faded red and green of his leggings and smell in the room suggested he hadn't bathed for some time. Piers stayed by the door. "What do you want?" he asked.

"Right now? Mead, but I'll settle for wine," Smogg laughed, got up and slapped him on the back. "We'll be fine friends if you stay so attentive to my needs!"

"I didn't mean…" Piers swallowed, keeping his temper in check. "I meant what do you want with me?"

"Let's head downstairs where the wine is and discuss it," Smogg said. Before Piers could react, he was already passed him and in the corridor. "Come on, otherwise you'll never learn how I got in," he added and laughed again as he went down the hall.

Piers hesitated. It was plain this strange little man wanted something, but he couldn't be sure what it was without the expected conversation. *That doesn't mean I dance to everyone's tune,* he thought. He shut and locked the door then went to the chair, sat down and waited.

After a few minutes he heard footsteps returning. There was a soft knock. "Are you coming?" said Smogg.

"No," Piers replied.

"But I need to speak with you."

"You broke into my room and assumed I would blindly listen to what you wanted to say," Piers said. "I don't know who you are, or what you want, but these theatrics do not impress me." He went to the window and looked out. The speck in the sky was much lower now and clearly identifiable as a bird, wheeling in small circles.

Smogg knocked again. "It is vitally important we talk."

"Why?"

"Because lives are at stake," he said, "including ours."

Piers sighed, got up and opened the door. "Explain."

Smogg peered up at him and glanced left and right. The conversation had attracted spectators; a man on the stairs and a woman lodger from down the hall. "Not out here," he said.

Piers grabbed the front of his tabard and dragged him in. With a squawk, Smogg fell into the chair. "We'll start again then. What do you want from me?"

"I've been sent to warn you," Smogg explained, keeping his voice low. All trace of his humour from before had vanished. "The Temple ritual being planned is dangerous. It needs to be stopped."

"Who are you and who sent you?"

"I already told you I'm— Oh, very well," Smogg pulled at his stained tabard and shirt sleeve, revealing a familiar brand on his wrist – the *caduceus* symbol – the sign of a sanctioned wizard. "I'm the same as you."

"You're a member of the Temple?"

"No, I'm not that— I mean, no, I'm not."

"Then how do Temple matters concern you?"

"My charge from the Church is to explore," Smogg explained. "I work with some of the greatest alchemical engineers who ever lived. They build portals, I test them. Over the last century we've established a network that stretches around the world. That's why I'm here."

"Who sent you?" Piers repeated.

"Fulk de Villaret. He has been invited to a counsel with the Pope."

Fulk de Villaret was the Grandmaster of the Hospitaliters, the other militant order of the Church and a direct rival to de Molay although both organisations had worked together in the past. Piers stared at Smogg. The man wore no white cross, the symbol of de Villaret's order. He pointed at the window. "The bird in the sky, is it yours?"

"What?"

"The bird, did you try to kill me last night?"

"No I only arrived—"

"Then why come to me?" Piers asked. He grabbed Smogg again, lifting him up so they were eye to eye. "What do you expect me to do?"

"I learned of your petition to the Pope," Smogg gabbled. "A friend in the administration told me!"

Piers sighed and released him. "I don't know whether to trust you or not, but I will warn you as I was warned. Don't try to stop this."

"But the result will be catastrophic. They don't know what they're doing!"

"Even so, the best we can do is let them to their business and look to ourselves. If you persist in your message, they'll kill you, and me. Then you'll stop nothing."

Brynfrid Vigdís sat waiting her back against rock, her legs drawn up against the cold. She stared out into white land and into white sky. Nothing here fulfilled the promise of *Eiríkr hinn rauð*. This was no place for farmers. The green of the stories never existed. The frozen soil blunted and broke spade and hoe, the chill wind made ice of the water for crops.

Eiríkr lied.

Six years ago she came, leaving behind her life in Nidaros as the southern god's priests built their stone houses and prayed to their one god. They arrived as traders first, but she knew the truth of them. The one contained many, who took their due for leading others to the path. The shrill songs they sang were just the same as the rites and rituals they sought to forbid; exhortations of faith, of magic.

She left after seeing their wares. The doubt they peddled, the talk of sins and confession. The ways of Odin did not bother with such ruin. Life should be celebrated before the end of days and the Ragnarok.

Brynfrid knew if she stayed amongst the fixed minds of the southern priests, she would waste away. She feared weakness more than death, so she left on a dragon boat to lend her strength to *Eiríkr*'s promise.

Only to find herself here.

In times past it had been better; farms, fields and dark leaf trees, a new kingdom for its red bearded lord who had been twice exiled. *Eiríkr* died, leaving a rich heritage for his people. His son Leif journeyed further into the unknown, bringing back wondrous treasures. Some said the old gods blessed him, but even he had taken up the southern religion, bringing the false faith to the kingdom of his father.

Brynfrid's *valkyrja* blood understood. This Greenland was the battleground. *Jötunheimr* sought to conquer before the end of times and only the strength of mortals would prevent them. Perhaps sleeping Odin lay under the ice, or away in *Ásgarðr*. Whatever the case, *Eiríkr* had brought warriors here, to guard the edge of the world. The southern priests might build stone houses to their idol, but here, Odin's truth could be seen, written in ice and snow.

Brynfrid's gaze roamed, seeking difference amidst the blanket cold. Her vigil was lonely, but filled with purpose. She watched the western plain where land became sky, protecting the people of *Vestribyggð*. Animal pelts kept the cold at bay, a chainmail skin beneath would turn back the blades of frost giants. Her own sword and axe were at her feet, wrapped in cloth and had served her well in battle, but they would stay idle if the *Jötnar* came. Next to them lay a long stave, passed down from her grandfather. He had been strong in the old ways and taught her the magic of Odin, though her blood could not sustain much of it. Sometimes he still spoke to her on the east wind. The stave would be her best weapon in a war of the gods.

A shadow flickered amidst the white, at first merely a shade, but it grew darker and larger, getting closer. Her hands went for the stave, but moved to the axe. No giant approached, instead, a man, wrapped in strange skins – a *skræling* of the borderland, the people who travelled between the realm of men and immortals.

She stood up, shrugging off snow and ice. The man waved his staff, changing direction towards her. He was short, dark haired and round of face, like all his people. Three steps from her perch, he stopped and bowed.

"Aguta bring word to the Austmann," he said slowly in the unfamiliar *norrœnt mál* language and waved his hands around, gesturing to the sky. "This all worse, not right. A god has awoken in the ice."

"The end of days," Brynfrid grunted.

Aguta shook his head. "Old god, not *Tuniit* giants, older, sleep in ice. Stirs now and brings cold."

Brynfrid chewed her lip. Odin would not use the magic of his enemies on his own people. Bergelmir the frost king wielded the cold and before him, the long dead Ymir of the first days.

"Cold brings hard times." Aguta pointed at Brynfrid with his staff. "Land freeze and force people out, force south, into Austmann lands."

"I understand," Brynfrid replied.

"Aguta not want war, people not want war, but they must live."

"Aye, people must live."

They stared at one another in silence for a time. Then Aguta bowed again, turned away and began walking back the way he'd come.

"What should we do?" Brynfrid shouted after him.

He turned back and stared at her. "Cold ends with sleep or death," he shouted in reply. "Austmenn must come north and bring death to a god or the god will come south and bring death to them."

Chapter 6: The Use of Rituals

They reached the outskirts of Vidin by nightfall.

Galina was tired. Faim had forced them to leave the woman behind amidst the ruin of the hamlet. Galina argued and Katya pleaded, but he'd been right. Though she lived, the woman hadn't moved except to shake and moan as she huddled on the floor. Her eyes remained shut, hidden away with her face behind bloodstained hands. They couldn't carry or move her, so they'd simply walked away.

Faim made some attempt to talk to them both, asking about the village and the family. He didn't appear to be listening to the replies, just staring ahead down the road. Galina understood what he was trying to do and answered when she could, but Katya didn't speak. She stared at her feet, like she used to when she wasn't really there.

They'd walked without speaking, each step an effort to banish what they'd seen. Thankfully, they saw no-one else until it grew dark.

Moonlight illuminated a black silhouette of the city ahead. Lantern lights and torches speckled the dark shadow of its ancient walls and keep. Galina heard stories of such buildings but had never seen them. It would be morning until she got a chance.

"We'll stop here for now," Faim said, leading his horse from the road and into the trees.

"But it's right in front of us!" Galina protested.

"Folk who enter after dark are remembered," Faim replied. He laid his staff aside and with a groan, sat down on a protruding rock and pulled off a boot, shaking it out before doing the same with the other. "You should start a fire."

Galina seated herself on the wide end of a fallen tree branch opposite, but made no move to gather wood. The sky was clear, but the details of his thin face were obscured in the dark. She glanced at her sister, who'd also stopped and sat on the wet ground. "You need to help her," she said.

"Help?" Faim sighed. "This is her journey, not mine."

"You should have helped the woman too."

"You cannot make someone want to live."

Galina glanced at Katya again. "Will she—"

"She just needs time," Faim said, "and she has you. Your little village is far away. The wide world is vast and dangerous. You have each other, more than others have."

"Why not help them?"

"We return to the same question," Faim stood up. "You need to accept my answer."

He pointed at the tree branch on which she sat, gestured and spoke a word that slipped from her mind as soon as she heard it. She felt the thrill of power and blood red flame sprang from the limb furthest from where she sat. Galina leapt up and rounded on him. "You could have warned me!"

"As I said, we need a fire," he continued to stare at the flames, his fingers becoming claw-like. The fire remained at one end of the branch. "Controlling it is much more difficult. I spent years perfecting my abilities. Your sister struggles with this every day."

"You think I don't know?"

"You do not understand." Faim returned to his seat on the stone, but continued to stare at the blaze, his gaze focused and intense. "You view your sister's gift through your own, which you accepted long ago. Occasionally, you explore your abilities, but they never endanger others. You know power, but you do not comprehend its price. You are both selfish and jealous. You do not help or encourage her, perhaps because in your heart you believe you are the lesser creature."

She went for him, cooking knife in hand, slashing and stabbing at his thin face. He caught her hand with surprising strength, dragging it down to the ground. She bit his arm, but he did not waver or cry out. A bony knee on her wrist opened her fingers and the blade was gone. Then he let go and stepped back.

"In this world you care for each other," he said, drawing back his sleeve. Red blood dripped from his left wrist. "I had no-one and was much the better for it." The bite mark was deep in the forearm. He placed fingers into the wound spoke another word and rubbed at the flesh. Another thrill and Galina saw the blood smear and cuts vanish. "When I met you both, you were wary and distrustful, the right instincts around people with power. Why now are you concerned with me, when your sister should be your charge?"

She couldn't meet his eye. Her wrist throbbed painfully and guilt ran through her. As far back as she could remember, no-one but her sister had been allowed to touch her more than was necessary. *I provoked this, I lost control.* She looked at Katya, who remained sat on the ground, her head bowed. "I don't know what to do," she confessed. "What should I do? What do you want us to do?"

"I told you, I am no teacher," Faim said. "But you must stay safe and help your sister master what she is. Otherwise, she will destroy you both."

The darkness of the cavern under the bishop's palace seemed more threatening the second time Piers experienced it.

After Elbo Smogg left, he sat in his room for a long time weighing up whether to attend the ritual or not. In the end he realised it wasn't a choice. If he stayed away, the assassin would track him down. He had to be there and be seen to be there.

He arrived at the palace early and went to the hidden spiral stairwell. The light faded as he descended until touch and sound became his guides. This time there would be no pointless gestures of magic. He would be prepared for eventualities.

Piers counted each step to the bottom and felt his way around the room. He sensed he was alone. The runes etched in each stone spoke of ancient power and he found newly worn grooves arranged in intricate patterns. Containment spells, woven as a cage, breached only by the narrow arch that led to the staircase. The preparations both reassured him and gave him clues of what to expect.

He wished for his staff and hat, but bringing such devices here would raise questions. Instead, he carefully re-read the most powerful protection rotes he knew, ensuring his invocation would be perfect if he needed them.

Footsteps and voices echoed down from above. He backed away from the noise, until he had the wall at his back…

…And sharp steel on his throat.

"Keep it quiet sir," whispered an old rattling voice in Latin. Piers recognised it immediately. "Just stay here with me, near the wall."

"You're the priest who guided me here the first time."

"Indeed I am."

"Did you send the bird to murder me?"

"I sent it to *warn* you and now I'm repeating the point." For emphasis, the blade against his neck shifted, nicking the skin. "You've seen what I do with this? Let's not waste your precious gift out here on the tiles, eh?"

Piers realised his mistake. Somehow, the man had concealed his own nature when they'd first met and now, concealed himself in the hall when Piers believed he was alone. "What will you do with me?"

"You'll find out."

The footsteps became louder. The light of a lantern spilled into the chamber, illuminating the man who held it. He wore coarse robes. Behind him came an assortment of others, men and women, wearing Temple vestments. Dark sackcloth shadows flanked them, more servant priests holding more lanterns. Piers counted fifteen then twenty and then lost count. He had not thought this many Templars existed in all France.

"If I shout out—"

"You shout, I'll drive the knife through your throat and name you Judas."

"I've betrayed no-one."

"But you came close, which is why we need eyes on you, to ensure this evening goes well."

The double doors at the far end of the room opened, revealing the candlelit chamber beyond. For a moment, Piers thought he'd been seen, but the shadows along the wall would not be banished and resisted. The gathered crowd moved through the entrance as one, their booted steps an echo of purpose.

"We'll follow last," the old man whispered in his ear. "You'll take a seat with me alongside. You'll keep quiet and participate in the ceremony when asked. At the end, we'll return here and talk again."

Piers didn't reply, there was no need. The crowd thinned, the knife vanished and a hand shoved him in the back. "Move."

He stumbled forwards, joining the back of the group. The ceremony chamber was as he remembered it with one addition. A wooden arch stood in the circle dais. The black wood shaped symmetrically and covered in runes of varying sizes. Piers could smell its power, an intoxicating heady air that demanded attention.

His companion nudged him towards seats in the upper tier, over the entrance and opposite where he'd sat before. He fumbled up the steps, without taking his eyes from the construction, which was surrounded by priests. As they reached the top, he found it easier to breathe and managed to turn away, scanning the packed benches for familiar faces, but found none. Specifically he searched for Lady Eleanor, but there was no sign of her.

From this vantage point he could not see the armour, but near the doorway, he spotted one person he recognised.

Elbo Smogg.

The little bearded man had changed and wore the same black robes as others around him, but his jutting beard was unmistakable. He hung back in the corner near the wall.

"Sit down," the old priest whispered.

Piers turned to him. "Something's wrong," he said.

"We know all about your doubts, sit down and be proved wrong."

"That's not what I mean," Piers leaned over and lowered his voice. "Someone's here to disrupt the ritual."

The old priest glanced around. "Where?"

"Over there, I—"

At that moment, a horn sounded and Grandmaster de Molay appeared at the chamber entrance, causing everyone to stand and making Smogg impossible to spot. Ten escorts flanked the grandmaster as he took up his chair in the expectant hush, his back to Piers. On cue, the assembly sat. Piers looked for Smogg again, but he had disappeared. He turned to the priest. "You need to go after him."

The old man measured him with a long stare. "Like that would you? Free reign to interfere, just when you want? We had high hopes for you. A shame to see all the effort go to waste."

"I'm not lying, you need to—"

"I need do nothing."

Below, a procession of figures appeared. Dirty prisoners chained together, dragged into the chamber. Piers saw men, women and children, all proclaimed unbelievers, pagans and heretics. They were pulled into a circle and forced to their knees between de Molay's chair and the wooden arch.

"We will perform the ritual as taught by our guide who showed us the way," de Molay announced. "The blood and the body of misused gifts will form our vessel. Our blood will guide it and make it whole. By purifying the souls of the damned, we will ride to heaven's gate and demonstrate our worth to Our Father."

The Grandmaster stepped forwards and accepted a golden cup from an attendant. A flash of steel opened his palm and blood dripped into the bowl. He passed the cup to another, who did the same. "Accept our offering, Lord and Av," de Molay intoned. "A pledge of the gift you granted us, that we might journey to your side."

Beside the arch, Piers spotted the Italian he had spoken to before. The man took the cup and repeated the ritual. Afterwards, he took it to the nearest benches where men and women did the same, each taking up the chant – *Lord and Av.*

It took more than an hour for the cup to reach the upper tiers. It came to the old priest first who repeated the ritual and stared at Piers until he offered his palm. A wide 'x' slashed through the flesh made him gasp, but he didn't wince or draw back. He turned his hand, letting the blood drip into the cup, already nearly full from the ablutions of others.

The cup disappeared, leaving Piers nursing the wound. He pulled a thin piece of cloth from his pocket and wound it around his hand. "You enjoyed that."

The priest gave him a gap-toothed grin. "Of course."

On the dais, Templars interspersed themselves amongst the prisoners, causing some to wail and beg, flinching away. Piers caught sight of the cup, re-appearing in the hands of the grandmaster's attendants. He accepted it, raised his hands, quieting the murmured chant to speak to them all.

"Our father, who art in heaven, hallowed by thy name. Thy kingdom come, thy word be done, on earth as it is in heaven. Give us this day our daily bread and we shalt give bread unto your people in your name. Give us your true blessing and we shalt raise up those who bless you."

As the assembly murmured its assent to the familiar prayer, de Molay moved into the centre of the dais, standing between the prisoners and the arch.

"As your soldiers, we deliver unto your care, the evil of heathen, heretic and faithless. Gathered here are the tempted, to be taken into your care and for your correction. We do this in the cause of your word, to bring Heaven to Earth. This is our purpose."

As the assembly echoed his final line, de Molay turned to the soldier nearest to him and nodded. The sound of steel being drawn brought a hushed quiet, each soldier positioning themselves behind a prisoner.

Then the screaming began.

Swords hacked at the kneeling supplicants. Men and women, blessed with gifts, but condemned for their lack of belief died on the stone floor of the chamber. Piers gritted his teeth, watching the pathetic scene. These people were traitorous souls, betrayers of their inheritance, but that didn't make the act any more palatable.

Somewhere below, the cheering began, scattered at first, but gathering momentum. In the heart of the temple, the living had been transformed into objects and then finally into the dead. The smell of piss and shit intermingled with the heady air of power.

Piers wasn't sure which part he abhorred more.

De Molay stood amidst the gore, immobile and resolute. Blood spattered his clean robes. He held aloft the cup and poured its contents onto the centre of the dais.

"Father, we beseech thee, open for us a path to your blessed realm. Open this gate that we might know your glory and better understand your word. We beseech with the power of the gift you grant us."

Piers realised his fingernails were gouging into the hard wood of the bench. He'd witnessed the opening of portals before, but never concentrated power like this. He glanced left and right. There was no sign of Smogg, the old priest and everyone else on the row were enthralled by the ritual. Quietly he murmured his own incantation, feeling the runes in his clothes awaken.

"Receive us father, let us open a door to the blessed realm!"

Thunder rumbled from above, resonating through the roof of the chamber. An impossibly devouring wind, stole through the space, a charge of blackness amidst the legion of candles, pulling at clothes and flesh. Piers saw the Italian he'd spoken to in the Pope's chambers step forward and kneel in front of the grandmaster, his hands grasping each of the wooden arch poles and shouting something incomprehensible. Noise in the room gathered pace, a roaring that drowned out the chants and exhortations.

Then the Italian began screaming, a sound that chilled Piers to the bone. The space inside the wooden arch went black and seemed to suck up the light around it. At that moment, the courage of the hall broke and people began rushing toward the solitary exit, tripping over each other in their haste. The void between the poles was impenetrable; a vast nothingness – *nothing* – and he realised what that meant.

There is no god here, no heaven, no hell, only darkness.

Piers could feel the power of the blackness reaching out to claim him, to claim them all. It was a tempting horror, a nothing pure and blank. It defied his senses and any attempt to be explained. It was pure void, endless insignificance.

Piers glanced around. He struggled to breathe, the air thin, where it had been thick before. He was alone on the upper bench. The old priest had gone, fleeing with all the rest. The armour stand fell to the floor with a crash and sections of the strange suit scraped across the floor towards the emptiness. The runes on the dais floor throbbed and the bodies of the prisoners were dragged towards the black. Everything that came into contact with the darkness vanished, claimed by that terrifying absence. People on the nearest benches were forced to grab hold of their seats as the strange wind seized them, pulling them towards oblivion. One man slipped and screamed as he flew through the arch, swallowed by its mysterious depths.

A gnarled hand touched his. Piers turned to find Elbo Smogg at his side. "I told you!" he warned. "We have to get out of here!"

"How?" Piers yelled back. "The way out is down there, we'll be sucked through!"

"We have to try!" Smogg said. "It'll only get worse!"

Piers nodded. He slid from the bench to the stones and followed Smogg, crawling on hands and knees towards the end of the row. They began a descent to the doors, keeping low and grabbing the end of each bench as they climbed down. He snagged his cut hand, re-opening the wound and heard more cries of despair as people slipped to be dragged away.

A tortured ripping noise made him glance up. A bench near the arch tore loose from the stone and dangled towards the void. "The whole room will collapse!" he shouted.

"It may at that!"

When they reached the row above the doors, Smogg grabbed his arm. "We can't go any nearer," he said. "Our only chance is the roof."

Piers stared at him in confusion until he realised what he meant. They would have to go over the doors, lowering themselves into the passage beyond. "The minute we jump, we'll be dragged away!"

"Then we can't jump."

Smogg scrabbled along the row over the exit. He placed his hand on the rock and his eyes lost focus. For a moment, nothing happened, but then a vine sprouted from between the stones, growing at an impossible rate. Tendrils of the creeper were immediately drawn towards the arch, but others spread and multiplied, anchoring the plant to the roof of the doorway. As the growth thickened, Smogg grabbed a handful of stems and pulled at them, then judging it safe, he swung from the stones and with surprising agility, began to climb down to the floor.

Piers watched him carefully, mindful of being bigger and heavier. The plant continued to grow as Smogg scampered along, but strands were becoming fragile as it exhausted the power of the spell. Thin strands snapped, flew through the air and disappeared into the dark between the wooden poles. The draw increased moment by moment, the creeper couldn't hope to—

"Your turn!"

Smogg was on the floor of the passage. Piers took a deep breath and lowered his feet onto the creeper, gritting his teeth against the pain in his cut palm. The plant shivered, but held his weight. Quickly he started downwards, hands and legs shaking with effort or fear.

"Hurry!"

The vines were dry, hairy and abrasive. Some came away as he clutched at them, but others held. He made it from the ceiling to the wall, the strange sucking wind, dragging at his clothes with every move he made. He didn't look up or down, just at the plant and stone in front of him. When his right foot touched the floor he stumbled and fell, gasping for breath.

The wind pulled at him as he struggled. Ignoring the pain in his knees and with one fist clenched around a thick plant tendril, he turned his back on the black void and tried to get off the floor, but his feet kept slipping on the stone.

"Help me!"

The vines began to wither in his hand. Piers saw whole sections from where he'd climbed fall to pieces and drift away back into the chamber. He focused on them, trying to add his own strength to the spell, but it wasn't one he knew. Smogg was ahead, some distance down the passage with other people around him. He turned back, but didn't move.

Then the stems snapped and Piers found himself flying backwards towards the wooden arch.

A hand grabbed his wrist, yanking him away. A low boom echoed out as the chamber doors slammed shut. The roaring wind dropped to a murmur. Piers crashed to the floor. He glanced around. The spider-web of runes from before were glowing. They covered every surface, shining from the walls all around him.

"Gaveston!"

A woman's voice, shouting his name. He stood up and limped down the passage as the runes grew brighter and brighter. He reached the far end to find a whole host of people waiting there.

"Close the passage!" someone yelled.

The crowd moved back into the outer chamber, which was also beginning to glow with light from the patterns on its walls. The doors were locked and barred. Ten or more figures clustered around a huge stone and began to roll it in front of the entrance, sealing it for good.

The crowd settled into stunned quiet. The roaring noise from the assembly chamber remained as a low murmur, but it was contained and the strange wind had disappeared.

"Piers."

Lady Eleanor stood in front of him, her lips set in a serious line. "Are you injured?" she asked.

"I don't understand," Piers said. "You weren't in the chamber."

"No, I wasn't."

"Why?"

She smiled without humour. "Perhaps I took your advice?"

"But you were so sure I—"

She held up a hand. "Sir, there are more matters at stake than you can know. Your assistance has been appreciated, now it is time for you to leave."

"Leave? After what we've just—"

"You will never speak of it, on pain of death." She turned away before he could answer. He stepped forward to go after her, but found a gloved hand on his shoulder, a soldier in blood flecked papal livery. "This way, wizard," the man said.

For a moment, Piers considered resisting. His mind burned with questions, but he realised he wasn't going to get them answered amidst this nervous crowd. He lowered his head and allowed himself to be led away.

Chapter 7: The Right Thing in the Rain

Deep into the night, Gurda gazed out from the battlements of Horažďovice.

It was cold and her breath steamed into the air. Clouds were gathering in the east. They would bring rain or sleet, which suited her perfectly. Watch fires lined the ground below, marking the pickets outside the moat. The army of Rudolf I, nicknamed *Král Kaše* – 'King Porridge' surrounded the fortress as they had for weeks previous with little change, but this was the first time she'd seen them, the first time she'd been here.

"Identify yourself!" shouted a voice in German.

The soldier on the wall levelled his polearm threateningly. She held up her left hand, palm open, whilst leaning heavily on the walking stick in her right. "My name would mean nothing to you," she said in the same tongue, "but I am here to break the siege."

The soldier stepped forward, eyeing her uncertainly. He was older than she expected, physically as old as her; a long grey beard and shaking hands betraying his fear. "You shouldn't be up here," he mumbled.

"I won't be for long, I need a way down to them," Gurda waved at the watch fires. "There must be a secret tunnel or a gate."

"I'm to bring all trespassers to the sergeant at arms."

"Then if you cannot help me, take me to him."

She was escorted from the wall to the courtyard, an uncomfortable journey with her knees and aching body. From there, they walked to a command post near the postern gate and she was asked to begin the conversation again, this time sat on a wooden stool talking to a man behind a table.

"Sergeant, you lose nothing by letting me out."

"You may be a spy, sent to assess our defences."

"If I am, how did I get in?" She tapped her walking stick on the floor. "I am no dextrous assassin or circus tumbler. If you believe I broke in, you must alert all your sentries. However, since I want to leave, your conclusion makes no sense, unless I have been here a long time and only now have information that will betray you," She shrugged and leaned in. "Surely *Král Kaše* would pick a more capable spy?"

"How can I believe you?"

Gurda sighed. "Sergeant, if you trust me this siege will end tomorrow or the next day. The army of Rudolf will evaporate before your eyes and Bohemia will be free to choose a new ruler."

"And how will you accomplish this feat?"

She smiled at him. He'd been educated and knew his letters, as indicated by the parchment and quill on the table, but underneath he remained a barbarian, with all the same superstitions and fears of his ancestors. Outside she heard the first sounds of rain and the wheezy breath of her escort pretending not to listen in. "Sergeant, do you pray?"

He blinked twice, plainly not expecting her question. "Of course, the Lord God is my saviour through his son Jesus Christ, what does that—"

"Do you remember the priest talking of revelation?"

He looked nervous. "The end of times?"

"Yes. If you thwart me, the people you protect will suffer. Your prayers and confessions will be worthless because you obstructed a servant of the divine. What would strike down your enemies, will fall upon you."

"But how can I trust what you say?" the resolve in his voice had weakened, taking on a pleading tone.

She smiled again. Her hands went to the buttons on her shirt, opening it from the bottom, and lifting it up to reveal the flesh of her belly. The smell of infection filled the air. The sergeant's face went white. She understood why.

"How are you still alive?"

"Faith," she lied. "I have work to do and you are delaying me. Allow me to leave. If you do not, the mark will be left here and the end will begin with your people."

Matters went smoothly after that. Following his master's instruction, the old soldier opened the postern door. As she slipped through, Gurda began a spell, weaving together what shadows she could find. The rain helped, discouraging sentries on both sides of the siege.

She walked slowly down the embankment and into the moat. Its waters were still and fetid, too deep for any human to wade and swimming would draw attention, so she let herself sink to the bottom and walked. The frailties of her body made her slow, but she could still surpass the strength of humans.

She reached the other side and passed through the picket line. Rudolf's pavilion was not hard to locate and the shadows protected her approach. She kept away from the entrance and walked to the back, sitting down in the mud by the embroidered canvas. There were more guards here, walking around the tents, but she waited and gradually their attention went elsewhere.

She removed a few pegs and crawled inside the tent.

"Given name?"

"Galina."

It was raining. A wooden roof held up by four pillars sheltered a balding official sat at a table. His quill scratched out the responses on a long parchment roll. When her name was recorded, he glanced up and his gaze went to Galina's left. "What about her?"

"Katya, my sister."

More scratches on the roll. "You cannot write?"

"No."

"Then I have made marks for you," He turned the sheet around and pointed. Galina could see two neat 'x's on the page next to a shape or pattern of ink. "What is your business in Vidin?"

Galina stared at Katya, but the girl's eyes remained fixed on the floor. "We've come seeking work," she said.

The official's critical gaze went over them both. Galina remembered that look – cold and impersonal. "I daresay," he replied then his eye went to the line stretching out behind them. "Move on," he announced and waved. "Hurry up now."

Putting her arm around her sister, Galina led the way along the cobblestone road and into the city.

She'd woken up that morning to find Faim gone and wasn't surprised. The argument spelled the end of their relationship. She couldn't work out what he'd gained, but somehow she knew he didn't need them anymore, at least for now.

Vidin was a strange place. The early morning cold and drizzle didn't prevent crowds. People were everywhere, going about their business in the wet mud and damp. She felt suffocated by them. Her eyes roamed the streets, seeking shelter and a place to catch her breath, but the buildings loomed overhead, powerful stone blocks, taller and larger than anything she'd ever seen. Noise came from everywhere, she couldn't get her bearings.

Then a boy ran into her, his head barrelling into her stomach. She recoiled instinctively. In her village there would have been an apology, tears and a look of shame. But here, the child hardly paused and dashed off, disappearing down an alleyway.

For a moment, Galina felt sorry for him. *He'll be cursed for his ignorance,* she thought. The instinctive dogma she'd been taught about corruption and the purity of her old blood were difficult to reconcile with Faim's words. But then Faim's very existence defied that explanation. His gifts were greater than Katya's but he clearly didn't share their faith. *How can he be chosen and not believe?* If that were possible, perhaps she and Katya weren't as special as she thought and the boy would be fine.

She turned around. There were more people in the street than she'd ever seen in her life. How many of them had gifts? The old man sat by the artesian well? The merchant with the heavy cart and attendants? The bored official sat at his desk? The city militia man leaning against the gate? *How many?*

She turned to her sister. Katya's eyes remained on her feet, her expression dull and vacant. "We need to find somewhere to rest," she said. Katya didn't respond, so she took her hand as before and led her to the well. The old man eyed them for a moment, but turned away as they passed.

Galina took both of her sister's hands and knelt at her feet, gazing up into her vacant face. "I need you," she confessed in a whisper. "You've always turned to me for advice, but I don't know what to do. This place is all so much."

In response, Katya blinked, but stayed silent. Galina sighed then remembered the riverbank. She withdrew her hands and reached into her carry sack, pulling out the thing she'd made; a short stave about two feet long. The interlocking branches and twigs held together by their own twists and turns. Ash from the burned house filled the gaps, giving it a strange mottled appearance. "This is for you," she said. "It's not finished, but I think it will help. I studied Faim's staff. I think it helps him control his gifts," she held out the wooden object. "Please take it, we're stronger together, stronger than anyone."

Katya didn't reply for a long time, but then gradually her eyes changed. The lost and faraway expression faded away as she journeyed back, until Galina met her gaze, sensed her recognition. She reached out to touch the stave and touched her sister's hands. "Together." She whispered and smiled.

Galina's eyes filled with tears. "Yes, together, for good," she replied.

All magic has its price.

Cooperation and the sharing of knowledge amongst wizards remain essential to our effort. The studies of Aquinas, and others prove our worth as do the mechanisms we construct to enhance and refine the gift.

However, the greatest of our constructions are churches. The refined power of faith and belief from the mortal, codified through our written instruments empower the gifted. The shared belief of the masses provides power. Individually, they are insignificant, but in their thousands, they are mana to our sacred warriors.

The holy orders are blind to the true war. The crusades are a foolish waste of resources in a squabble over definition. The heathen is our true enemy, an enemy whose weakness we can exploit.

We must find those with the blood who deny us and sacrifice them, using their power for our own purposes. The wielders already made a path to eternity, we of lesser gift, but keener mind, can transcend as well, if we are empowered, but this cannot be a selfish cause. The pledge must be for all, to bring the world to its destined paradise.

Guido Cavalcanti.

Timeline of Significance

1307: King Philip IV of France accuses the Templars of magic and heresy. Philip has the Templars arrested. Some are tortured and executed. King Rudolf I of Bohemia dies of dysentery, besieging the rebel fortress of Horažďovice in Bohemia, leaving no children. Edward I dies campaigning in Scotland and as a consequence, Piers Gaveston returns from to England from exile.

1308: Edward II leaves England to marry. Piers Gaveston made regent. Later that year, Gaveston exiled for the second time.

1309: At the request of King Philip IV, Pope Clement V officially moves his court to Avignon, away from hostility in Rome.

1310: Giotto di Bondone an Italian artist unveils his painting – *The Ascension*. The Knights of St John conquer the island of Rhodes.

1311: The aggressive sultan of Delhi, Ala-ud-din, of the Khalji family dynasty, conquers the southern tip of India, putting the whole of India under his rule. Piers Gaveston pardoned and returns to England.

1312: Issue of the *vox in excelso*. Piers Gaveston captured and 'executed' on the road near Blacklow Hill.

1314: Jacque de Molay is executed and curses the pope and the French king, Phillip IV. Dante Alighieri publishes *La Divinia Commedia*. Pope Clement V dies. Phillip IV dies.

1315: Crops fail in a cold season throughout Europe, heralding the beginning of the Great Famine (1315-1322).

1316: Ascension of Pope John XXII.

1317: Total Lunar Eclipse (21st September). Philip V crowned King of France. The Pope decrees *Sancta Romania* against spiritualists.

1318: Go-Daigo becomes Emperor of Japan.

1319: Earthquake in Ani, Armenia.

1320: Pope John XXII authorises Inquisitors to prosecute sorcerers.

1321: A drought begins in Japan. Dante Alghieri dies from an illness while returning to Ravenna from a diplomatic mission in Venice.

AD 1324 – The Mustering

You will never know truly how hard things were.

After we came to Vidin, you were not yourself for some time. The moment of focus and clarity that came when I took your hand soon faded. You withdrew, plainly damaged by what happened at the village and what you did with your magic.

The first few nights we slept in the street. The cold stone houses were shelter from the wind, but offered little warmth. The watchmen moved us on and made threats about being sent back through the gates. I fed you, cleaned your clothes and bathed you in the river when I could. Occasionally, you would return to me for a while and talk, but you'd barely remember it.

Some days, strangers were kind and gave us scraps. On other days, I learned to pick the discarded fish from the catch in the early morning and to cook on the rubbish fires. At times, I had to leave you so we would eat, but then you had already left me.

One day I came back to find a man about you, whether he wanted your blanket or your body, I'll never know. There was a blinding flash, he screamed and burned up right there in the street. Afterwards you went far from me, your slack mouth refusing food and water.

I thought you might die.

But you did not and came back for a time in the spring. Those days in the sun I remember and treasured. I blocked out the cold and hunger, remembering only you, your fragile smile and gentle face.

Weeks became months. I found shelter in the stone houses of the Church. I listened to sermons and learned the ways. Eventually the priest called me to him and asked of my life. I told him little, but saw something in his eye. He gave me work and coin. At times I brought you with me. We sat at the back and I learned of their Heaven and Hell, with this world as a place in between. The people are not so different to us, but believe the path to good is through their priest. I remembered Faim's words and wondered whether the man might be of the old blood.

It was in church I met Milen. He smiled and pressed a coin into my palm as I worked in the dust. His touch was strange to me after all our years being untouched. A few days later, he asked me how I was and how you were. I told you of him and his gentle way. I smiled at him and he became kind.

Letters to Katya – Galina Purvanova.

Chapter 8: We are Angels

A dry day. Hino Suketomo sweated under his monk's robe in the noon sun.

He waited in the shadow of a wooden fence outside the servant's entrance to a wealthy home – the Tokimichi residence. The street was dusty and surprisingly quiet, but he kept the hood around his face. It would not do for the Emperor's *dainagon* to be found in these streets meeting strange associates, so a disguise was required; one complete enough to ensure nothing aroused suspicion, meaning he could not wear the *tachi* sword of his house. Without it he felt naked and vulnerable.

But Hino knew people were watching. Jiro Katsuchiyo, the bushi assigned to escort him lurked somewhere close by, though not near enough to draw attention. Keyo Tokimichi's people would be watching as well. The servant's door would be guarded and others would be concealed in the street. This was welcome, but further observation would not be.

A man appeared at the end of the road, walking towards the Tokimichi house. Hino eyed him as he approached. He was taller than most Japanese men and moved with the ease of one accustomed to long distances. His clothes confirmed his identity, the foreign dress of an African or Arab. A formal conversation between this man and the Emperor Go-Daigo's chief counsellor would be the subject of inquiry. Powerful nobles would use such information to imply his corruption and petition for Hino's removal, less he 'affect the Emperor'. Such games were the obsession of petty minds. Hino understood the fragility of his place, but the Emperor had sent him here and required that he meet an assortment of individuals who others might deem unsuitable. In some ways this day and this man was no different than the others.

The man stopped in the middle of the street ten yards from where Hino waited. He kept his eyes on the ground but didn't move any further. Hino muttered a curse under his breath and walked over to him.

"Greetings *Suketomo-sama*," the man said. He was painfully thin with a long face and the tanned skin of desert lands. "I hear you wish to speak with me?"

Hino moved closer and kept his voice low. "Indeed *Faim-san*, but the middle of the street—"

"Is the perfect place for two individuals to learn trust," Faim smiled, revealing shrunken gums and exposed teeth, yellowed and blackened in places. His sunken eyes and bony frame gave him a haunted look. Hino had seen similar expressions on starving children in the orphanages.

"There are more comfortable places – seats, food and drink that befit your stature…"

"I require none of these and prefer the comfort of the open road," Faim replied. "What is it you require?"

Hino hesitated. Such conversations were not meant for street corners, nor should they be delivered in such blunt sentences, but the stranger's question gave him little choice. "You have exceeded the request you were given," he said.

Faim nodded. "Indeed, my efforts prove more effective than I thought."

"We require you to stop," Hino added.

"If the Emperor requires this, he should tell me himself."

Hino frowned, his hand aching for a sword that was not there; the old blood in him burned. "You know this will not happen."

Faim smiled again. "Your people have been sleeping whilst oppressors assume control of their lives. Your Emperor feels this. These usurpers stand between him and his nation. I act to awaken them, you cannot control their enlightenment."

"Your methods are excessive," Hino said. "Most of Japan has been without rain for three years."

"And you believe that is a result of my work?"

"You and the spells of your followers, yes," Hino replied. He stepped closer. "I did not conclude the arrangement between you and my master, but it falls to me to end this work. The Emperor wishes you to leave Japan."

Faim stared at him. "Your master wishes the *bakufu* regime undermined. My work will do that and has already done much, but change is not something you can impose or govern, it is a necessity that all of our blood be free and understand the slavery of your kingdom."

"You speak of the end of all law and organisation," Hino said. "The Emperor does not want this."

"Then your Emperor should know better the people he hires," Faim laughed. "I will leave and the effort will end. There will be a price."

"Name it."

"No, instead I will arrange it to be paid," he stepped back and bowed – a mocking gesture with no shred of courtesy. "Inform your master if he wishes to speak again, he must use his own voice." With that, he turned his back and walked away.

Hino watched him go and glanced around. The street remained deserted. He walked back to the servant's entrance and looked again, seeing no-one at first, but then a gleam of metal caught his eye from across the street. A figure stumbled out of a doorway and ran in the opposite direction. For a moment, Hino considered going after him, but decided against it. Instead, he recited an old incantation under his breath and made a hooking gesture with his left hand.

The figure froze in midstride and fell to the ground.

Hino slipped back through the door. As expected Tokimichi guard stood to attention as he passed. He beckoned him over. "There is a person lying in the street. Bring him into the house and to a room. Keep an eye on him until I return."

The man hesitated for a moment before bowing and slipping out of the door, leaving Hino alone. He walked back to the house and to his guest room, shedding the monk's robe and pouring a cup of cool water from the jug on the floor. He sat down and sipped thoughtfully. The meeting had been successful; he had gained the agreement he had been asked to obtain. *What will it cost me?* He wondered. *What will it cost the Emperor?*

The palace had no name.

Janak scrubbed its floors. He was old now, much time had passed since the first times he remembered as a child. He recalled little of anything else. For most days, from then to now, he scrubbed, stopping only to fill his troughs from the well, cleaning stone, tile and trammels of all things left behind by those who lived within these halls.

He was unclean, named 'untouchable' by birth and so cleaned to wash away the dirt in his soul.

In the first days he learned to keep his eyes down and ears open. Men of wisdom and counsel did not tolerate the stares of those beneath them. Whip scars remained on his back from those times. He never screamed and so never invoked sympathy or malice. Years later, they took his tongue as a precaution. He did not miss it; there was no-one he would speak to.

They gave him clothes and food, so long as he cleaned. The exquisitely painted tiles became stories that filled his mind. Others like him worked in different chambers, men and women made equal by their mixed blood and inherited sin. He avoided them and they avoided him, for each knew association increased their unworthiness.

As he worked he learned of the world through the fragments. All manner of people came to the city through its gateways, travelling from faraway lands. Some spoke Urdu, but many others did not and their words were strange, but the inflection and passion remained similar. Some part of his mind catalogued and ordered the words, seeking repetition and phrasing. In time, he learned Latin, Cantonese and French by listening; the travellers who spoke each he recognised by their feet and sandals as he scurried from their paths. He saw women's feet in equal number to men. When he took meals in the tunnels, he heard them murmuring together in the vast stone chamber.

"Our agreement will bring much for both our peoples. Maps that show routes of trade and travel make the world smaller for those who cannot use magic as we do."

"Indeed, but you must remember to leave out the secret places, like Teku Benga…"

He struggled to remember when the voices first became urgent and angry, but there was a marked change. In the later days, he barely recalled laughter in these vast halls. Feet hurried on their way, with less and less casual visits. The vibrant community of the masters became a tense counsel. The rooms were full or empty, never anything in between.

"Ala-ud-din is the only leader who can resist the Mongols and unify our kingdom."

"He is an unbeliever and not of the blood."

"We will use him and when we are done, bring in others who are more suitable."

Janak aged and the rooms became harder to clean. As a young man, he washed everything in two days, but he was no longer young. He learned the cunning ways of the old, to be busy when watched and to perfect the tiles that would be examined, leaving the less used places till last, or not at all. In these times it was all he could do to prepare the meeting chambers, but no-one looked at his work, their bare feet and sandals replaced by hard boots and hard minds.

"You must control these fanatics!"

"We are trying to, we have—"

"Trying is not enough! What are these rumours they have opened a portal you cannot close that seeks to devour the world?"

"I assure you these are lies. We have the matter in hand!"

He slept on the same stone every night, in the lowest chambers near the ancient tombs. As a child, being close to the long dead sultans and kings frightened him, but the Brahmin masters tolerated no complaint and told him how privileged he was to be near such royal blood and how others like him would sleep with no roof in the rain. He could not touch the resting places, but by being close to pure blood, his soul had the best chance of being reborn amongst the *chaturvarnya*, when the time came.

"You must accept our rule. It is the way of things. If not, the death of your people will be on your hands."

"We will not agree to these terms, we must—"

"Please, do not dishonour yourself, this is not a negotiation."

"Then why are you here?"

Janak knew these days would be his last. At night he shivered on the sleeping stone and could not get warm when he woke. Once, he found his left arm held no strength and his face became numb. When he went to the well, he dropped the pitcher of water, slipped and fell to the floor. He lay there for a time as the sensation spread to his legs, believing this would be the end and he had won his right to a new life, but when he awoke, he was not born anew; the tiles remained cold and dusty from neglect and his belly rumbled with hunger.

He worked harder, fighting the weakness of age. He was the last left and saw no feet or others of his kind. He caught rats and ate them raw, not daring to sully the floors of the palace with the smoke and ash of a fire. When he couldn't catch rats, he fasted and prayed.

In some chambers he found bloodstains and worse, but no people. As he washed away the defilements, he wondered if the Brahmin masters had died? If so, they left nothing of themselves. Perhaps the other untouchables had worked harder and already been delivered from corruption.

At times he felt a presence with him. It made him look around cautiously from the corner of his eye, expecting to see someone watching him work, but no-one appeared. He came to understand the presence, riding behind his eyes and seeing what he saw in each room. The visits were regular at first, but gradually died away.

Eventually the silence became his friend, waiting everywhere for him as he crawled around the halls. He could not walk far anymore and struggled with the troughs and pitchers. His clothes were gone, rotted from his back or used as cloths for the floors. Naked and old, he cleaned with bare hands and saliva, rubbing away each stain and blemish in a smaller and smaller circle.

One evening, knowing he was alone, he looked up and finally saw the beauty of the grand chamber; the huge domed ceiling and painted characters rising from the ground to high above at the top. His gaze lingered upon all manner of creatures, each with their own story, like the figures on the tiles under his feet. By looking he had sinned and deserved the whip, but he felt no shame or guilt at seeing such wonders.

In the centre of the room, he found a massive spherical rock, held up on a pillar. Carved into its surface were green shapes in recesses of blue. A whiteness adorned the top, like a crown of painted hair.

He awoke one morning after that unable to move from the stone where he slept. He tasted blood in his mouth and found breathing hard.

After a time, he gave up trying and closed his eyes…

Tuia knew no peace.

He crouched in the trees; miles from the stone arch he had spent his life watching. Now he watched something else. Below, a long line of prisoners from a nearby village shuffled past, dragging and carrying huge lumps of rock. Around them, men with spears, mantle clasp cloaks and feathered headdresses. They were stern of countenance and purpose, leading the procession onwards to the north.

These new people did not worship Si. Instead, they named her *Mextli* and themselves Mexica. They followed many gods of wind, sun and more. Their words were strange, but Tuia could make himself understood if he chose.

Tuia had travelled north after his time as watcher of the gate ended. He remembered the day the woman came through and turned her magic upon the arch, cracking the huge lintel and ending its power. Quietly, Tuia followed her and after three weeks, his journey led him here.

The broken stones being transported by the prisoners were the remains of his charge, scattered amidst other carved rocks. The woman remained at the head of the procession. She was different to the others, shorter, with an angular face and narrow eyes. As they journeyed on, she discarded her strange clothes and took up the feathers and mantle of the followers who joined her, revealing a lattice of scars, the worst upon her back and arms.

She took up a spear like the Mexica soldiers and called out the largest of them, besting him easily. His corpse was drained that night, the blood boiled for a feast and the body burned. After that, the Mexica obeyed her without question.

Tuia spied on them all from above in the branches. He made his way from tree to tree, taking care to avoid their scouts and watchers. At times, groups would go off and return with captives until eventually, the gathering grew huge. Tuia wondered what he hoped to gain by following them, but he had nothing else. The arch had been his life; a

75

strong magic, broken in an instant. He would find the source of this new power and attain its worth or he would kill the woman in revenge for taking the purpose of his life.

He was not a young man. These days, the carving of wood gave him no comfort. His hands, not as strong as before, would shake at times. The time he spent in trees, awake and asleep, planted aches in his joints. As they journeyed further from land he knew, he became hungry. The plants here were different and he struggled to find the right ones to eat.

One morning they came to a vast lake. A temporary village of shelters clustered around a collection of wood and broken rock. Tuia lost sight of the woman, but studied the people. They were a mixture, some black as night, others pale like milk and a host of variations in between. The majority were short and brown, wearing the feathers and mantle like the warriors.

The prisoners were set to work on breaking the larger stones. People busied themselves everywhere. From a great tree on a hill above the shore, Tuia saw the stones being loaded onto rafts attached to ropes then pulled out into the waters, disappearing into the mist. At times, people were placed on the rafts instead and taken away.

At night, the prisoners were fed then gathered up to sleep in a large pen guarded by soldiers. He spied the cooking fires and his belly rumbled. He waited and when it was quiet, stole down into the camp. In the embers he found slivers of charred meat and scraps dropped on the ground. He collected up what he could and snuck back into the trees.

When he returned to his tree, he found the strange woman sitting where he had sat. He stared at her and she stared back.

"You take everything from me," he said at last in his own language, "first my stone, now my seat."

"It was never your stone," she replied in the same tongue with only a slight hesitation. "You were its guardian while its purpose remained. That purpose is over now."

"Who are you?"

"I have many names, most would mean nothing to you." She waved at the valley below. "They call me *Teotl* which in their tongue means magic. It is more of a title than a name. Others call us *Egregoroi*, which means watcher."

"Why do you need stone?"

"Because the age of old things is past, we need swift strength if we are to survive the coming storm," the woman sighed. "The old ways are slow and sure, but there is little time. The new path will be ruinous and wasteful, yet brings power we can use. The stones of the arch will be added to what we make and find a new purpose, as will all those who venture across the lake."

"You send your prisoners across the lake," Tuia said. "No-one returns."

"Most are sacrificed," the woman admitted. "But this is necessary. We are building a city, the last city before the end of days. It will save those who are worthy."

Tuia considered this and the woman. She sat as he had; the bare skin of her arms and legs showing the scars he noticed before, but this time, up close he saw just how many and their variety. These were not ritual wounds, they came from war. "You are accustomed to getting your way," he remarked.

The woman inclined her head in assent. "I am not a builder," she said. "My gifts destroy, yet in this purpose I find a chance to be free. I am willing to help builders for a time, if they bring me towards what I seek." She got up and approached him. "Tell me, what did you do with the crosses Odoric gave you?"

Tuia frowned, but reached to his belt and pulled out the last of the wooden keepsakes and held it up. Three sticks in a perfect intersection of height, width and depth. "The old ones were wrong," he said, "a confusion of the message."

"May I?"

"Yes."

He dropped the object into her outstretched hand. She smiled and turned it over, studying the axes. "A prophetic warning given thirteen centuries ago, misremembered and turned into a religion. How did you know to fix it?"

Tuia shrugged. "I just did, I am a worker of wood. Sometimes it speaks to me."

"You are gifted. This is why you were chosen to guard the arch. You will find new purpose in the city, one better suited to your talent."

"You aren't going to kill me then?"

"No."

Tuia should have felt relieved at the admission, but the woman's demeanour belied any assurance. Restrained violence oozed from every pore of her.

They sat for a while staring for different reasons. Finally she spoke again.

"We removed your gateway to prevent others coming here unless we want them to. We removed all gateways from these lands, save for the one across the lake. Odoric will not come here again. He and his kin stand for the old ways. They would not understand what we do."

77

"And what is it that you do?" Tuia asked. "What will you use this power for? What do you offer?"

The woman smiled. "Immortality."

The washbasin water clouded quickly with dirt and Katya sighed. Seventeen years since she arrived in Vidin and took a job with Milen at the Prancing Horse and it was getting harder and harder to keep the old tavern clean. The wooden tables and chairs were mopped and dried every other night, the stone hearth swept, cleared and refilled, the ale purchased and restocked, the wine watered a little and rebottled. All things that needed doing, all things that needed more than one person to do them.

She wiped a metal plate and caught a glimpse of the stretched face reflected on its edge; her face – hardly changed since the day they arrived. Galina carried her years a little more and now people believed she was the elder sister. She'd married Milen more out of necessity than love, so they gained a purpose and a place to be. The second son of a wealthy merchant, he'd been good to them both, accepting their story with quiet forbearance, but he had none of the old blood in him. His thirty odd years were now fifty odd years and he too looked like Galina's father, not her husband.

The years were not kind to most people. Seven failed harvests stirred talk of judgement and the Lord's wrath. Katya kept away from such conversations in church and the common room.

Muffled coughing noises came from upstairs. Katya bit her lip. Six rooms were available for lodgers, with only one currently occupied, but the coughing didn't come from there. Instead, it came from the room Galina shared with her husband. When he'd first got ill, she'd thought herself cursed and remembered Faim's words about her causing sickness to her Father, how her magic affected him and made him sick. Death seemed to follow them wherever they went, but these days disease was everywhere and few survived. The corpse cart bell rang on the street every morning and evening. People prayed more and sinned less, but no-one rightly knew the cause.

Footsteps on the stairs and Galina appeared, a hint of crow's feet around her dark eyes. Plainly she hadn't slept. "He's worse," she said.

"How long?"

"A day maybe two at the most."

"Is it us?"

She'd asked this question every time they learned of someone dying.

"I don't think so," Galina said. "I think it's the same as everyone else."

"Am I doing that too?"

"No, if someone is, then it's intentional and far more powerful than anything we could manage." She faced her sister and their eyes met. "Since those days, you've learned to control yourself. I sense that about you."

Katya nodded, accepting the answer, but something instinctive within her squirmed. Magic lingered here in some way, a magic she didn't understand. "We should ask the priest," she said.

Galina's expression darkened. "*They* are no friends of ours."

"All the same, he may know more."

Katya watched her sister weigh up the idea. They both remembered what they had been told and saw that night in the abandoned hamlet, the woman shivering on the ground. They had not seen Faim since, but his mistrust of the Church remained with them and echoed their own upbringing. In Vidin, they held regular services in their stone house. Both Galina and Katya attended, more to prevent talk than anything else.

"If the priest has knowledge he would share, unless he has reason not to," Galina said. "If we reveal ourselves, we'll gain trouble, not answers."

"Then what do we do?"

"I'm not sure."

They took a table and sat together in silence for a time. After a while, Katya got up, found a stopped bottle of watered wine and brought it back to the table with two clay cups. Galina accepted one gratefully.

"If he dies, we'll not be able to stay here," she said. "People already wonder why you are not married. The talk will worsen."

"Talk worsens anyway," Katya said. "Many are dying to this plague; people seek answers and see sin as the cause. Those who are different are sinners. I see the looks and hear the whispers."

"Perhaps we should leave?"

"Where would we go?"

"Back home?" Katya missed her family, her father especially. If he'd recovered, the old blood in his veins might keep him alive for many years yet. But the moment she mentioned the idea she knew it was wrong and silently accepted Galina's shaking head.

"We cannot walk away every time something happens."

"Then we must try magic."

Galina sighed, reached for the bottle, poured herself a measure and drank, leaving nothing in the cup. "I tried charms and herbs as we were taught. I prayed and wished, asked others and taken up their remedies. I bled him and tried to find the source of corruption, but it eludes me. What else could we attempt?"

"Perhaps it is time I helped," Katya said.

"That could be dangerous."

"Do we have another choice?"

They stared at one another, Katya noting the changes in her sister's face. There was a trace of age and the lack of sleep enhanced it. The old blood they shared manifested in different ways. Faim had been more interested in her gift than Galina's insight. She never thought their differences might separate them.

"We've hidden your power all this time," Galina said at last. "Faim told us others would come if we didn't."

"On the Sabbath, the priest spoke of the plague being a mark of sin," Katya said. "Merchants from Sredets say it is there too and in all the outlying villages. We cannot run; there is nowhere to run to."

Galina nodded and stood up. She held out her hand. Katya took it and followed her up the stairs to where Milen lay in his marital bed. The large hearty man Katya remembered was now shrivelled into a sweaty, feverish patient. His skin glistened like parchment and his were eyes bulging and staring as they both entered the room.

"It's all right, he can't see you," Galina said. "I'm unsure of what he actually sees, some waking dream that tortures him alongside the other afflictions." She sat on the stool beside the bed and touched a finger to his balding temple. "He burns constantly, as if the evil is setting fire to everything within. When he speaks, he claims to be cold."

"When I last used my gift properly, my anger and fear brought fire," Katya recalled. "It drained away when Faim mentioned the woman being in the house."

"Can you remember how?" Galina asked. "Can you concentrate and bring forth the magic?"

Katya approached the bed, going to the other side, next to a bowl of water on a small table. She knelt down and stared at Milen's eyes. They were raw. He didn't blink or focus, the fever ravaging his mind as much as it devoured his body.

In seventeen years she'd mostly kept to herself, experimenting with her gift in small ways, so as not to draw attention. She started with the rotes Faim had taught her. A few weeks after they'd settled she'd learned how to produce sparks to light candles and conjure small gusts of wind. Each time she succeeded, she practiced hard to repeat the same action and thought. It was difficult to remember things precisely and the raging flames were never far away when she lost control. Priests learned to read and write. She guessed they would have books recording their achievements to pass on to new initiates – another reason for her to learn her letters.

Katya stared at Milen and tried to focus on the strangeness, conjuring up images in her mind of him when he was healthy, but it was hard. The smell of infection and rot blocked her, as did her natural caution. She remembered the rote she'd cast on the small bush tree across the street outside, making it grow a little taller before catching fire. *Could I use that?*

"I can't see what do to," she said. "I don't have your eyes."

She felt Galina's hand in hers. The steady mind of her sister gave her immediate reassurance and heightened her percepience. Their connection from childhood renewed itself. Katya brought power, Galina direction.

Together, they sought out the disease and the faint stirrings of Milen's breath. Quickly, Katya realised she could not break the infection, she had not mastered such a use of her gift, but with her sister's help, she understood Milen.

Her lips moved, uttering sounds she didn't comprehend. Magic came to her, pouring from her fingertips into him. His heartbeat steadied, his breath strengthened and colour returned to his face. She looked into his eyes and watched him blink and focus. Then frown in pain.

Galina grabbed her wrist and snatched her hand away. "That's enough," she said.

"I'm sorry," Katya stood up. There were tears in her sister's eyes. "I didn't mean to—"

"I know."

Milen sat up slowly and gazing at them both. "What did you do?" he whispered.

Katya flinched under his scrutiny, but Galina took her hand again, squeezing her fingers tight in gratitude. "What we were born to do," she said. "Help people. Help you."

Chapter 9: They are Demons

"Ho! Man! We've horses, attend!"

An English voice speaking French. In response, Piers Gaveston shuffled out of the stables, keeping his hood up to cover his face. A long grey beard meant most folk wouldn't see his face; an important consideration for a man who died twelve years ago and doubly important amongst these people.

He recognised the blue striped livery of Aymer de Valence, the second Earl of Pembroke; once his jailor and now the advisor of his former king, Edward II of England. Twenty horses and riders would fill the Inn to capacity. The soldiers would be grateful of the barn, the earl and his companions would lodge in the guest rooms.

He took the bridle of the first beast and led it to a stall. The earl remained on his horse whilst his steward spoke to the Innkeeper, Jacque Renarre. He could feel the eyes of Pembroke's groomsman on his back. Gradually, the man's caution faded as each animal settled. The Englishmen were wise to be on alert. Relations with France stood on the edge. Pembroke's mission might bring peace or war.

Gaveston busied himself with his work. He helped bring stew to the soldiers when they were settled and drew more water from the well. The earl asked for bread and mulled wine. Renarre fawned around him and his attendants as the cook and servants brought what was asked. Gaveston burned to speak to his old acquaintance, to find some way to help the man still considered King of England, but there would be no chance yet for a discreet conversation.

I'll have to wait.

The hours wore on and the shadows lengthened as the day drew to a close. Gaveston eschewed his own bed and loitered around the stables. Pembroke retired at sunset, a guard posted to his door. His steward remained with the other attendants. Gaveston stayed outside, noting the candlelight in the earl's room. A group of soldiers stayed up, talking outside the barn around a fire; too many eyes all around.

He went back to the stables and hunkered down in a corner. Horses kept the place warm, the smell of straw and shit became part of his life in the last twelve years, after being left by the road at Blacklow Hill to die. He'd been in the custody of Pembroke, but kidnapped by other barons who determined his guilt. *A man condemned for loving his King...*

The prophecy of the *sibylline* witch had come true. King Edward I died on campaign in Scotland at a place known as Burgh by Sands. Piers returned to England to renew his allegiance to the newly crowned Edward II. Elevation to an earldom followed, along with the role of royal counsellor. But long before that he'd sensed the shift in things. After Avignon and de Molay, a mark remained against his name. Support shifted from Edward to his wife Isobella and his son, the Black Prince. Piers kept his oath to never speak of the ritual, but it no longer mattered. The Church would find other reasons to kill him.

He'd abandoned his family, his name and everything else, selling rings to obtain passage to France. Then he took up a new life, travelling as much as possible, working for food and lodging. It was a life the *caduceus* training prepared him for. Those strong with the gift lived long lives, outlasting their peers. Eventually, the road or the cloister became the only realistic choices until those who once knew them were long dead.

He could not return to a cloister, so only the road remained.

The moon rose and the shadows drew in. Piers ran through what magic he knew. His staff and book were long lost. Only the spells he remembered perfectly would be useful. The power did not come easily anymore, not since the day he'd seen the void through the portal under Avignon. *God does not exist, he never existed. We are all alone.*

A flicker of movement across the road drew his attention. At first he thought it was one of the soldiers gone to relieve himself, but the figure who emerged from the woods wasn't anyone he recognised. A large, stocky woman, walking with a stick approached the entrance to the Inn, her limping gait slow, but purposeful.

He stood up and stepped out of the stables towards her, glancing left and right. The soldier's fire had burned down and no-one seemed awake. The candlelight in the upper windows had gone out.

"Who are you?" he called out to the woman.

"I might ask you the same," she replied, coming to a halt a few steps in front of him. "You're in my way."

Piers made no move to step aside. "The Inn is closed to visitors," he said. "Come back in the morning."

The woman shook her head. "You would be wise not to detain me, stablehand."

He sensed the magic in her then, a boiling cauldron, fed by hate, seething just beneath the surface of her calm. "I can't let you—"

The world went white.

In Kyoto, the mid afternoon sun began to dip on the horizon when the first shouts were heard and Hino Suketomo knew what they meant.

We are betrayed...

He stood up on the wooden *engawa* outside the Tokimichi house, the folds of his black *sokutai* rustling in the faint autumnal breeze. The household bushi soldiers were already running to the compound gate; as a guest of the house he would be protected, but it was only a matter of time.

"It seems they know you are here *Suketomo-sama*," said his host Keyo Tokimichi from the doorway.

"It seems so."

A crowd gathered in the streets to watch the *bakufu* break down the doors. Already some tried the walls, to be forced back with long spears.

He wondered who might have elected to betray his mission. The politics of Japan had become complex in the last decade. The Emperor Go-Daigo had sent him into the country to seek out and meet with those who were prepared to stand against the shogunate. Minor nobility, wealthy merchants and mercenaries stitched into a coalition ready to turn on the council who ruled in the Emperor's name, but not by his wish.

Above the games of those in power lay the game of wizards. The uneasy truce between the Emperor and the shoguns kept the country under stable rule and safe against the threat of the Mongols, but it would not last, it could not last. So, the Emperor had chosen to act first.

One by one he recalled the faces invited to the secret meetings, remembering names and opinions. It was a gift that came from the old blood, a talent that made him an ideal councillor. Now he was *dainagon* – first council to the Emperor, a worthy emissary to his allies and significant prize to his enemies.

He glanced at his discarded staff on the steps. Its power would enhance his own, but only delay the inevitable, leaving behind a story his Emperor would not want. He did not wear his family sword as the Emperor expressly ordered he should play the part of a monk. To be captured without it would be shameful.

"Respectfully *Suketomo-sama*, you may make of use my grandfather's blade if you wish—"

"No, but thank you, such an act would be honourable, but it will not placate them," he turned to face Keyo Tokimichi; an old man, no doubt with memories of the golden times before the *bakufu* and split succession. "They are aware of my presence. To not be here implies guilt. To be dead, implies the same. You may do as honour dictates, of course."

"My thanks *Suketomo-sama*."

Alone, he picked up his staff. There would be a use for magic here, but only a subtle one. He closed his eyes, and repeated the phrase he'd been taught, casting his mind away into the sky.

A moment later, the rook landed on his shoulder. He coaxed it to his arm and clipped a small message tube to its leg then cast it back into the air, projecting a clear picture of where and to whom he wanted it to go. The bird flapped its wings three times, gained altitude and glided away over the wall, just as the gates were forced open.

"I am here, *Suketomo-sama*."

Hino looked around. Jiro Katsuchiyo, the bushi assigned to escort him, appeared from inside the house. He wore his full set of armour, including the fierce *kabuto* and face mask. His hands were tucked in his belt, close to the hilt of his curved *tachi* blade.

"Offer them the terms," Hino said calmly.

"Can they be trusted to agree?"

"We will see, but it is discourteous not to offer."

Jiro nodded and strode forwards towards the milling crowd, Hino a careful two steps behind. As they approached, the Tokimichi bushi moved aside and lowered their weapons. The *bakufu* soldiers outside did the same.

"Honorable *Suketomo-sama* wishes to leave the House of Tokimichi and return to his own lands," Jiro declared.

"This is not acceptable to us," someone shouted in answer. A foreign woman stepped forward. Hino recognised her from the meetings, but couldn't recall her name. An *onna-bugeisha*, she wore a simple kimono, carefully cut to allow room for movement and carried a six-foot naginata, its curved blade catching the afternoon sun. "We will fight, champion of Suketomo. If you win, your master may leave."

Jiro nodded in response and the bushi of both sides cleared a space around the gates. Hino stepped back as well, eyeing the woman and trying to recall what he knew of her. Nothing more than the memory of her face came to mind. She had betrayed them, but he had no idea why.

Jiro drew his sword and took a step forwards. In response, the woman adopted a fighting crouch and gripped her polearm in both hands, but did not advance. The expectant crowd quieted and Jiro took another step, but still the woman didn't move. Her eyes remained fixed on a point on the floor in front of where he stood.

Jiro raised his sword and moved forwards again, this time, bringing the weapon down in a high arc towards the woman's head. She dodged aside, but the blade nicked her left shoulder, tearing through the kimono and making a small cut in the bunched muscle. Around the thin line of blood, Hino could see many other scars. Plainly she had fought many times before.

"Thank you," the woman said. Hino wondered what she meant, but then she moved forward on the balls of her feet, nimbly evading Jiro's attempt to crowd her. The naginata flicked out, its curved blade scoring the paint on his left greave before she brought the wooden shaft up to block another katana cut and circled away.

Jiro stalked her down; a flurry of strikes were exchanged, the katana cutting gouges out of the naginata, but the polearm held. In turn, Jiro took a succession of blows, one slicing into the flesh along his thigh.

Hino sensed power in the woman. She all but glowed as she moved around, impossibly fast, seeming to know where and when Jiro would strike, evading and parrying the katana with a twist or turn at exactly the right moment.

Then Jiro grabbed her wrist, dragging her towards him and thrusting the blade into her chest. She gasped and coughed blood into the dirt. Jiro let go and kicked out expecting her to slump to the ground.

But she didn't. She reversed the naginata and jabbed the blade into his throat, all but severing his head from his shoulders.

Jiro fell backwards and crashed to the earth, his body thrashing before she stepped forwards and rammed her weapon into his chest, cracking the armoured plate and the breast bone with impossible strength.

The woman stepped over the body and stared at Hino, a widening red stain spreading across the front of her kimono. "You will come with me," she announced through bloodied teeth.

Unable to speak, Hino could only nod and accept his fate.

Two days later, Milen was dead.

Galina couldn't stop crying. She hadn't loved him, but she had grown to care for him. The way he gave up part of his life to share with her and Katya meant so much. When she'd confessed her reluctance to be touched, he accepted her choice with a rueful smile. In seventeen years, he never once tried to persuade or force her to change her mind.

He had been an honest and good man.

She went downstairs to find Katya asleep in one of the large chairs near the smouldering hearth. She looked exhausted. Every night, they'd used the magic, repeating their efforts to help Milen rally. The previous evening had been busy and he was well enough to work for a little while before growing tired and returning to bed.

Galina walked over to her sister and gently shook her awake.

"He's gone."

Katya nodded. "I think I felt it, or dreamed he passed. What do we do?"

"We leave or we stay," Galina said. "Maybe we'll be let alone, as people turn to their own problems."

"Teach me to read," Katya said.

"What?"

"Teach me to read. You learned some letters from father when we were children and have practised since. I need to write to remember what I've done."

"More experimenting may not be wise," Galina warned. "We'll attract attention."

"If we aren't prepared for when we are discovered, it won't matter," Katya said. "We need to be able to defend ourselves and help others."

Galina felt the tears returning. "Milen was a gentle soul."

"If I knew more, perhaps I could have helped him."

There was a knock at the door to the common room. Katya got up and opened it. Their only lodger, a middle aged German woman, was there.

"My apologies I did not wish to disturb…"

"No, its fine Gurda, what do you need?"

"I thought to make breakfast. Perhaps I could cook for you both?"

Galina sighed. "That would be… nice… I'm sorry I didn't sleep…"

"Of course, leave it to me."

Gurda negotiated her way into the kitchen and busied herself without question or complaint. She wore a simple green cassock, tied around her stocky body with a thin rope. Her hair was a mixture of grey and brown, bundled up into a ponytail. She'd arrived at the tavern three days ago with few belongings and paid for two weeks, mostly keeping to herself, with an occasional venture out into the city.

Galina took her sister's hand. "You want to stay," she whispered. "But it will be dangerous. Our best chance is to leave, go back to Bregovo and see if they will accept us."

"I'm not leaving," Katya said.

"There is nothing for us here."

"There is everything for us here. We didn't come for Milen, we came to be more than what we were. We've made a life here, but we've hidden what we are. Perhaps it's time—"

"Time you embraced your nature?" Gurda said, emerging from the kitchen carrying a tray with three steaming bowls, *bob chorba* by the smell. "The world is a difficult place for women alone without friends."

Galina frowned at her. "How long were you—"

"Listening? For most of the morning and at times in the days before that. You are the reason I came here." Gurda put the tray down on a table and drew up a chair. "Come eat, I mean you no harm."

Neither sister moved. Galina could see Katya flexing her fingers and guessed what she might attempt. To forestall, she moved forwards and took a seat. "Who are you?"

"I am who I said," Gurda replied, dipping a wooden spoon into her bowl and slurping down the contents. "I did not lie to you."

"But you didn't tell us the whole truth," Katya said. She stepped to the empty chair, but didn't sit. "You are of the old blood."

"I am."

"And you know what we are."

"Yes, as I said, I came here for you, although you hide yourselves well and took some time to locate," Gurda continued between mouthfuls of *bob chorba*. "I had to be certain of you and be sure you were ready for what comes next."

"And what would that be?"

"To learn of the world and your place," the bowl was empty. Gurda tipped it sideways to spoon up the dregs and then pushed it aside. "You said it yourselves. You built yourselves a mortal life here, but you are not mortal, you are gifted. You are starting to understand what that means. People will grow old and die around you. Some, like Milen, you can help for a time, but not for long. There will be talk, whispers about your solitary ways and the like. Eventually the Church will come here and you will be marked out." She grimaced. "In the south lands, the papacy names us sorcerers and witches, passing laws to have us hunted down and burned according to the directives in their book." She favoured them both with a bitter smile. "Words, like many things are granted power by those who believe in them." She tapped a finger on the table and fixed Katya with a stare. "Come, your soup grows cold. You must eat before we leave."

"Where are we going?"

"As I said; to find your place in the world."

I urge you your holiness, to empower our cause. The heathen and heretic walk amongst us, provoking the wrath of our Lord. You have given us sanction, but now we need active support. The churches of the faithful must ring out in denunciation of the devil's practice.

We have seen omens. People starve all across the land as sin rampages unchecked. The witch we hunt here is but a symptom of what lies ahead. Armies of demons rise from the east to consume the light of our faith. We must be strong and true. Only by purging dissent and heresy can we be forged as true soldiers of the Lord. We must carry his banner to the maw of the beast, so that we may cleanse the world of its taint.

Richard De Ledrede – Bishop of Ossory.

Chapter 10: The Stones

"*Suketomo-sama*?"

Hino glanced up from where he sat on the cold stone floor of the prison cell. A woman stood at the door, carrying a staff and dressed in the strange clothes of another land. She was beautiful, in a way that many women were in drawings and paintings, pristine, perfect and different all at the same time. She was not Japanese, but he recognised her immediately and smiled.

"Lady Rani, you are a long way from home," he said in halting Urdu.

She remained at the door, eyeing him with a look of pity. He accepted it. He knew what he was, a man in rags with a black eye, broken fingers and toes, a frustration to those who wished harm to the Emperor. His lodgings were stark and odorous, a full bucket waiting to be taken away and rice cake scraps littering a straw bed. "I asked the *bakufu* to release you to me," she announced. "I will take you to other lands, where you can do no further damage to them."

"What did they say?"

"They are deliberating, but want admissions from you, implicating the Emperor."

"That will never happen."

She nodded. "I understand what you want, but we cannot permit it. A war would undermine our efforts for everyone."

He smiled again. "War is already here. If I had succeeded, the disturbance would have been minimal. Others want what I want and what the Emperor wants."

"Then petition for reform," Rani urged, "not this."

"It is too late."

She sighed. "People fear change."

"People fear the loss of power," he replied. "Change must come if the path of the old blood is to reach its end. We cannot achieve *nirvana* without change."

Rani sighed again and a line marred the perfection of her forehead. "You are strange. Nobles of your land usually value honour and death above these things."

Hino smiled. "Your experience teaches us all. My death is certain. What it achieves in this life remains in question."

"So you sacrifice yourself for this."

"Your own moment of ascension was similar according to the legends. I may yet attain the eternal state. I am respected by those around the Emperor."

"The longer you remain here, the more likely they will forget you."

Hino shrugged. "And what of it? How long since you vanished from the lives of your people? You are forgotten whilst others you remember ascend and dream."

She let the words hang between them in the damp air for a long time. Finally she spoke again. "The day of the martyr is long past for you. Do you hear what they say? *Let Lord Suketomo be struck down.* They care nothing for you."

Hino shook his head. "There is always a day for martyrs. Do not think other religions monopolise such things."

Rani stepped towards him and knelt down. "I need you alive," she said in a low voice. "The point is proven here. If you disappear with me, your supporters will not believe the *bakufu* when they claim you left Japan."

"Your plan is agreeable if I make no admission," Hino said. "If the shoguns agree to that, I will come with you and learn the ways of other gods."

"I would prefer you kept your own faith," Rani said. "You are far more enlightened than you realise."

Within an hour, Katya and Galina had gathered clothes and packed their belongings. Gurda did the same. She moved slowly up and down the stairs, getting in their way at times and leaning on her stick as she went. When everything was ready, her gathering of possessions was the smallest of the three.

"When you travel as I do, you get a better idea of what you need," she said, smiling at Katya's confusion. "Don't worry about me."

Another knock at the door interrupted the conversation. Gurda went over and opened it, letting in an old man in a hooded cloak. Katya recognised him as the corpseman who drove the cart on the street. "Katya, Galina, this is Obydiah, he is here to help with Milen."

The old man bowed. "My sympathies to you both," he said. "I came on foot and wasn't followed. The house will remain unmarked and no folk will learn what transpired."

91

"Are you from the Church?" Katya asked.

"You mean are we sanctioned wizards?" Gurda shook her head. "No, we hold no allegiance to them."

"Do you know Faim?"

Gurda smiled. Despite her dour face, the expression was warm and reassuring. "Yes, although I have not seen him for some time."

"Did he send you to us?"

"No."

"Then why should we trust you?"

"If I were here to kill you, I would have done so already."

A tense silence ensued. Obydiah drew back his hood, drawing stares from them all and breaking the standoff. He appeared older than Gurda, but moved lightly, like a young man, and was long-faced and bald with wisps of white hair above his ears Light guileless eyes made him seem honest. "I'll take your husband away and bury him deep, so the dogs won't find him. Whilst you're gone, I'll keep an eye on the place too. Can't be too careful."

Galina frowned. "Milen's family will wonder—"

"We have a plan for that," Gurda said, cutting her off. "But, if you're both ready..."

"We're leaving now?"

"Yes."

Katya picked up her belongings. Reluctantly, Galina did the same. They followed Gurda through the door and out into the yard.

A misty overcast morning greeted them, with few shadowy shapes of people outside. Gurda gestured and they made their way towards the harbour. The mist rolled from the Danube into the town and they walked straight into it, Gurda taking care on the uneven portions of the road.

Katya glanced at the houses as they passed. Some bore the plague mark on their doors, a cross daubed in blood red paint. As they neared the riverside, she saw more and more people huddled on the ground, or watching them from alleyways. Their looks of hunger and despair invoked feelings of guilt and shame in her. She drew her hood up and focused on the road.

Gurda led them from the main street into a darkened alley between two tall houses. "From here on, the world gets smaller," she said and lifted her walking stick above her head. It seemed to grow in her hands, until it became taller than her, a mass of writhing vines and worm-like bodies, undulating in her grip.

A flicker of movement in the shadows drew Katya's attention. The air rippled and flexed like water. She felt power here; a strange dislocated sensation, as if she were in two places at once.

"Follow me," Gurda said. She walked toward the distortion and disappeared.

Galina gasped in surprise. Katya almost ran, but managed to control herself, sensing her sister's panic. She looked at Galina and nodded. *If we hesitate, we'll never go,* she thought.

Boldly, they both stepped forward and vanished.

Piers Gaveston awoke in darkness, shivering.

He was soaked through, propped against a slimy stone wall, his right arm bent at an awkward angle. Twitching his fingers sent shooting pains through everything. *I've broken bones then,* he thought.

Slowly he raised his head to peer upwards. A small circle of light illuminated some of the brick work and he realised where he was. *I'm in the well.* The revelation didn't bring much comfort, nor did noting his position propped on a ledge, his legs dangling below. The water level reached his knees and gave no indication of its depth.

He guessed he'd been pushed in and been lucky to land on the shelf, otherwise he might have drowned. As it was, the landing had caused injuries, probably enough to prevent him climbing out.

That meant a slow death.

Ignoring the pain, he shifted around, levering himself into a sitting position. He thought about magic; in this state his only hope for escape. The limited number of spells he remembered would need a plan attached to them and also a clear head.

He recalled the last time things were this desperate, kneeling in the road at Blacklow Hill, a sword stuck through his chest. With the second blow about to sever his head, some instinct brought out his magic in a raw utterance of power, killing both of his captors.

Here, such an answer wouldn't help.

His thoughts turned to what he'd given up, his wife Margaret and new born daughter. He'd seen her for a few days after his return from exile, days he would treasure. *Will she have the gift? Likely I'll never know.*

He thought about Edward. They'd become friends as soon as they'd met. Piers knew what he was being asked to do by the Church, to manipulate the prince, but the task never came between them, not until the end.

Now he was alone and Edward was king, surrounded by men like Pembroke.

Aymer de Valence was honourable. By all accounts, Edward trusted him now, otherwise he would not have been sent to France, but he would never be the King's confidante. *Not like I was.* Piers could reason with the man, if he got out of the well.

He took a deep breath, stilling himself, searching for the magic. The process was difficult. The ritual in Avignon had shattered his faith, meaning he no longer accessed the vast stream of power other sanctioned wizards used. He could not tap a source he did not believe in. *The sleeping eternals in the tombs of Rome are deluded, no God exists; no paradise waits for the dead.*

Instead, he had to reach inside and draw from his own sense of self and certitude. In any weaving, an amount of the wizard's own energies would be used, but the benefit of being part of the Church meant the support of thousands affirming their belief. Those without the gift could not comprehend the power they held as a massed congregation. Wizards within the faith were able to access that power, which was why the religion had been built as a structured hierarchy. The path to God and heaven lay through priests, ascending toward the pinnacle, the papacy, *the voice of the Lord on Earth*, that was the doctrine, the lie and illusion.

The spell opened like a flower in his mind, floating petals unwrapping into bloom. The surge of power flowed through him, warming his hands and feet, awaking fresh hurts and injuries, things that required attention.

Piers grabbed his left wrist with his right hand and pulled, hard. Splinters of bone in his forearm ground against each other; he heard screaming and realised it came from his own throat, but he was too far gone to stop. The bones must be aligned correctly or the magic would heal them as they were and he would never regain full use of his limbs. Piers was no expert, but had healed himself several times and knew what to expect. He turned his attention to his hand and did the same, straightening his broken thumb and index finger. Then he felt along his body, pushing and prodding at ribs and hip, probing for internal damage, his hands passing over the puffy scar on his chest. This time, mercifully he found nothing worse than the arm and some cuts and bruises.

With a groan he let the spell go and sagged back against the slippery stone wall, exhausted.

Galina stumbled as she stepped into the distortion. For an instant she sensed a between space, a cold nothing or nowhere, but then it was gone and the shadows of the alleyway seemed to draw back, revealing something startling.

She was no longer in an alleyway at all, no longer in a town. Instead she found herself standing on a grassy hilltop under a sunny sky. The thin green shoots gave off an earthy smell, as if she had awoken in the early morning dew. The air had a crisp feel, a freshness that banished any thought of rest and demanded attention.

"Where are we?" Katya asked.

"The Giant's Dance," Gurda replied, her staff writhing and contracting into the walking stick it had been before. "We're a day or so from the south coast of England. This has always been a place of power, from the earliest days."

Galina blinked and looked around. Standing stones surrounded them. Each was at least eight foot tall, arranged in a circle and bridged by a lintel of almost equivalent size, making a perfect ring of archways. She turned all around and caught sight of a familiar flicker from the one behind her.

"These are portals," Gurda explained. "This is a nexus of entry ways, used by those powerful and skilful enough to navigate them. From here we can go to any number of locations across the world."

Galina approached the arch, touching the stone gingerly. A faint tingle of remembered magic thrilled in her fingers and for a moment, she glimpsed writing on the pillar's surface, but then it was gone. "Who made these?" she asked.

"Lesser minds like yours," Gurda said, "those with the eye of the gift, but little ability or power." She waved her hand at the stones. "These passages were crafted long ago, by people who are long forgotten. It is said this site is dedicated to an old Goddess of the Moon. Some gifted hag of the blood, no doubt. In the last two thousand years, hundreds have been constructed, enabling wizards to travel vast distances in little time."

"Why did you bring us here?" Katya said.

"To show you what is possible," Gurda pointed at the archway they had used. "For now that door is connected to the old Dunonian passageway in Vidin, but it can be shifted elsewhere as well. I will teach you the spell that opens these and how to move them. Each requires a different touch, but gradually you will master them all." She hobbled toward another archway and passed through it, onto the grass beyond. "The stones are harmless unless invoked, although this place can be busy, come!"

Galina followed her out of the stone circle. "If I am a lesser mind, why are you bothering with me?" she asked.

"Because of the bond you share," Gurda replied. "There are many with the gift remaining unaware, living mortal lives as mortals do. Some in their ignorance age and die as mortals. Such a waste! But you two, one with the power, the other with insight, you are special and different. That is why I brought you here."

"What do you want?"

Gurda smiled. "To win your loyalty to my purpose and not see you murdered by the Church."

By nightfall, Piers reached the top of the well.

The vine spell he learned from Elbo Smogg all those years ago proved successful in helping him climb, but left him exhausted and starving. The use of magic drained him utterly and he collapsed in a heap on the ground.

He lay there for a while, gazing at the stars and shivering. The gift made him stronger and less frail than ordinary folk, but the same weaknesses would end him as it would anyone else. Only the most powerful transcended their mortal form and became eternal, to live forever as a guide to all humankind. He smiled bitterly, *the chosen of a God who never existed.*

He stood up on wobbling legs and stumbled towards the house. There were no lanterns lit and moonlight gave everything a greyish cast. When he got to the door he discovered a painted red cross on the wood. Inside windows were broken, tables turned over and everything ruined. He remembered the woman. *What has she done?*

Piers' fatigue vanished. He went to the stables. The horses were gone. The lifeless body of Renarre lay in the straw staring up at the sky. He'd been stabbed in the chest several times. Piers knelt down and closed his eyes.

He returned to the house. He found flint, steel and a candle. Nursing the flame he went upstairs to Pembroke's room. Less had been disturbed, but the sheets were bloodied and the earl's clothes were in a pile on a chair. *What happened?*

He picked up a long cloak and wrapped it around his own wet garments then checked the other rooms – all empty and abandoned. A lady's necklace and rings had been discarded on a table. He pocketed them, and went back downstairs. He lit a fire in the hearth with the flint and steel, righted an arm chair and sat back to think.

The woman intended harm to the earl, that much was certain. The bloodied sheets and Renarre's death meant she'd probably killed him.

Without Pembroke's mission, England and France would go to war, *which must be her plan.*

As his clothes dried, Piers wondered what he could do. The events were beyond him, even if he crossed the distance to England and alerted Edward, the effort would mean nothing, but his heart ached to go anyway. If Pembroke's soldiers were alive, they would head back. A journey to Paris and King Charles would only see him branded a liar and found by the Church inquisitors.

His thoughts turned to the woman; stocky, overweight and middle-aged, more at home in a mill house or on a farm than murdering earls. She had the gift and would be anxious to leave the region. *She'll make for a portal,* he thought. *She may have come here through one in the first place.*

When he was dry, he got up and went to the kitchen. He found the room in a worse state than everywhere else; the stores emptied all over the tables and floor. *They were looking for something. Poison?*

He collected up the unused stale trenchers, biting into one. It was hard going and tasteless, but it was food and by that count, better than anything he'd eaten in more than a day. Three disappeared before he acquired a knapsack to stow more. They would serve for a short walk. He picked up a knife, slipping it into his belt, before reversing the earl's cloak to conceal its emblem, then stepped out of the Inn and into the darkness, making for Amiens, the nearest town and the most likely place the woman would have gone.

The trail would be cold, but still there.

Chapter 11: Giant Dances

"And how do you intend to win our approval?" Galina asked.

"Watch and judge for yourself," Gurda replied.

Katya felt a tingling in her hands. She looked over her shoulder at the stones and the space between the pillars they had come through rippled. A man in robes appeared and stepped through into the grass circle. She recognised him as the priest from the local church. He glanced at the other archways before catching sight of them on the hillside. He smiled and made his way towards them.

"I had hoped to catch you, it is time we had a proper conversation I—"

"Come no closer," Gurda warned, placing herself between him and Katya. "We know what you are."

He halted and the smile became strained. "You brought them here I take it?"

"I did."

"To what end?"

"So they can choose for themselves."

The smile disappeared. "There is no choice to make," the priest said. "The lonely existence of parasites like you is no comparison to the kinship we offer. By working together, we further everyone's path toward heaven."

Gurda gave a bitter laugh. "Ah yes, your pyramid of faith, proclaimed to all religions; the blind mortals sing and chant, invoking their God through their prophets and priests. You all share in this soup of lies, promising them paradise for their life of confession and honest tithe!"

The priest's expression hardened. "You mock me."

"You peddle a mockery to the world in the name of morality! What proof is there a better world exists at the end of your promises?"

"Both of you stop!" Katya shouted and surprisingly, they did, turning towards her with matching expressions of curiosity. "You're fighting over us, as if we're to be owned," she said. "What makes you think we'll accept either choice?"

"Because I offer you the truth," the priest said. He glanced at Galina. "I helped you, gave you a life when you were cold and alone on the streets."

"And for that you expect me to serve you?"

"No! That's not what our path is about, let me explain!"

"Then do so," Katya said.

The priest straightened his shoulders. "You know me. My name is Petŭr, I was raised in Sredets as a boy, before being taken into the Church when I came into my gift. The elders schooled me in channelling my talent and taught me of its origins. We are the Angels, descendants of the Lord's chosen, granted magic in this world that we may serve him better. By leading the mortals in worship, I gain his favour and his aid," he raised his right hand, which began to glow. "I humbly walk with the trust of nations, the support of thousands; we will deliver our people to the Promised Land."

"You have been lied to, priest," Gurda spat. "Your ancestors lie in tombs, dreaming of a paradise that does not exist!" She took a step towards him up the hill and raised her walking stick. "You call me a parasite, but in truth, you are an institution of parasites, following the direction of the mad and deluded!"

"And the alternative? A lifetime watching your friends and loved ones die? Of being vilified for being different?" Pietr's hand grew brighter and he clenched his fingers into a fist. "Outside of order and purpose there is no legacy, you will fade and be forgotten."

"And this is where you fail," Gurda said. "I know your ways. I was once one of you. Other paths exist beyond your rigid world." She stepped into the ring of stones, her walking stick, expanding once more. "This place was built by people who worshipped different gods and dreamed different dreams, a vibrant world with many voices. In your reality, we are condemned to believe ourselves unworthy of our lives, continually yearning towards a perfect world we will never achieve." She pointed at Katya. "You would condemn these women to a world of self-doubt."

"You wrong us."

"No. I see you clearly!" Gurda raised her staff and spoke guttural words. Katya flinched as power surged through the air, focusing around her then splintering into six points on the grass, two of them next to Pietr. "Worship is not the only source open to us, priest!" Gurda snarled. The hilltop groaned as dark wood trees ripped themselves out of the earth, their branches hooked and spiky, grabbing at the priest's arms and legs. He screamed as his robes tore and the coiling limbs seized him, digging thorns through skin, flesh and bone.

Then he vanished.

The vicious trees remained, their limbs groping the air for something, anything. To Katya, they were unnatural; leafless and animated, like the worst thorn bush you ever saw, if it was capable of wanting to hurt you.

Gurda grunted disconsolately. "I might have guessed."

"Is he dead?" Galina asked quietly.

"No, he escaped. A little trick sanctioned wizards can use if they're prepared, a spell that ports them to somewhere safe. Utterly draining though, we'll not meet him again," she turned to Katya. "It wasn't wise to let him talk."

"The alternative was to accept what you tell us," Galina said. "Faim told us to make our own decisions, not blindly trust anyone."

Gurda sighed. "I am not Faim. He would have the eyes of the gifted opened and the Church starve, yet this provides no answer, only suffering. Time turns and we must act to change the course. With Faim's freedom, you wasted yourselves in a mortal life, a snare to capture the ignorant. How do you think Pietr followed us?"

"He tracked your magic," Katya said, "when you brought us here."

"My spells would not have roused him, despite the burden of bringing your sister," Gurda said. "The death of his creature however..."

"His creature?" Katya glanced at Galina, whose face paled in shock. "You mean Milen?"

"Yes," Gurda also stared at Galina. "Your dead husband and benefactor, a tool of the Church."

"That's not true! He loved me!"

"Only as much as you loved him."

The depths of night. Hino raised his head from the straw mattress. Keys rattled and the door to the cell creaked open.

"Quickly, *Suketomo-sama*!"

He rose from the bed. A hand grabbed his arm and led him swiftly into the dark corridor, along to the end and down a staircase. His eyes were used to the gloom, but the speed they were going made his injured feet unsure. He stumbled and the hand let go, he fell to his knees on the stone floor.

"Get up, quickly!"

A black shadow stood above him. Hino blocked out the pain and struggled up in answer. There was a shout and footsteps behind. He turned to see *bakufu* bushi arriving bearing torches, their curved swords drawn.

The shadowed figure moved fast, throwing blades with both hands. The knive caught the first two pursuers, one in the throat, the other, the leg. They both went down.

Hino ran the other way and didn't look back, passing through a series of rooms into a large open courtyard. A solitary candle lit the space and Lady Rani stood at the far end, beside a wooden frame set against the stone. The air rippled within it.

"Hino!"

He didn't need to be told. He sprinted towards her, eyes fixed on the distortion. More shouting followed; then orders and screams of agony. Then something slapped against his right leg, driving him to the left. When his foot came down again, pain shot through him and his leg refused to bear his weight. He stumbled again, but caught himself, limping the last few steps and diving head first into the frame, towards the wall, trusting the magic…

…and found himself flat on his face in grassy mud.

Hino glanced up to see the rising sun from a hilltop surrounded by standing stones. Strange waving trees guarded two of them, gradually crumbling away as he stared. He felt the pain in his leg again and rolled over. An arrow was sticking through his calf. He clenched his teeth, fighting down the pain and panic. Lady Rani appeared in the stone archway he had passed through. She waved at the rippling air and the portal spell ended. Then she knelt at his feet.

"Can you walk?"

"I fear not."

Her hands on his leg were cool and gentle until she grasped the arrow, snapped off the end and started to push it back through the flesh. He almost screamed, but kept his mouth clamped shut, so the noise came out as a long whimper. The shaft popped out, making the pain even worse if it were possible, but then her fingertips brushed the wound, soothing the hurt. He caught her mumbling words and felt the tingle of magic. "You'll live," she announced as it faded. "We need to get moving."

He stood up again, favouring the leg. "Who was your companion?"

Rani smiled, "Someone brave." She held out a bundle of cloth. He took it, finding a wrapped *tachi* inside. His family sword. He stared at her.

"How did you…"

Rani pressed a finger to his lips. "You know what I am and what I am capable of. Come." She hurried to another arch, Hino a step behind at his best pace, noting the expanding ripple as she cast the spell and went straight through. He followed…

Tuia stood on stone – the platform of a large unfinished structure – a hollowed four sided pyramid, built with huge blocks. He'd watched them being made, some were gigantic bricks, others fusions of the broken rocks transported from the other side of the lake to this strange island.

Torchlight surrounded him and below, the workers chanted. The phrases were an incantation and prayer, proclaiming their faith to the Gods who brought them here to build this city, the last city of the world.

On one side, a set of steps reached down to the ground. Already the building was taller than houses, at least three times the height of the largest in Chimor. On the steps were prisoners. They shuffled forwards, flanked by soldiers in mantles and bright coloured headdresses. Some of them were the people he'd followed through the jungle. Each flash of recognition struck a blow against his resolve.

Tuia turned away and drew the knife from his belt. A wide blade, curved and with a hooking point, unlike anything he'd ever owned before. The woman had given it to him when he'd sworn the oath she demanded, nicking his chest with it to seal their bargain in blood. He knew what it would have meant if he'd refused – *execution.*

The second wound the knife made was in her wrist. She made him drink of her. That night he dreamed of power.

A lifetime ago he'd carved wood into shapes. This knife was made for a different sort of carving.

The platform wasn't quite flat, but raked slightly at the edge on all sides, descending to the centre. In the middle was a small round hole, no bigger than a baby's head. Beneath Tuia he could hear expectant voices, waiting.

The first prisoner stepped forward; an old man, naked, grey haired and fearful. He wore a clay symbol on a cord around his neck. Tuia grabbed it and snapped the string, dropping the keepsake into the hole, provoking a shout in response. Then he seized the man by the hair, dragging him into position, forcing him to kneel and tipping his head back.

The hook of the knife tore into the soft skin of the man's neck. He made a gurgling gasp and bright red blood poured out, soaking his emaciated chest. Tuia reversed the blade and drew a second line from collar bone to penis, opening the man's flesh and pushed him forward, to fall, face first onto the stone.

Blood pooled and ran into the cracks between the stone, the angle of the platform driving it all to the centre, to the hole. It dripped through, running down onto the people below...

Who cheered.

Carefully, Tuia licked the blood from the blade and kicked the corpse from the platform, to fall onto the ground below. He gestured to the mantled guards who pushed the next prisoner forward, a child no more than ten, his stare an accusation.

The guilt came back, but Tuia ignored it and brandished the knife, stepping towards him.

Chapter 12: The Ancient City

"You're safe now."

Bright sunlight made Hino blink back tears. The pain of his wounds had faded and he stared into the smiling face of a little boy, his little boy, Kumi.

"Where am I?"

"I don't know," the boy replied.

Hino tried to raise his head, to take Kumi in his arms, but he couldn't move, only stare. "You're not really my son," he realised aloud.

"No I'm not."

"Then who are you?"

"Someone who cares." The boy's hand stroked his forehead. "Relax. They will need you and without my aid you will not be able to help them."

For a moment, Hino thought about asking more questions, but Kumi's expression had become serious, the hand on his head was insistent, and his eyes strained in the light. Time to let go, sleep and let the healing begin.

He closed his eyes.

At the monastery of Sado Island, a boy stood in front of the middle gate.

A monk came to meet him. "Is there a reason that you wait here?" he asked.

The boy stared. A solitary tear ran down the side of his cheek. "I am the son of Lord Hino Suketomo come a long way on foot to be with my father at the last."

The monk stared at the boy for long moments before inclining his head. The boy did the same. Without another word the monk turned away and disappeared inside.

It began to rain. Heavy droplets that soaked the boy's shift and sandals, but he did not move or seek shelter, he stayed and waited, waiting long into the afternoon.

Eventually the monk returned. "Homma of Yamashiro will see you," he said and opened the gate.

The boy walked down the path, following his guide to a small hall. Another robed man knelt in the centre of a wooden floor. He stood, turned and bowed.

"I am Homma of Yamashiro and you are the son of *Suketomo-sama*, Hino Kunimitsu also known as Master Kumawaka."

The boy nodded. "Where is my father?" he asked.

Homma frowned and his gaze slipped to the floor. "You may not see him," he said.

"I am here to be with him."

"Nevertheless, it cannot happen."

The boy cast himself to the floor to catch Homma's eye. On bloody knees, he clasped the robes of the monk. "I beg you... please," he said.

Homma pulled away and went to the door. "You will remain here, until I decide what to do with you," he said.

When he was gone and the door closed, the boy let himself cry.

At dawn, Piers reached the small church. He felt better than before, the trenchers in his knapsack had vanished. Bland fare, but fuel to his exhausted body.

He put a hand to the wooden doors and found them slightly ajar. He pushed gently to ensure he made the minimum noise and slipped inside.

The two lines of pews that greeted him were empty, just as well. He walked between them, his footsteps soft and careful, reaching the rood screen. Once there, he touched the wood, exploring it carefully, trying to find magic.

A small thrill went through him as his fingertips brushed the arch to the left of the aisle. *Here!* Quickly he traced along the whole section, ensuring there were no imperfections or breakages. This was the portal and it had been used recently.

"How may I help you my son?"

The priest's voice over his shoulder was calm and gentle. Piers froze, gripped with indecision. A sanctioned wizard left to monitor this church would quickly overpower him with magic, but if the man was an innocent...

He didn't turn around, but his hand went to the handle of the knife he'd taken from the Inn kitchen. "I came to pay my respects, father."

"Then why are you here and not seated as others would be?"

Piers turned slowly. A priest was standing between the pews, some distance away with a lantern, wearing clothes he'd hastily thrown on and staring blearily. Piers raised his hands, palms open, fingers spread. "I didn't mean to disturb you father," he said, taking a step towards him.

"The Lord is always watching, but his servants need their sleep," the priest said with a tired smile. "What troubles you so much that you must be here at this hour?"

"When a man is troubled, sleep is the last thing on his mind," Piers replied. Another two steps and he stopped. "I must lay my sin aside before I can rest."

"Confession is not something I can grant you now, I—"

Piers dived at him and grabbed him by the throat, driving him backwards and into the wall. "Forgive me father," he said then dashed the man's head against the stone. His eyes rolled and he slipped to the floor, unconscious.

Piers went back to the rood screen. *Have I the strength to activate it?* he wondered. A portal spell on his best days as a sanctioned wizard had been difficult with the power of the Church behind him. Now, as a faithless heretic, the cost would come from him alone.

I have to try.

He traced the line of magic, trying to focus on the previous spell. The trace remained faint, but he managed to grasp it and spoke the words, sensing the air tense and ripple.

Will it hold?

Gritting his teeth, he stepped forward.

Galina sighed with relief when, finally, light welled out of Katya's hands, illuminating the rock around her.

"Well done," said Gurda, her voice laboured, betraying her exhaustion. "The cave entrance should be around to the right."

After the priest disappeared, they'd transported from the hilltop through a different arch. When they were through, Gurda ended the spell and sat down, declaring she needed a rest and bidding them keep quiet for a time.

Galina seated herself and tried to get comfortable, She'd shut her eyes, only to be shaken awake what seemed only moments later. Then she waited, whilst Gurda instructed Katya in how to use her magic to make light.

They were in a hewn cave. Writing lined the rough walls, mixed together with paintings and symbols. Galina saw a strange cut groove in the stone, running upwards in a rectangular shape, like a doorway; the exit of the portal perhaps?

"What is this place?" she asked.

"Somewhere forgotten," Gurda replied. "Abandoned when the great orders discovered what is happening to the world." She got up from the floor and Galina caught sight of bare skin beneath the sleeve of her thin dress. Her arm was covered in pustules and swellings. Gurda looked at her and jerked the garment back into place.

"Are you all right?" Galina asked.

"I'm fine," Gurda snapped. "Tired, owing to the effort of dragging you with us, I only hope you prove to be worth it."

"But… you are unwell…"

"The infections I carry are no concern of yours."

"They are if you afflict us."

"I will not."

"How can you be sure?"

"Trust me." Gurda moved past them both, feeling her way along the wall into the darkness. "Hurry," she called.

Galina glanced at Katya who shrugged. "We need to know, otherwise we're trapped here."

"Agreed."

The passageway curled to the right and opened out into a wide hall of smooth marble stone. They found Gurda in its centre. A florid gesture from her and candles around the room sprang into life.

"Behold the council chamber of the orders," she announced, "now a relic to their fear. In this place, the wizard lords of all religions came to discuss the future of the world."

Galina stared. The room was larger than any she'd ever seen. Light reflected from the floor and more painted pictures covered the walls. "Why abandon such a place?" she asked in wonder. Her eyes alighted on a strange stone sphere in the middle, held up at eye level by a vertical pillar. "What is this?" she asked.

"Our world," Gurda said.

"The world is round?"

"Yes."

"In our village, the elders told us the world is flat," Katya said. "Which should we believe?"

Gurda chuckled and sat down next to the sphere. The two girls did the same. Galina noticed there were pins in the object, metal needles, sticking out in different directions. "The council of orders built this to represent the centre of all things. Around it circle their ideas of the domains in existence, places like heaven on the ceiling, purgatory on the walls, hell on the ground and many others. The spiritual kingdoms of all religions are depicted here."

"But this is all the artifice of the last two millennia. These halls are much older, built in a time before people sought dominion over each other, when those with the magic stood apart, leaving the different peoples to rule themselves," Gurda fixed Galina with a stare. "But then, legends say these ancients chose one people over all others because that people offered them worship as gods. As you know, worship conveys power and the old ones could not resist the lure. This began the age of humanity and their spread across all lands."

"Through power, the ancients discovered a way to shed their mortal forms. Humanity prayed to them and revered them until they became the gods they once aspired to be."

"But the ascended ones fell into slumber. The reverie is a world of dreams, but those within perceive the dreams as real." Gurda gestured around the chamber. "Some say they visit other worlds and places, which is where these realms come from."

"Over time, some ancients became too close to their charges. The old blood mixed with that of mortals and much was lost. Yet, this blending brought new insight. The children born to gifted and mortal cannot wield power, but they can perceive it and understand how it works. Their keen minds developed our understanding, enabling the construction of devices to enhance the magic of wizards." Gurda tapped her strange walking stick on the tiles. "Items like this." She smiled at Galina, but the expression didn't reach her eyes. "You made something similar did you not?"

"Yes."

"Show me."

Slowly, Galina drew out the half-finished stave she'd made at the river seventeen years ago and held it out. "I couldn't find any more pieces," she said.

"You weren't meant to," Gurda replied. "By this method, a staff can take years to construct. The fragments must resonate for it to work. Some are never finished."

"You could have told us this story back at the tavern," Katya said. "Why bring us here?"

Gurda turned on her. "Would you have believed it? You'll see shortly," she said and smiled as if laughing to herself about a private joke. She cleared her throat. "The mix-blooded have a mind for structures and patterns. So it was that they began to stratify the worship of the mortals. To begin, they created pantheons, with elaborate rituals for each god. Later they constructed the monotheistic religions, placing those already in reverie at the top of their hierarchies. It is not known if there ever was a true creator, but many faiths speak of this and teach mortals that the path to this god is through their exalted servants; the priests, the cardinals the—"

"The wizards," Galina finished for her.

"Exactly so."

"But you were part of this," Katya said. "You said you were to the priest who followed us."

Gurda nodded. "Yes, I was."

"What changed you?"

"Two things. The first was our mutual friend Faim. After an encounter with him, I learned to question what I was being told. Faim has this way of opening your mind and freeing you of preconception. He left me hungry to learn the truth for myself."

"He told me he wouldn't be my guide," Katya said, "that I needed to find knowledge on my own."

"Better to be shown to make your own choice as I promised," Gurda said, "another reason why we are here." She raised her walking stick and pointed to the wall. "To the left of me is another passageway, go there and down the steps to the end. Explore the room, come back and tell me what you find."

Katya got up and walked into the shadows. Galina got up as well, but Gurda motioned her to remain. "Not you, we have more to talk about."

Galina sat down again. "You didn't answer my question from before. Why is this place abandoned?"

Gurda pointed at the roof. "Seventeen years ago, far from here, a small group of wizards performed a ritual to open a portal to heaven. They failed and instead opened a door to nothing, which being nothing, began to pull everything into itself," she frowned. "I don't rightly understand it and I wasn't there, but the portal never closed and continues to devour everything it can reach. The orders learned of this and tried to fix what had been done, but failed. They met in this chamber trying to work out what it meant and eventually determined the truth."

"What truth?"

At that moment, Katya emerged from the passageway, her face pale and expression grave. "There's a man lying on a stone," she said. "He's dead."

"How long?"

She swallowed and struggled to keep her voice level. "I don't know, but no more than a few days."

"Good," Gurda said. "He was the last. They may yet come back, but I doubt it." She closed her eyes and muttered strange words. Galina recognised the signs and the building tension in the air. What spell was the woman casting now? What could she possibly want to—

"*Orisinizi!*"

The voice came to her, echoing out of her long forgotten past, she turned around and found herself grabbed and hugged by small arms and legs.

"*Juje?*"

"*Juje!*"

Katya joined them, her embrace encircling them both.

Chapter 13: Revelation

The boy, known as Hino Kunimitsu and Master Kumawaka waited on Sado Island to see his father.

He could not count the days. He dwelt in the personal hall of Homma the monk and to make a tally mark in the small room might offend his host. When it grew dark, he slept on a thin rug. When it became light, he rose.

Each time he awoke, he found food beside him. With nothing else to occupy him, his intention turned inwards. He meditated, studying his magic and the ways it might be expressed. He exercised, remembering his father's wisdom to train the body while young, so he remained flexible, supple and strong.

He was thirteen years old, not yet a man, but making the decisions of one. His mother had begged him not to come here, he had begged the monk called Homma to let him see his father. Now he could do nothing but wait.

In the fading afternoon, Homma returned. He brought with him a leather sack drawn closed with rope. "Master Kumawaka, I am able at last to resolve our differences," he said.

"What day is this?" the boy asked.

"The thirtieth of the fifth month," Homma replied. He held out the sack. "As you requested."

The boy accepted the gift, drew it open and reached inside. His hand closed around something hard and dusty. He pulled it free.

He held the blackened thigh bone of a man.

"The counselor's death was honourable," Homma said, "performed by my brother Saburō with a clean blade befitting his rank."

Sudden shock weakened the boy's fingers. He almost dropped the burned remains, but to do so would sully his father's name. Instead, his grip tightened and he stared at it. "Father," he said. "Unable in the end to be together, I behold you now, burned into ash and dust."

Homma bowed. "Your purpose here is ended," he said.

The boy did not reply.

Hino opened his eyes.

He lay fully-clothed in a soft bed, unlike anything he'd ever slept in before. The padding beneath him made it feel like floating and helped him recall the dream. For a moment his son's smiling face was there again and he smiled in turn.

"Good, *dainagon* you are awake," said a voice in accented English.

Kumi's face faded away and Hino raised his head. An older man of European descent dressed in red robes sat on a wooden chair at the foot of the bed.

"My thanks for your efforts, Cardinal," Hino said, recognising the garments.

The Cardinal smiled, bringing more lines to a careworn face. "What little rest we granted you helped. I commend you on your powers of recovery."

Hino returned the smile, his gaze drifting to another figure in the room. A woman, also European, stood by the door. She wore the long ornate garb of a *caduceus* wizard, belted at the waist. The hood was drawn back from her face and the mask hung loosely around her neck. "We have little time," she said.

"We have some moments," the Cardinal replied. "*Dainagon*, I am Cardinal Giovanni Colonna, this is Lady Eleanor, formally of Aquitaine."

"*Always* of Aquitaine, Cardinal."

"Of course, my apologies, Lady."

Eleanor smiled. "A fine welcome for guests, a shame more do not come here."

Colonna sighed. "Those days are past I fear."

"We need to bring them back," Eleanor replied. "What is abroad is beyond us, we need the counsel of others with the knowledge we lack."

"We approached the old orders many times," Colonna said. "Few remain true to the alliances and the purpose which once held us all together, but you are right."

Hino inclined his head to them both. "You must call me Hino, *dainagon* is no longer a title I hold. The Emperor abandoned me on the moment of my capture."

Cardinal Colonna rose from his seat. "I accept your gift not to remain on ceremony. Hino then. Can you walk?"

Hino swung his legs over the edge of the bed and cautiously lowered his feet to the ground, putting weight on each in turn, before attempting to stand. His injured leg did not protest and when he bent down to examine the wound there was barely a scar.

He raised his head again. "Where is Lady Rani?"

"Your rescuer left shortly after leaving you with us," Lady Eleanor replied coolly. "She believes you will be useful."

Hino shrugged and bowed. "I will try," he said.

"Then get dressed," Cardinal Colunna said, pointing to another set of robes. "We need you."

Hino nodded and did so, strapping his *tachi* scabbard to the belt of the garments and following his hosts out of the room.

Eventually, the *juje* released them both and Katya stepped back. The little man hadn't changed at all since they'd last seen him – around four foot tall with thin spidery limbs and a shock of hair.

"You are proper *orisinizi* now!" he crowed. "Proper three!"

They all looked at Gurda who scowled. "Such nonsense," she said. "Dwarf, have your people returned?"

"Some are here," the creature admitted. "Nervous of you. Believed all had left."

"They did," Gurda said. "We are here for the seal."

The *juje* nodded and took a step towards the far end of the chamber, but Katya stopped him with a gentle hand on his shoulder. "What is the seal?" she asked Gurda.

Gurda stood up and gestured to the stone sphere, her fingertips brushing the metal spikes. "As I said, the ritual to heaven made a hole in the world. This needle marks the location and is driven through to determine the corresponding location on the other side. Six places were located by the orders before they left, forming an intersection in the centre of the sphere—"

"A seventh seal," Galina said.

"Yes, exactly a seventh seal."

Katya stared at the globe. "This place is one of these locations?"

"Yes, that is why it was abandoned," Gurda pointed through the doors at the far end of the room. "Events are already in motion. Through there is the ritual chamber, we believe it will break open and become a rift, like the one in Avignon."

"Where it started?" Katya asked.

"Yes."

Galina frowned. "But why involve us? We haven't the strength of the people who fled. What could we possibly do?"

"You are *colonnazi*," The *juje* said proudly and smiled, as if the word explained everything.

"You are twins," Gurda answered, "one with power, one with insight. In all I read, such a birth is unprecedented. It would be recorded in a legend or story."

"So you believe we can stop the end of the world?" Katya laughed, but could force no humour into the sound.

"Perhaps we deserve an end?" Gurda said. "Each day inquisitors murder more gifted people like you. The orders strangle change in favour of their past masters and use the weapons of sin and guilt to make their congregation shout into the void after our long lost creator. Mayhap it is time for transformation and a second chance for others, like the *dvergr* or *jötnar* of legend? I brought you here to show you what transpires. Now you make your own decision of how you intervene." She pointed toward the other side of the chamber again. "Go there, see what you find and make your choices."

Katya stared in the direction Gurda indicated and glanced at her sister. For a moment they were children once more and shared the same thought – apprehension at what might await them. She walked over to Galina and took her hand. "Come on, let's go."

"She's not telling us everything," Galina said, eying Gurda.

"Then we'll go and talk about that."

They stepped forward together, reaching a half open door. Katya pushed it wide. The shadows retreated from her light and a circular room revealed itself. There were no pictures here, just etched symbols on every inch of the stone. She recognised repetition in places, but once again, her lack of reading made the knowledge unobtainable. The whole room smelled of power, the air hazy with it, making her feel lightheaded. "Can you make sense of this?" she asked Galina.

"A little," her sister replied, kneeling in the corner. "There are many layers. There were different writers placing messages over the top of others, each imbued with an enchantment." She traced her fingers over the indentations. "There is one repeated rune. It appears in the upper layer and the oldest work at the bottom – a circle with a cross inside... I think..." She raised her head and looked at Katya. "I think it's a warning."

Outside the room, they heard a muffled shout and scream then the door slammed shut. Katya ran to it immediately and pulled on the handle. It didn't budge.

"We're trapped," she said.

Accompanied by his hosts, Hino made his way carefully down a wide set of stone stairs.

Having spent years at Emperor Go-Daijo's court, Hino had access to a vast library of information on the different magical orders of the world and recognised a competent bureaucrat as a kindred spirit. Cardinal Colonna was that and more. The Colonnas were old blood, Italianate royalty, closely associated with the *Summa Magiolaie*. Giovanni himself was a scholar of magic, his gift not being strong enough to invoke power. Whilst the family did not hold the papacy, in the absence of the Pope and the Curia, they controlled the Vatican.

Lady Eleanor was more of a mystery. He knew the name, but little else and as they walked, tried to recall anything he had read from the journals of the Emperor's missionaries to different courts and councils. He could sense the power of her gift.

"All knowledge of the spell cast in Avignon has been eradicated. The membership rolls of the Temple of Solomon were assiduously kept and with your help, we eliminated every loose end."

"Apart from me."

"You are no loose end, m'lady."

They made no attempt to explain their conversation, so Hino pieced together what he could. He remembered a story of magic in the vaults of the Avignon palace, but couldn't recall the details.

"What about a reversal of the ritual?" Eleanor asked.

"Our best minds contemplated this ever since the event, consulting each eternal as they awoke," Colonna said. "We are no closer to understanding what was unleashed."

The corridor below led to an arch, Hino followed his hosts through and found himself in a vast empty hall. The wooden rafters of the ceiling were high above and arches decorated the walls. At the far end, sculpted trees of stone framed panels of glass, which illuminated the chamber. He stopped and stared.

"What is the purpose of such a place?"

Lady Eleanor turned and smiled at him. "Welcome to my home," she said. "This is the hall of lost footsteps. It is in these spaces we come to understand power."

They walked across the floor and as he followed, Hino thought he understood. The sound of each step he made disappeared in the enormous space, making him feel insignificant. He saw more passageways and a raised stone level. "I held court here," Lady Eleanor said, "sat in a simple wooden chair. Nothing else was needed. That life is over now."

"The demonstration is well executed," Hino said. "I am brought here and abandoned by my rescuer into your care. I am given no explanation of purpose and disturbed by mysterious dreams. What do you wish of me?"

"Rani left you with us because you are a powerful wizard, Hino," Cardinal Colonna said. "Your political life is over, as hers was and as Lady Eleanor's is. Your face is unknown in these lands; useful to us."

"Lady Eleanor is stronger than I."

"Perhaps," Colonna replied. His eyes narrowed. "Seventeen years ago a spell was miscast and cannot be reversed, a spell that threatens the stability of our world. A cabal of wizards planned this. You met one of them in the streets. He called himself Faim."

Hino held his gaze. "I answer only to the Emperor," he said.

"I care not for the reason behind the meeting," Colonna said, waving his hand. "Your politics are not our concern; keep your loyalty as you wish."

Hino shrugged. "Very well, I met an outlander to end his service. Sometime after this people came for me, one of them was of the old blood and had betrayed us."

Eleanor turned to him. "You are sure? Could it not have been some spy from the *bakufu*?"

"The *bakufu* are not stupid. A spy of theirs would quietly arrange my capture or assassination, not bring an army to the doors of the Kyoto residency in which I was staying," Hino replied. "Someone wanted to provoke conflict, humiliate the Emperor and begin a war," he frowned. "There was a woman, scars all over her. I saw her at the secret meetings before. She duelled with my escort, toyed with him before the end."

Colonna bit his lip. "Scarred you say? All over, apart from the face?"

"Yes, that's it."

The Cardinal nodded, his expression grave. He produced a handful of parchments from his robes, knelt and spread them out on the floor. "These commissions and reports were for an assortment positions in the first crusade to establish Outremer in 1095," Colonna explained. "At the time, the expeditions were not given such names, but the papacy under Urban II and the eternals wished to see a projection of Christian power in the east. The mission drove a wedge between the eastern mystics and the orders here. At the time, the senior council was concerned about the number of illustrious noblesse being sent into the unknown, so appointed a set of powerful escorts to journey with them. These wizards were amongst the most gifted of our kind and took positions in the entourages of the Kings and princes sent forth." Colonna divided the

paperwork on the table. "Many of those who went were killed, as the sorcerers of the enemy targeted them, seeking to remove our eyes and ears, but a few survived. I remembered one description when you mentioned a scarred woman."

Hino bent forward over the document. His Latin was not perfect, but good enough to manage the words aloud.

"A woman from the furthest lands, small in stature, but within her chest beats the heart of a lion. She walks and fights as a man, her body covered with the scars of her enemies..."

"What you said, reminded me of this," Colonna said. "There are more accounts of the individuals given positions and sent to Jerusalem, but this woman appears many times in the writing, where the fighting is worst. There is also an ominous sign which always disturbed me."

"What is that?" Eleanor asked.

"There is never an indication of what side this woman fought for," Colonna replied. "She has no name or title; she is mentioned only as 'the warrior' and features in every description of a major battle."

"It must be the same person," Hino said. "That would make her more than two hundred years old, strong in the old blood and in her magic." He tapped a finger on the parchment. "It would seem choosing a side is less important to her than the war itself. The woman I met lives for conflict and proving her mettle. Perhaps that was the reason for her betrayal?"

"It might be," Eleanor said, "but these parchments cannot be a complete account of what transpired."

"In three hundred years, why has this woman not transcended her mortality?" Hino asked.

"She is plainly no longer a believer in our path," Colonna said, "and as such a dangerous enemy." He reached into his robes again and produced another rolled script. "A further account of her appears here..."

I am sent to you as a messenger. The only reason I live is to deliver my recollection and the mark as I was told.

We arrived at the designated time; all those who had been sounded out and spoken to, our thoughts and opinions weighed and measured before discreet invitations were issued. Instructions were given to a place dimly remembered, a forest grove once dedicated to the first gods, lost to the archives of all religion.

117

I make no bones at my disenfranchisement. The dream of the Manual Alchemical and the path of the orders is no longer my dream. I went looking for a new way, expecting to find others of like mind and at first, I discovered exactly that as more and more people appeared in the nexus grove while we lingered.

To be there announced betrayal, so trust between us remained a fragile thing. Who could know the heart of each man or woman? We were Judii, and all that bound us was our presence, until our hosts arrived.

They came through the portals from north, south, east and west, on horseback, wielding staff and sword. From the north a starving man on a pale horse, from the east a physician upon a donkey with the mark of the caduceus. From the south came a bone collector and from the west a warrior marked by her foes.

Before we knew it, they set about us, spilling the old blood of those nearest to them. In response, the magic came. I have never witnessed such power and never will again. Wizards fought to live and to escape, casting thaumaturgies all around in their panic.

The horsemen made short work of us, until a last dozen remained, surrounded in the middle of the grove, far from the gates and survival. At that moment I cast aside my staff and abandoned all hope, surrendering to their sinister purpose.

Perversely, they spared us, charging us all with a message, but not before ensuring our fate. The physician came to each of us, practising magic I will not speak of, lest its art go further. You can see the evidence of her festering work upon my body; my life is over. Our gifts protect us from the sickness of mortality, infection does not trouble us in the way it ravages humanity, but this... mark is made for us, a plague crafted to destroy the old blood.

A warning we were told to pass on. "Remember the old ways. There are more powerful paths than religion." Then we were ushered through portals, sent back as messengers to you all.

This is a pestilence made by magic. It was a gift to me that I grant to you.

"A warrior marked by her foes," Eleanor said, pointing to the phrase on the parchment. "It cannot be a coincidence."

Cardinal Colonna folded up the parchment. "In four days, every member of the interrogation committee had become sick. Thankfully we were able to isolate them all within church grounds and when we knew they would not recover, intern them."

"You mean, you buried them alive?"

"Yes. They were walled into a reverie chamber sixty feet below the Sant'Apollinare," Colonna explained. "No cure could be found to their illness, if we had not acted…"

"Everyone here would be dead," Hino said.

Chapter 14: Traps

The spinning white of magic, a moment between places, where the self fractures into a thousand shards, consciousness strewn across reality, a myriad of dust stretched to span start and finish then recombined. Awareness re-emerges with purpose, thought and volition. The traveller understands who and what he is and what he is doing. He remembers a life full of love and loss, with feeling and experience that shapes a man, making him.

Piers Gaveston emerged from the portal in the dark of a narrow alleyway. He stumbled out into a cobblestone street and heard the cry of gulls. A harbour town or city perhaps?

It began to rain. He walked down the road towards the port, seeing the coast stretching out to the left and right. He cast an experienced eye over the boats. None of them high-masted ships, suggesting the settlement lay on a river or lake.

He retraced his steps back up the hill, trying to focus on the magical trail that brought him to this place, but too many other souls had been here. One memory of pain dwarfed the rest, could it be the woman? He wasn't sure, but followed the echo, a hand on the knife at his belt all the while.

The echo took him into the poorer quarters. In another alleyway he found a man lying in the dirt. He wore the bloodied and soiled robes of an orthodox priest – out of place for this part of town. The man barely breathed. Piers knelt down and touched his fevered brow, bulging eyes and shaking hands. There were puncture wounds along the man's arms and legs at regular intervals, some sort of scourge – a barbed whip might have caused them, but there were no tears in the skin where the weapon would have been removed.

"You best be leavin' him. He's past help."

Piers turned. A cart had pulled up and a man leaned down towards him. Piers frowned – how come he hadn't heard them? The cart stank and was marked with a cross in red, its contents wrapped in a stained blank sheet. A corpse cart, out to collect the dead. The driver was grey-eyed and long-faced with a hood covering the top of his head. "Folk sent me to pick him up."

"But he's not yet passed."

"I seen the signs, 'ee will be shortly, best to get 'im buried in with the paupers as soon as we can."

Piers stepped away. The driver picked up the priest with surprising strength and carried him around to the back, tucking him under the cloths. Small bare feet stuck out from underneath, the skin blueing with decay – a child, no more than six or seven.

"A church man would have relatives and friends," Piers said. "Seems strange for him to be alone like this."

The corpse man shrugged. "All sorts end up in the pit 'o th' poor. Sometimes folk can't be found an' bodies can't be left. Tha's the law." He headed toward his seat behind the horse, plainly believing the conversation over.

Piers looked up and down the street but saw no-one. People wouldn't want to be near the dead. Superstition and fear kept them away in their houses, praying and confessing the sins that might mark them to be infected like those who had died.

The cart moved away, leaving him alone. He stared after it, wondering where to go next. *A strange town where no-one knows me…*

"Not wise to gawp."

He turned to find a young boy at his elbow and felt the point of a knife pressed into his back. His eyes went to his belt; his own knife was missing. Piers muttered a curse under his breath. "I don't have anything worth stealing, what do you want?"

"Ain't me what wants you," the boy replied and nudged him forward. "Get moving."

"To where?"

"The house over there."

Piers saw the door ahead marked with a red cross and sighed.

The dim sound of a church bell echoed into the hall from outside. Lady Eleanor glanced up and frowned. "We must leave immediately," she announced and without waiting swept towards one of the arched exits, Cardinal Colunna followed and after a moment's hesitation, so did Hino.

"Where are we going?" Hino asked.

"When you arrived, Lady Eleanor was about to make a trip to ascertain the validity of our concerns," Colunna explained over his shoulder. "A hidden city beneath the oceans of the east was once a meeting place for wizards. It was abandoned after a secret spell was performed in one of the chambers. Lady Eleanor wishes to visit the place and determine if what was done was the same as Avignon."

They reached a small chamber. A whispered word brought light to the candles on the walls. Lady Eleanor plucked a long staff from its resting place in the corner. She scraped the end against the stonework and began to chant, drawing a door shape in the wall. Hino sensed the spell complete a moment before the stones dissolved to be replaced by the familiar rippling vortex of a portal.

"Go, quickly!" Cardinal Colunna urged.

Hino closed his eyes and stepped through.

"What do we do?" Katya's voice rose to a hysterical pitch.

Galina looked around the room. There were no other exits, only swirls and patterns of writing, layer upon layer covering walls, ceiling and floor –*everywhere*. She crouched down amongst them, her study of them entirely different now her life depended on it. "These are spells," she realised aloud. "Protections crafted to contain anything in this room."

"Including us?"

"Once activated, yes."

The air in the room seemed even thicker than before, a cloying haze of magic, building into something, she couldn't tell what. The power gathered and swirled in the centre of the room, like a strange invisible whirlpool, moving slowly, but faster as she watched. "It's feeding on us," she said.

"We have to get out!" Katya shouted, she went to the door and hammered on it. "Help! Let us out!"

"No, wait!" Galina grabbed her by the shoulder. "Gurda wanted us trapped here; she's outside and not likely to release us."

"Then we—"

"No, we think this through before we do anything. Can't you sense the power in here already? It's like…" she swallowed past the lump in her throat. "It's like just before a big storm, but as if the storm is all here inside…" She blinked rapidly as her eyes filled and ran. "Can't you see?"

"I can't see anything," Katya said.

"There's magic here," Galina said. She walked slowly to the centre, giddy as she approached. She reached out, trying to touch or grab the strange haze, but it slipped through her hands. She could feel it against her fingers, like she would the breeze. "We need to make a choice. That's why Gurda trapped us."

"Is that how we get out?"

"I don't know," the swirling currents raised hairs on her skin. "If you use your power, you'll set everything off – the warding spells, all of it." She backed away to the door. "Whatever we do we should be here, that's our only chance."

Katya nodded and came over to stand by her side. "What do we choose?"

"The kind of world we want," Galina drew out the half-finished stave and lay it on the floor. The wood quivered in response to the magic around them. "If we stay here, eventually we'll be consumed by what's building up. If we break the seals of the room, we'll likely trigger it and be consumed anyway." She stared into the spinning torrent. "I don't think Gurda cares if we die. We must find another way."

"What did you mean about a choice?" Katya asked.

"I'm not sure. The restrictions we live with now or something new. A complete change, something we can't understand before it happens," Galina pointed to the door. "Perhaps a return to the early days, maybe that's why the *juje* and his people are here?"

"Can you stop what's happening?"

"I don't know where to begin," Galina said. The distortions whirled faster. She peered at them, trying to get a sense of what they could be. They reminded her of dreams. Faces appeared; people going about their lives in another space and time; some of them stared at her. She gasped. These were visions of the past – rituals, councils, sacrifices, all manner of events over the years. Some were *juje*-like figures, some were huge – twice the height of normal men.

A pattern emerged – a gradual build of magic from this place and others, making it a place of transition. There were glimpses of places underwater, on an island and a pyramid where a man cut the throats of prisoners and threw them into a dark pit.

The answer came to her – this was like a wound or a disease. She remembered how she had guided Katya's power to help Milen, how they hadn't known how to save him, but managed to slow down the spread of the infection.

"Katya I've got an—"

And then something stepped out from fragments and into the room, something solid and real.

The boy's name was Rag – at least that's what he called himself. He made Piers think of his own daughter, who would be a similar age now. He remembered her small face in her mother's arms when he'd last seen them. Thirteen years, twelve since his 'death' on the road.

At Rag's prompting he walked across the street and pushed open the marked door. The room inside was pitch black, unnaturally so. "Close it," rasped a voice.

Piers did as he was bidden. "We could have talked out there," he said.

"My people are not welcome in the sun," the low voice replied, plainly male. "We remain in the dark places of the world."

Clothing rustled in the gloom. Piers clenched his fists and fought down the urge to run. "What do you want?" he asked.

"You followed a woman here," the tone didn't change and came from the far end of the space. "You lost her trail when you arrived, but then found the priest."

"What of it?"

"You didn't fight when the corpse man came, so you intrigue me." Cloth rustled again. "Which side are you on?"

Slowly, Piers reached backwards then swiftly grabbed the boy's wrist and twisted the knife away from him. The child gasped in pain before Piers dragged him forwards and pressed the blade to his throat.

"Please no!" the boy yelled.

"I'm not one for threats," Piers said. "What do you want?"

Something rushed across the room. Hands grappled his, nails dug into his wrists and savage strength drove him into the wall. He thrashed against the sinewy grasp, but couldn't break it. *Impossible! No mortal could—*

"Watcher of the old blood, you are in no position to bargain in this place!" Fetid breath filled his nostrils and he sensed a face inches from his own. Lambent red glowed from eyes staring into his. "You are orphaned, bereft of purpose and support. You broke with your flock and found no power in the deep. That makes you weak and ripe for our use!"

Piers shut his eyes and relaxed as he'd been taught, letting the magic flow, but something got in the way, disturbing his connection. He felt sharp teeth on his neck, his eyes flew open and he cried out.

"No father," said the boy.

Abruptly, everything stopped.

"We can use him another way. Learn the Church ways from him without fear of them finding us. He'll be perfect for that."

The hands on his throat relaxed, the figure in darkness stepped back. "You're right, I forget myself."

Without warning, pain exploded on the side of Pier's head, his legs gave way and he fell to the floor as the blows rained down.

Katya stared at the creature and it stared back.

Its presence felt unnatural in the chamber, a violation of some law she'd never consciously understood, but instinctively accepted. Strange obsidian skin, back facing knee joints, a wedge shaped head and muscular shoulders, both covered in spiky horns. White eyes and teeth – fanglike, clawed hands, three fingers and two thumbs. All recognisable features for what they were, but none like they should be.

It stepped towards her.

Galina screamed a warning, but it was too late. The magic came forth without thought, an instinctive protection, shaping itself as Katya'd learned – *in fire*.

The black skin caught light. The creature howled and fell, a clawed hand reached out to her. "Please!" it begged as the flames took hold. Katya remembered Faim's words at the house – *innocent!* Once again, the power ran out of her like a wave and she stepped forward to grasp the outstretched fingers.

But it was too late. The creature burned away, turning to ash in her hands.

The room shook, the writing on the floor began to glow and she realised what she'd done. The fire spell had triggered the defensive wards, which meant whatever they were set to defend against…

…had arrived.

At first it looked like the distortion she'd seen through the portals, the same rippling of the air and wall behind, but then the space seemed to tear, revealing a blackness like the skin of the creature. Accompanied by a sense of wrong.

What have I—

The door to the room exploded inwards, knocking them from their feet. Two figures came through, both in long robes covered in symbols and writing strode into the room, light shining from them. A gloved hand gripped Katya's arm. She gazed into a masked face and the eyes of a woman.

"Come with me."

Katya was on her feet and running, Galina in front and the two strangers following. Outside the room she slowed and glanced behind. Their rescuers stood by the broken door arch, one wielding a sword, the other with a long staff planted in the ground in defiance of what lay

125

beyond in the room. As she watched, the walls of the chamber reached out for each other, shrinking the doorway gap until the room was sealed.

The woman turned towards her, staff in hand. Katya flinched. "I'm sorry," she said.

"No apology is needed," the woman replied and took her hand again, walking quickly to the other end of the room. Katya followed as best she could. Already the writing in this chamber was beginning to glow as well. They went past the sphere and back down the passageway to the cave room where they'd first arrived. "What happened to Gurda and *juje*?" she asked.

Suddenly, a cry came from the shadows and a small form threw itself at the woman. Spidery fingers clawed at her robes, teeth snapped, trying to bite and tear. "Hino!" the woman shouted.

In response her companion swung his sword, catching the figure across the temple. There was a flash, a scream and he disappeared.

"*Juje*!" Katya screamed, but there was no reply.

The woman glanced at her, eyes wide. "Did you know that… creature?"

"He was a friend."

"Then I am the one who must apologise," the other masked person said; a short man, speaking with a strange accent. "When we transported in, there was no-one here. We heard you cry out and found you in the room. What were you doing there?"

"Someone trapped us," Galina said before Katya could answer. "Will you take us with you?"

"We will," the woman said. "Then will come the time for questions." She stared at the cut groove in the stone and spoke a rapid sequence of strange words. The air rippled as the portal activated, she stepped forwards and vanished.

Katya followed quickly.

Galina went to follow her sister, but a hand on her shoulder tugged her back. She turned towards the man. "What's the matter?"

"You are not of the gift."

Galina swallowed and shrugged. "I can't do what Katya can do. Is that a difficulty?"

The man let her go. "It means we go together," she said. "Come on."

They held hands and walked into the wall.

Tuia's arms trembled as the sun rose and he lowered the knife.

Throughout the night, the procession of victims continued, a tortured differentiation of humanity ascending the steps towards their bloodletting and doom. Beneath, inside the temple, the chosen were anointed as soldiers empowered to bring about the world's end.

The tall mantled Mexica had been first. Then came the fur-clad Khamag and their lesser kin. After these, the other allies of Teotl and her council, a mixed collection of warriors from the corners of the world. Tuia saw the white skin he remembered of Odoric and midnight dark flesh. An alliance of power and change knew no boundary.

In the daylight he rested, as the workers raised the temple higher. At dusk he ascended and sacrificed them.

The guilt no longer troubled him. Faces blurred and smeared into each other. Only the knife remained constant. He treasured it, licking clean all trace of its victims between sacrifices. In the daytime, he slept with it held in both hands, a reminder to himself and others of his new purpose.

A carver of wood no more. Now a carver of flesh.

As Teotl promised, the magic awoke within him. He learned the ways of the old ones in shaping and directing it. The minions of ancient times came to him when he called, but the eagle remained out of reach.

Now, as his labours ended with another dawn, he felt the ground tremble. Some shouted in panic, but he did not.

He walked down the bloody steps into the growing city. A crowd had gathered in the square. People stepped away from him as he neared, fearing the knife and his dread purpose. They would never feel anything else for him – this was the price of power.

Ahead a group of figures did not step away. Instead, one of them turned as he approached – a gnarled old man in tattered robes with guileless eyes and wisps of white hair over his ears.

"Welcome brother," he said.

Tuia accepted his hand in a clasp of friendship. He bowed and turned to the next figure, a stocky woman who leaned heavily on her walking stick. She did not offer a hand, so he bowed lower. Behind her stood Teotl and to her he bowed lower still.

"You have done well."

"I act only as you instructed."

"No, you do more," she said. "I expected weakness, a crisis between your gift and the remains of your mortality, but you transcend such considerations and enchant the soldiers of our cause equally without flinching. Now the sign comes to us and we are ready, so we shall begin."

"What is to happen, great one?"

"Invasion."

Lightning flashed and thunder roared.

Beneath the charged heavens, the boy known as Master Kumawaka did not sleep.

In the days after his father's death a fever gripped him. He refused to leave Sado Island and was moved from the personal hall of Homma the monk into guest quarters. At night, they locked the door and a servant sat in the corridor.

As Kumawaka's body burned, so too did his soul. The anger shielded him from sleep, seething and bubbling in his veins.

Blood must pay for blood.

This was no child tantrum. His fevered mind struggled to focus. The monks obeyed masters who were unknown to him. The world of the *bakufu* and the Emperor had been his father's. He would find no peace following his father's ghost.

Kumawaka rose from the bed and on the balls of his feet, stole across the room to the door. He leaned close to the paper window and heard the soft snoring of the servant. He drew the broken blade of a knife and pressed it to the paper until it tore. Slowly, he cut out a hole.

A man could not fit through such a space, but a child might.

Head first he slipped through the gap.

At first, anger made his hands shake, but long deep breaths brought calm. The servant lay sleeping on the floor. Kumawaka eased past him down the hall and into the yard.

Outside, the wind and rain soaked his simple shift. He stayed close to the buildings, watching for other servant guards. He crawled under houses and crouched beside walls. Eventually, he found what he sought – the only lamp lit dwelling near to the north wall.

The place where Homma slept.

Kumawaka inched towards the light. Two *ashigaru* guards stood outside the door, both alert with *naginata* spears and swords. A child could not pass such warriors, but a gifted child...

In the shadows under the *engawa*, Kumawaka called forth the magic. Flickering wings caught the storm's light and a moth landed on his hand. A moment later, a second joined it, then a third and a fourth. He sensed more fluttering above and bent them to his will. The moths gathered, swarmed and poured themselves at the guards, who shouted and screamed as they drowned on insect flesh.

Kumawaka sprung from his hiding place. More shouts came from elsewhere but he ignored them, snatched up a sword, flung open the door and charged inside.

"Who dares to disturb—"

The blade bit into flesh. The speaker coughed and slumped against Kumawaka. The boy struggled, but pushed him off. Lightning flashed and he got a glimpse of the man's face.

It was not Homma.

Kumawaka's hands shook, his vision blurred and his breath came in gasps. He couldn't drag his eyes from the monk's dead face. *Who have I—*

"Saburo! Saburo!"

Kumawaka kicked over the lamp. Oil and flame spilled and spread across the floor. He leapt at the *shōji* window on the far side, crashing through it in a mess of paper and wood.

"Saburo!"

Fire spiralled into the sky as Kumawaka ran into the night.

Timeline of Significance

1326: The Ottoman Turks expand their lands from the northwest of Asia Minor. They conquer the city of Burs, about fifty miles south of Constantinople and Ottoman warriors cross into Europe to plunder. The Ottoman sultan, Orhan, allies himself with one of the Christian contenders for the throne in Constantinople, John Cantacuzemus, and marries his daughter, Theodora.

1328: King Charles IV of France dies. He is succeeded by Philip of Valois, who takes the title Philip VI. It is the end of the Capet dynasty and beginning of the Valois dynasty.

1333: Stability provided by the Kamakura shogun *bakufu* breaks down. Emperor Go-Daigo is joined by a number of warriors who are at odds with the shogunate ruling from Kamakura – the Hōjō family. The Emperor declares the end of the Hōjō shogunate, and the Hōjō shogun commits suicide. This marks the end of the Kamakura era and the beginning of the Kenmu Restoration.

1334: Conclave of Cardinals. Election of Pope Benedict XII.

1336: India suffers from drought and famine. The Sultan of Delhi does little to assist his subjects, and discontent gives rise to rebellion. Some Hindus proclaim independence from Delhi rule. A new Hindu kingdom, dominated by Telugu-speaking aristocrats, arises – Vijāyanagar – named for its capital. In Japan, the Kenmu Restoration collapses. Ashikaga Takauji leads the military class against the Emperor Go-Daigo. They capture the imperial city, Kyoto, and establish an amenable emperor from the northern faction of the royal family. Ashikaga Takauji names himself the new shogun.

1338: Philip VI of France intervenes in a dispute in Flanders where Edward III of England owns property and English influence has been dominant. Edward retaliates by declaring that he is King of France – by right of birth and family connections. Philip responds by declaring Edward's fiefs in France forfeited. War between England and France ensues.

1339: Bengal declares independence from Delhi. From fighting among Bengal's nobles, Malik Haji Ilyas emerges victorious and assumes the title of Sultan Shams-ud-din. The mass of Bengal's population converts to Islam. Sufism spreads through Bengal lower classes.

1340: The Tatars are ravaged by the bubonic plague. The disease is passed to Genoese merchants returning from China.

1342: Conclave of Cardinals. Election of Pope Clement VI.

AD 1344 - Invasion

These children are not the enemy, your Eminence. We found them locked in the warded chamber, trapped there as a sacrifice to what lies beyond these rifts.

They are an unusual pair. Twins – identical in most things apart from their gift. One is dangerously powerful, the other, perceptive. Between them they excel in both arts. With no training, the perceptive one, Galina, has constructed a resonating tool. In her own way she too is dangerous, but what makes them both unique to us is the bond they have, the hidden magic of twins that enables them to combine their talents.

It is possible whoever placed them in the warded chamber knew this and was attempting to use their skills to repair the worsening damage we have seen. But whilst talented, these sisters are unskilled and inexperienced, lacking anything but the most rudimentary understanding of what gifts they have and what these gifts mean.

Your Eminence, I request your dispensation to train them. I understand the misgivings of others, but in these times we lack options. Your intercession holds weight amongst the European councils. You will be listened to, over and above the refutations of our brethren in Avignon.

Time is a matter in all things. The predictions of scholars suggest six seals will open, just as the good book indicates. As you know, the locations of these seals could be anywhere across our lands or the lands of others. To monitor this requires the admission of responsibility from the Holy See, which we know will not be forthcoming.

We know not what order these seals will break and without unity of purpose, cannot act without incurring curiosity and questions over our actions.

The seventh seal has yet to be determined.

If there is a Creator out there in the darkness, then it is through their providence we have been granted these children. They may yet be our salvation.

Eleanor.

Chapter 15: Contentious Council

The light of the transportation spell faded and Hino blinked, adjusting his eyes to the twilight. The Giant Dancers loomed behind him and behind all the other delegations invited to the meeting.

The Grand Conclave of Orders – a gathering of wizards and magical scholars from all over the world, the leaders of every organisation commanded nations, religions and vast territories.

In the first days, before Hino's time, this august council met frequently, but was only attended by the most powerful of the old blood. Over time, those with lesser talents were accepted as some orders became larger and political power gained more status than skill with magic. Now, the scholars dominated, their gift with the making of portals, staves and all manner of other devices had become essential to every wizard. The religious structures that populated countries and continents were designed and administrated by those who could not use magic themselves.

Hino wore the formal mask and robes of a wizard escort. No staffs or other talismans were permitted. Next to him stood Lady Eleanor, similarly attired and in front of them, their charge.

Cardinal Giovanni Colonna.

The red robed priest strode forward to stand in the second circle. He was not a voice in this meeting, only the Pope's representative would be permitted to speak for their faith.

Hino was more concerned about revealing himself to the other attendants. On the other side, Ashikaga Takauji took his place as the voice of Japan, the position Hino once held. The Kyoto shogun was a powerful rival to Emperor Go-Daigo in a building civil war, but the Conclave did not recognise such disputes. Not far from him was the Emperor's loyal councillor, someone else Hino did not want to be discovered by.

His own son.

Hino Kunimitsu had become a competent wizard in his own right and now held position in the second circle. Like Colonna he was not permitted to speak. Kunimitsu's eyes roamed the faces of the attendants, making his father's heart swell with pride, but Hino could not reveal himself, if he did, he would break the protocols of the meeting.

And there were more important matters to discuss.

"The gathering will come to order," said an old man, walking into the centre of the ring, his voice soft, but carrying to everyone present. His name was Vyasa and he was older than anyone. He was rumoured to be eternal, having transcended centuries. He was never seen outside of the Conclave. A long white beard ran down to his ankles. He wore loose trousers and strings of beads, the dark skin of his neck and shoulders exposed to the cold English night, but it did not trouble him.

Hushed whispers ceased, all eyes turned inwards as ritual demanded. "The orders come here under the auspice of counsel," Vyasa said. "All assembled will respect this, on pain of exile."

The silence indicated assent and Hino noted a thin smile on the lips of the old wizard.

"The Conclave is called to discuss the matter of the seals. The papacy is to answer the continuing rumours of a portal breach beneath the seat of your voice." He turned to the red robed cardinal representing the Pope – Cardinal Bernard De La Tour, only two years in office and junior to Cardinal Colonna, his presence, a clear indication of political preference.

De La Tour stepped forwards. "His Eminence is in agreement with his predecessor, the heresy of the Temple was concluded long ago. Talk of continued tumult in our lands is false."

Hino looked around, thankful his expression could not be seen beneath his mask. Exclamation was not permitted in the Conclave and only the representatives were allowed to speak. Most had hoped Clement VI would abandon the denials of the previous pope, Benedict XII, but it seemed they were wrong.

Hino knew Lady Eleanor would be seething beneath her mask. Few witnesses to the ritual at Avignon remained, but she was one and had evaded several attempts to ensure her disappearance. He knew her account of events and recognised the similarities in what they had seen since.

"Emissaries sent by your order attended a disturbance in the abandoned council city of Isoloha, in the ocean depths," Ashikaga Takauji remarked.

"If they did, there was no sanction," De La Tour replied, his eyes fixed on Colonna in an accusatory stare.

"But you accept the correlation drawn in their report to this assembly?"

"We do not, we challenge it." De La Tour had warmed to his argument now and remained resolute in the face of compromise. "Whatever occurs beneath the waves is unconnected to our past."

"What about the trajectory evidence?" A woman spoke up. She wore furs and was shorter than those around her. Hino remembered her name – Aippaq, a witch from the furthest north.

"Such supposition is not evidence," De La Tour replied, "only supposition."

Aippaq sighed and glared at Vyasa who bowed slightly to her before speaking. "We have heard the answer. Without concert, we cannot act."

"The intervention in Isoloha should be welcomed," a man with long straight grey hair said. He was known as Great Shaman and came from the vast plains of the North West. "Without it, we might not be alert to the danger."

"What of the absences at our council?" Aippaq asked. "What of the gathering portents of war, plague, starvation and death? Are we to do nothing about these?"

"Such issues are for each domain," De La Tour said. "I do not seek to tell you how to lead your people, nor does my master ask advice on his own affairs."

"But absences are not an internal issue!"

"Then why should we be involved?" De La Tour asked. "I am a new voice to this assembly, but is it not our purpose to share knowledge and not to intervene?"

"If what we face is a coming doom, it will affect us all."

"Emissaries sent to these silent kingdoms without invitation may be seen as hostile acts." De La Tour shrugged. "Perhaps they do not wish to attend? There is no agreement amongst us for action, until there is, such talk is ill advised."

Aippaq appeared frustrated, but little could be done to counter De La Tour's answers. Hino glanced around the circle. None of the other voices seemed inclined to comment. If they did, they risked the ire of the papacy – a strong political power amidst the gathering and no-one else would breach the protocols of the Conclave. Hino gazed at their most obvious adversary – the Hadith of the desert kingdoms, but they were a small delegation and rarely spoke, making no motion to do so now.

"What if representatives from the orders gathered here were to investigate further occurrences?" Takhauji suggested. "There are many places in this world where our reach is weak."

"We would not countenance an unauthorised presence in our domains," De La Tour warned.

"But we are not speaking of the lands you claim," Takhauji asserted. "You cannot assert dominion over the unknown. Nor can you restrict the rights of any with the gift to use portals that exist in these other places." He raised his voice. "I move that the Conclave requests aid in investigating further disturbances similar to that seen at Isoloha."

"Seconded," Aippaq said immediately.

Vyasa turned to each representative in turn, bowing in response to every nod or shake of the head. He reached De La Tour last. The Cardinal flinched under his gaze, glancing left and right as if trying to determine the direction vote before voting himself. Finally, he shrugged.

"There is no objection," Vyasa proclaimed. "The move is passed."

Beneath his mask, Hino smiled. Takhauji could not be trusted and would have his own reasons for proposing such an act, but the agreement would help Colonna and their cause.

"We shall recess," Vyasa announced and the whispers started once more. Hino kept silent. A small concession had been won. But whoever opposed the Conclave had nothing to fear as yet.

The bells of Stensnes' church rang out across the quiet ice.

Brynfrid glanced up from where she chopped wood. She'd never set foot in the place, but the time for worship was long past. Otherwise, the bells would only sound as a warning. *Warning from what?* She shaded her eyes and scanned the horizon, seeing nothing.

The chimes ended, then a man screamed and stumbled out of the church; the priest, his cassock torn, his chest bloodied. He collapsed in the snow. After him came a man in a hood and a tattered cloak, his hand outstretched. Brynfrid didn't recognise him. She shouted and ran towards the building, noting two men ahead of her doing the same. As they got close, the arched doors behind him burst wide and a creature the size of a large wolf leapt out, grabbing one of the men. It had three heads, and bore him to the ground. The other swung a sword at the stranger who dodged aside and pressed his palm to his assailant's chest. A second scream echoed out and the man collapsed.

Brynfrid reached them and spat out words of power just as her grandfather had taught her. The wolf-like creature vanished, but its prey remained, bleeding out, red into the white snow. She felt exhausted. "Who are you?" she rasped at the strange man, brandishing her axe and getting a good look at the wrinkled face under his hood. The man smiled in return.

"To this place, I am death," he replied.

A growling came from inside. Brynfrid snuck a quick glimpse, taking her eyes from the man for a moment and saw shapes moving in the shadows. "I do not fear death," she said, but took a step back. She could feel the power this man wielded, it far outstripped her own. She remembered where she had left her staff, back in the house. "We are not your enemies."

"I agree," the stranger said. "This would be so much easier if you were."

He advanced towards her.

You come for a story then? Gentle children.

The story to be told is one of the past. A tale of the world, that you might understand your place within it.

Perhaps you have stared out into the night and wondered, what is up there? Are we alone in this great space?

Above you and around you, stare into the dark far from our home, the vastness that lies beyond firmament. Somewhere you can only glimpse, blurred through mortal eyes blinded by the world's dust.

Gaze upon the stars. These lights are each travellers, countless vessels and creatures, journeying through the deep. Pick one and follow its path. Some of these are kin; other children of the Leviathan.

If you listen carefully, you may hear them sing.

The world turns at the centre of all things. In most ancient times, travellers came upon it, and were trapped. These travellers were fickle, yet as with all life, curious. Creatures from the void clustered around this bright gem and found a way into its sky and thence to the earth. They discovered a world, which at first could be whatever they wished. A place made real by the life and power of those who came to it. The land lived and breathed, changing with the passion and purpose of its new people. It grew a light of its own, becoming a refuge for the weary and a realm of story and tales.

Later, these visitors found they were not alone.

The travellers took forms that pleased them. Separated from the deep, they forgot who they truly were and became locked within these physical shapes. They aged and changed and learned the lessons all children learn; to live, to love and to lose.

When it came, mortality horrified them. Their energies were bent to end its curse. Some burrowed far into the ground, others back into the heavens and further, into other places. They found another darkness, and forgot themselves. As they drank of corruption, so it changed them, and for the first time, they knew evil.

And so they lost their light.

Chapter 16: The Provenance of Sons

With all matters discussed and concluded, the gathering of the gifted broke up.

Hino Kunimitsu watched them go. He maintained an impassive expression – right hand on staff, left by his side – but assessed each in turn. The plethora of humanity's magicians, a sight to marvel and something he had never seen before. Skin, eyes, hair, height, breadth and more; a range of colours, some of which he had not believed possible. Masks covered many, but he caught glimpses of faces and noted the whispered conversations after the forum. It was plain there were numerous concerns.

Ashikaga Takauji and his retinue remained apart. A solid group who refused speech, referring people to their shogun, who stared ahead, ignoring attempts to engage him. Their unity was a reflection of Takauji's reputation. He demanded respect and obedience from those he trusted, rewarding them in equal measure.

He was also Kunimitsu's political opponent.

Eleven years ago, Emperor Go-Daigo had rewarded Takauji's soldiers for their part in the Genkō War. Takauji had betrayed the Hōjō clan shogunate and fought for the Emperor. He accepted his gifts with courtesy and hidden purpose. Three years later, he captured Kyoto for himself and raised his flag for the northern pretender, Kōmyō. Three years after that, Go-Daigo died peacefully.

Like his father before him, Kunimitsu remained loyal to the southern court and Go-Daigo's son, Go-Murakami. Takauji supported Kōmyō in name, but most acknowledged Takauji as the real lord of the north.

Portals flared as wizards, attendants and officials departed. Kunimitsu stayed where he was, watching Takauji. Eventually, even Vyasa the eternal mediator gathered himself to leave.

Kunimitsu glanced at his own companions. Two gifted bushi stood either side of him, their masks carefully drawn to hide their identities. Behind them sat Toki, the court scribe, who continued to embellish his scripture of the august meeting. Four to Takauji's eight.

Kunimitsu knew the truce of the Conclave would be maintained so long as Vyasa was present. After he left, the matter became unclear.

Honour suggested no violence would occur, but if there were no witnesses and no remains, a death might be explained as a portal accident. Asking the old man to remain was an imposition that would betray weakness and division amongst the kingdom's representatives. *Perhaps I should have left,* he thought.*But then I would have wasted this opportunity.*

Vyasa inclined his head to them both, moved towards one of the stone arches and, with a flash, disappeared.

"Master Kumawaka."

Kunimitsu gazed at Takauji, careful to betray no reaction, but inclined his head in respect. *"Chinjufu-shōgun,* no-one has called me that since I was a child."

"Nevertheless, your legend precedes you – the boy and his vengeance upon the traitor monks." Takauji said. "It is a shame we have not had a moment to talk like this before."

"A matter I regret also."

"I am sure."

A faint breeze stirred the grassland around them. Beneath his robes, Kunimitsu shivered, but kept himself outwardly calm. "The Emperor has many enemies," he said.

Takauji nodded. "Indeed. A matter we must be vigilant against. All this talk of a coming doom is a matter for *gaijin.* My proposal asserts the Emperor's righteous concern, but if these rebels exist, then we must expect them to already dwell in our lands and it is those we must seek out."

"I concur, *chinjufu-shōgun.*"

"The righteous Cardinal already resents what has been agreed," Takauji went on, "but he cannot risk being uninvolved. He will send emissaries to us. We shall be ready for them."

Kunimitsu nodded. "What of us?" he asked.

"What do you mean?"

"We stand in a unique position," Kunimitsu explained, "under the truce of conclave and outside the Emperor's lands. Many of the oaths that bind us both within our own domain do not apply."

Takauji frowned as he considered the words, but then he smiled broadly. "I had thought your great moment already passed when you took your justice at Sadogashima. Now I see there is more to you than the silent blade."

Kunimitsu bowed. "You honour me."

"What do you propose?"

"Send away your attendants and I shall send away mine. Then we might speak apart from our burdens and rank, at least for a short while."

Takauji nodded. "Yes for a short while. Very well it will be as you suggest."

"Thank you *chinjufu-shōgun*."

The town of Sredets lay to the south of Vidin. A strange place on the intersection of the different principalities, full of merchants still coming to terms with their new freedom under the rule of Tsar Ivan Alexander. It was smaller than Vidin, but fast becoming an important trade centre.

For Piers Gaveston, life in Sredets was the same as Vidin, where he'd been acquired. After the altercation with Rag and his strange father he had remained their captive. He didn't know how long it had been. The manor house they lived in now, accommodated many people 'collected' by the pair.

I deserve this fate.

Piers considered running away many times, but never attempted it. Self pity and shame kept him where he was. What good could he do otherwise? He accepted confinement. Others who'd played the dangerous games of court had been shut up in towers and monasteries, or executed in grisly rituals. To be reduced to a monotonous existence as the slave of another paled by comparison. Those born to the dirt, scratched out lives with their hands and teeth, with no hope of betterment in their mortal years. At least fate had given him a chance and memory of privilege. He didn't warrant another.

I failed all those I tried to help.

He drank wine and the memories blurred. Some days, he was the one slaying the heathens and opening de Molay's portal, or murdering Aymer de Valence and Jacques Renarre.

There was a fog about his mind, one that he could not shake off. It numbed him and made him feel remote from himself. Perhaps this was the reverie that others spoke of during his *cadeucus* training? He was sure it wasn't. God had abandoned him, there was no God, no Gods, no enlightenment and transition to a higher self. There was only this dark existence.

And blood.

His imprisonment wasn't without benefit. By day, the dusty rooms were all but abandoned. The mark of plague kept away visitors and he was free to roam the halls as he wished, unless called to tutor his student. They became a familiar refuge for his mind. The shapes and contours of the walls a reassurance of existence. The one thing he could not do was leave the grounds.

Lessons with the boy – now a young man – were a challenge. Rag grew up slowly, after two decades he was still mistaken for a child at times. Were it not for regular showy demonstrations of his power, Piers might have believed him completely ungifted. He had no aptitude for letters or runes and soon became impatient, sullen and distracted. But twenty years of continual study gradually refined his gift. The magic did not come quickly to him, but he made slow and steady progress.

Piers knew the price of failure, of becoming no longer useful to the boy and his father. Each night he was reminded of it.

Rag's ghoulish companions went about their own business, rarely sharing anything with him. Over the years, faces changed as they were no longer of use. More always appeared, vagabonds acquired from the streets or children taken from homes. They burned the furnishings to keep warm and squabbled amongst themselves, but once they arrived no-one left.

The father saw to that.

In the daylight hours he slept somewhere beneath the house. At night he would frequent the windowless chambers under the ground floor and summon the house guests to him one by one. Piers would be last and would descend into a pitch black room. The conversation would always be the same.

"How is my son?"

"Learning, as always."

Clawed hands gripped his. Teeth would brush against his wrist then bite down. They were sharp, plainly grown or filed that way. He could always feel the blood being drawn out and steadied himself against the dizziness that followed. Afterwards, the wipe of a long wet tongue would staunch the wound and when he returned to the light, he found no trace of injury.

He would sleep after that in the room he had been given, knowing he would not be disturbed. Each morning someone would be missing. Some days, Piers' found himself praying he would be the one to vanish. At least that would bring about an end.

No-one spoke of those who had disappeared. Instead, the other guests huddled closer around their fires and Piers went back to teaching the boy.

Only today he couldn't find him.

He walked from his room as usual and through the ransacked halls towards the west wing. It was bitterly cold, but he hardly felt that. A group of people squatted around a makeshift fire in hall corner as they always did. They ignored him, apart from one man who caught his eye. He was painfully thin and dark skinned, like a Moor. Piers flinched from that stare and felt the man's eyes bore into his back as he hurried away to find Rag.

The school room had once been a family chapel. The wooden chairs had disappeared, broken up as firewood. The stone sides under the windows were scrawled on with charcoal sticks, where Rag practised the symbols Piers tried to show him, but otherwise the room was empty.

The lessons had become a brightness in Piers' life. He knew his teaching the boy was forbidden and the Church would execute him for it, but then they had so many reasons to order his death and he had few left to counter them. When the time came, he could not see himself resisting. For now, talking and playing with magic in small ways was a pleasure. He took pains to withhold anything that might be dangerous, training Rag in parlor tricks that could amuse and entertain, but not much else.

Where are you boy? Piers wondered.

A scratching noise at the door made him look up. A short figure stood staring into the room, its face human-like, but not human. Two tiny eyes above a snout nose and a mouth full of canine teeth. Thin arms and legs stuck out of ragged clothes tied at the waste by a length of stained rope.

Piers had seen such a creature before, but only in a book as a child while being instructed in Avignon. A *gobelin* – one of the world's ancient monsters, summoned by the earliest wizards to bring mischief to their enemies. It was possible this was a remnant of that past; a lonely survivor, drawn to the house by the smell of magic or brought here by someone with the old blood.

Piers bit his lip. *What have I done?* The Church and other orders forbade a summoning like this. No place existed for gobelins amongst the heavens of the creator god, they were unpredictable and cruel. A wizard who called one would be punished. He raised his hand towards the creature and wracked his clouded mind for a spell to drive it away.

But then Rag appeared behind it smiling. "Do you like my new friend?" he said and laughed.

Piers lowered his hands and let the magic ebb away. "I did not teach you this," he said, half trying to convince himself.

Rag shrugged. "No, but we spoke of the eagle and the lion. I tried those and nothing happened. Then I did something different and he appeared," he laughed again. "What shall we call him?"

Piers kept his eyes on the gobelin. "He already has a name. I told you before, everything has a name."

"Yes, but he can't talk and tell us," Rag replied, evidently pleased with himself. "He's good at hiding and stealing things. I thought we might send him into the city tonight."

"Your father should be told."

Rag gave him a defiant smile. "There's a lot I don't tell father about," he said. "You need to decide whether you're going to tell him."

He walked away and the gobelin followed, leaving Piers by the window.

When the last of his attendants had left, Takauji gestured to one of the great stones on its side. "Come, let us sit."

Kunimitsu approached him and dropped to his knees on the ground. It was a gesture designed to convey respect, accepting they were not equals. Takauji seemed to appreciate it and seated himself on the fallen rock as a warrior might, in an open stance, ready to rise at any moment. His gaze took in Kunimitsu's attire and he frowned.

"I note you do not wear a weapon. What became of your family *tachi*?"

"It was lost to me on Sado Island," Kunimitsu replied. "The monks never returned it."

"A final dishonour to you and your father."

"Indeed."

"We are a pair you and I," Takauji said. "Each of us has made decisions of our own interest which some may see as disloyal."

Kunimitsu shrugged. "My concern is with what you said. How troublemakers prevent peace in our land. The portents of doom are talked about everywhere. While we remain divided, we are ripe to those who would exploit us."

"You are full-blood are you not? A wielder of the powers?"

"Yes I am."

"My mother was like you. The gift did not manifest in me. My way is earned through sweat and work, but I know of the paths – the ways your people gain sustenance from the devotion of others. I know how your legend feeds you."

Kunimitsu flinched. "The story is not of my doing."

Takauji leaned forward. "No indeed, but you profit from it. You sup from the teat so that you might live like these *gaijin* cardinals and kings." He laughed, a bitter sound. "You will outlast us all Master Kumawaka!"

A red flush crept across Kunimitsu's face. "I did not ask for this conversation so that you might insult me."

"No? Then why did you ask for it?"

"Give up your claims. Renounce your northern pretence and return to the Emperor's grace, he will reward you."

"I offer you the same. Abandon the son of the traitor and accept out legitimate ascension."

"I cannot."

"Then you have my answer as well."

Kunimitsu sighed. "Surely you see how we are manipulated? Hundreds will die in the name of each court if we do not prevent it. Others profit from our conflict, not us."

"Perhaps your magic grants you a second sight, but I will not trust it. My tail has turned enough. I placed my faith in your master's predecessor and he treated me with contempt. I will not give such a pledge again." Takauji stood up. "Go find these silent wizards you speak of who stir up trouble and suck the bones of our kingdom, just as you did when your father was condemned. They are the legacy of your gift, not mine!"

Kunimitsu swallowed a bitter retort. "This conversation is over then?"

Takauji strode to one of the stone arches. By some unseen artifice, the magical sheen of a portal appeared in the air before him. "We never spoke," he said. "We never met."

Chapter 17: The Abyss

A vast flat landscape under a cloudless sky; the air stirred by a restless unnatural breeze, bringing up dust to coat the clothes and mouths of travellers.

And travellers there were – seven figures bent under the weight of their burdens, following an ancient track into the featureless expanse. To the eagle, a journey without an obvious goal, unless to die and be forgotten.

In the centre of the column, Galina stumbled and cursed. This land was not meant for habitation. The strap of her pack rubbed her shoulder as she walked. Dust caked her face and got in her eyes. She drew up the hood of her cloak and kept her mouth covered with cloth, yet still her throat complained with each breath and step. It would be a while until they stopped, but she was already wishing away the time.

Ahead, the broad back of her companion. Ibrox moved along as if nothing troubled him. Galina had never met a man like him. Tall, muscular, and with darker skin than she'd ever seen, his white-teethed smile was infectious and a welcome comfort at their brief stops.

Next in line would be Katya and in front of her, Lady Eleanor, placed in charge of their mission. She followed their bearded guide, Elbo Smogg.

At the back came Hino, former *dainagon* to the Emperor of Japan and Magno, a Genoese soldier. Physicallly, they were as different as possible for two men to be, but the cultured Japanese counsellor and the Mediterranean military man had become fast friends in the last two weeks, a bond of mutual respect.

Over the years since Galina's rescue, Hino had earned her trust. He was a wise soul and honourable to a fault. At first she'd found his quiet ways intimidating, believing that he secretly judged her progress under Lady Eleanor's patronage, but she'd come to realise he was as nervous as she, coming to live in an unfamiliar land full of strange customs and rituals. When he visited her, she welcomed the company of a kindred soul.

Magno she did not know and had only met on this journey. Genoa was a port city a few days from Rome. The captain was a half-blood, like her, and incapable of much magic, but with a mind for devices and a sailor's dexterous fingers. He had light brown hair and eyes and walked oddly, with a rolling gait, as if he were permanently aboard ship. There was a sadness to him at times. Galina wasn't sure why.

No portals would short cut this journey, so they all learned to rely on each other, something Galina still found uncomfortable. On cold nights, with no fire for fear of being seen on the wide open plain, the only warmth would be from other sleepers. She lay awake then, conscious of the people pressed against her, remembering the village teachings about touch as a child. She knew differently now, but that didn't change the instinct and didn't help her rest.

Ahead, someone whistled and she glanced up. Through the dust she saw three figures standing together. Had time passed so quickly? Ibrox moved to join them, she followed.

"We're here," said Smogg. His unkempt beard jutted out from beneath his hood. He wore the same church cloak as all of them, but underneath was a stained tabard and mismatched boots. To Galina, he was the strangest of them all and most aloof. These surroundings suited his dishevelled appearance. "Forty yards further on would be the boundary the last time I was here, but I judge less now, perhaps fifteen steps or so, by the ground."

He tapped his staff into the mud and Galina glanced down. Interlaced fissures ran everywhere underfoot, widening in the direction Smogg indicated.

"Do we go now?" Katya asked.

"We'll wait for sundown," Eleanor said. "Let's make camp here. It'll lighten our burdens for the descent and mean we have something to come back to."

"Be better to get off this plain, highness," Magno said as he joined them, his eyes scanning the horizon. "We're easy to spot."

Smogg grunted. "We've been followed for two days. If they want us now, they'd be here. They'll hold off till we're done and likely want what we learn."

Magno shrugged and bowed. "As you say," he said and that was that.

They fell to, preparing a place to while away the remaining hours and rest should they return. At Eleanor's instruction, a full camp was to be laid out. No sense in taking things where they headed, only what was essential. Galina spread her bedroll as she'd done every night on the journey, only this time her hands wouldn't stop trembling.

Twenty years in a monastery in the centre of Rome had changed many things in her life. The monks were patient with her, they needed to be; she and Katya were the only living souls to have looked into a rift.

147

After the rescue, Eleanor and Hino took them to a small cloister. They'd been given separate rooms and been kept from each other for many days. The questions from strangers were constant, courteous but painstaking. At night, Galina sat by the wall of her room, knowing her sister was the other side doing the same, desperate to touch and feel the closeness they'd always known. She sensed the anger in Katya and feared it would explode.

But Eleanor had returned and summoned them both to a meeting hall where she announced they would be trained.

At first, Galina resisted the idea. She still clung to the faith of her far absent people and the word of the elders. Katya had been taken away again, to learn different lessons. The tenets of the stone singers remained strange to those she was raised with. She remembered Faim's words. To him, they were the enemy. She sat and listened to the teachers, but said nothing. Eventually Lady Eleanor met with her about it. "Why will you not accept instruction?" she asked.

"You cannot change who I am," Galina replied.

Eleanor smiled at that. "Do my instructors have keys to enter your head?"

"No."

"Then learn from them and believe as you wish," she urged. "You will find many who are helped by the Church keep their own counsel."

From then on, the classes became easier to digest. Once they confirmed her lack of ability with spells, they brought her objects, liquids and powders. Gradually, she began to understand her talent and found peers like her, who could see the potential of things. She learned the word *alchemy* and discovered there were many different disciplines. Some alchemists were skilled in making portals, some brewed potions and others made devices. "It is the alchemy that advances our understanding of magic," Eleanor told her. "Without it, we would remain creatures of instinct alone, unable to refine or improve."

But whilst the lessons improved her understanding, they didn't help with controlling her own gift. It defied prediction, she could see the power in items, but had little control over what she made from them or how they might go together. Given a pile of resonant objects, other practitioners could craft tools to design and purpose, but she could not and she was slower than them, taking hours and days to work through the tasks she was set.

"Patience," Eleanor had said. "Your blood grants you a life far beyond that of mortals. Understanding of your magic can come quickly or slowly. The greatest of us are still learning what we can do. Give it time."

148

Only now, there was no more time and they were here, in this strange land. She had been brought along because she had seen the other side.

And she might have the chance to do so again.

The sun hugged the hilltops in the west. As the others pitched tents to be used on their return, Galina went back over what she'd experienced. She remembered the white eyes of the creature before it burned and the ashes in her hand. Ever since when she'd washed and scrubbed her palms they never managed to feel clean.

She thought about her village again and dreamed about her father dying, four years ago. She'd had visions of his end prior to that. He'd lived a long and happy life and she knew he was at peace when he passed.

"What can we expect?" Eleanor asked Smogg.

The little man shrugged. "As you know, the first rift in Avignon sucked up everything around it. The warding runes contain the breach within the room. We cannot access the chamber anymore, but must guess it remains the same. The second rift in the Tarkian temple was similarly contained. With this one... well there's nothing here and we couldn't prepare."

"If it continues to rage, surely all of this island would have been consumed," Hino said. "If we are as close as you say, we would sense it."

Smogg shrugged. "This place was once fertile farmland. When I was last here, I saw the rift consume earth, rock and dirt, it turned and twisted like a whirlpool, eating everything."

"There's not much we can do to prevent it," Ibrox said.

"We all knew that when we agreed to come," Eleanor replied, but Galina caught a sidelong glance aimed at her and blushed.

"I'm not... I mean, I don't..."

Eleanor cut her off with a wave of her hand. "Let's get moving."

They stood and arranged themselves. As Galina fumbled with her cloak, Katya took her hand and squeezed it – a small gesture, but one that lightened her worry. She tried to smile in response, but her sister slipped away to a place beside Eleanor.

They walked as a group in the failing light. Magno gave out steel lantern boxes, lighting the candles inside. Galina held hers as high as she could, keeping her eyes on the cracks in the earth. They widened gradually, until the ground fell away in front of her and she stopped.

On the edge of a pit.

Shadows swathed the sheer cliffs below, but the depths glimmered with an eerie blue light. She recognised it, remembering the rift in the ruined city ritual chamber again.

"Must be four hundred feet or more to the bottom," Smogg said.

Magno pointed. "There's a path down," he said, "cut into the rock."

Smogg grunted. "Wasn't there last time, someone's been here before us, and recently, otherwise it'd already be gone."

"We'll use it," Eleanor decided. "Single file, we go slowly and carefully. Keep ropes handy in case we need them."

They arranged themselves as before, Smogg in front, probing the cut rock with his staff as Eleanor held her lantern over them both. "This has been carved out," he said, "must have taken an incredible amount of power or people."

Ibrox nodded. "No rogue wizard is capable of this," he said. "Whoever came here has many friends, or slaves."

"A member of the council perhaps?" Magno suggested.

"We worry about that another day," Eleanor said. "At present we mind the here and now."

Slowly, they made the descent. Galina kept her eyes on the rock side. The stone was pitted and scarred, the layers of mud and clay baked hard, as if subject to heat and dryness. No plants grew here, no grass or moss that she might have seen on a natural cliff. The blue glow got brighter as they went further down, flickering shadows along the hewn wall. A hand touched hers and she turned. Ibrox smiled and passed her a rope. Behind him, Magno secured the end to the top of the face with a stake. Galina tied herself on and hurried down the track. "Hino?" she called. The Japanese man turned and accepted the line, doing the same and passing it on.

When they were all attached, they continued.

At halfway, Galina risked a peek over the edge. Flickers of blue in the gloom, a strange lambent glow, like nothing she'd ever seen. It moved like thick soup, or turning mud under a plough in the field, seething amidst the darkness. She began to feel warm, despite the shrinking sunlight from above. The familiarly prickling sensation along her arms confirmed the presence of magic. She wondered why they weren't already dead.

"There's a door down here!" Smogg called back.

The rope went slack as the group hastened to join him. After a steep slope, Galina found herself on a wide ledge in front of the entrance Smogg had mentioned. Two doors, half circles, cut into the rock face and carved with an unfamiliar symbol. "What does it mean?" she whispered.

"It means someone knew what would happen here after all," Eleanor muttered. She stared upwards and Galina followed her gaze. The sky had darkened and the glimmer of torches on the ridge was unmistakeable. "We go through or we go down," she said. "Thoughts?"

"Down," Hino replied. "That's why we came."

Eleanor nodded. "Then no sense in waiting."

They moved on.

...We came upon the settlement late in the day, although time does not matter out here so much. The sun remained high throughout our time, banishing sleep, though any rest would have been difficult in this place.

Vestribyggð looked as if it were awaiting its people. Dinner remains on tables, livestock left grazing in pens and fields, but not a soul in a bed or about a house. The streets empty, all folk gone as if erased from the world.

We explored further, sailing upstream to the Stensnes' seat. Here we learned the cause for silence. The great church lay in ruins, broken a time in the long past. Fresh gravestones we found in the yard, though the soil hard and untended.

As you know, this land named green by Eiríkr hinn rauð is no garden as he claimed, yet the cold here at Vestribyggð could not be kept from the breast. We burned wood and oil, but still the chill held us. The silence stilled tongues and made us weak with caution. We sensed eyes out there in the quiet. Perhaps it was the Thule folk? But those attuned to such things thought not and spoke of Brynfrid Vigdís' tale all those years before, claiming the rise of an old god in the ice.

We remained for a week and more, making an inventory of what was left. I reminded all those whispering heresy of their duties to our church and state.

All items we could take aboard we took, to assuage the debts of tithe and tax.

I would caution any seeking to return to Vestribyggð. A doom besets that place. Anyone wanting our Lord's grace in the afterlife should avoid those becalmed ruins...

Ivar Bårdssön – Letters to the Bishop of Bergen (AD 1344).

Chapter 18: The Third Seal

As they neared the bottom, the rock wall became smoother and the ledge narrowed. Fifty feet from the ground, Katya found herself edging along on her toes. Ahead, Elbo Smogg asked them to stop, unhooked his tether and began mumbling unfamiliar words.

"No!" Galina shouted. "Don't cast any magic here!"

Smogg stopped immediately and peered up at her. "You might be right," he admitted gruffly, "my thanks, young lady."

He struggled onwards, eventually, reaching the bottom without incident and turned to help Lady Eleanor down. Katya followed, wondering what Smogg had been about to cast.

During the journey, she'd marvelled at the ease with which the wizards handled magic. Her own power remained a mystery to her, a flood gate which she continually fought to control. Her lessons with the priests had not gone well, even after she'd overcome her distrust of them. They explained techniques by which she could access her gift and taught her the ways in which other gifted students had profited from them. She had some success, but none of the methods worked consistently.

The lists of spells were interesting and she'd noted how certain expressions were mentioned but not explained. Very few creatures could be summoned, according to the books and there was no mention of *juje* or anything like him in those scripts, but when she read the expanded histories, there were references to other folk who were strangely inhuman, but no explanations of where they came from or how to call them, only a caution that they were not to be trusted.

The authoritative tone of the writing was occasionally difficult to reconcile with the conciliatory words of her occasional mentor, Rani Padmini. They'd been introduced to one another by Hino and quickly come to recognise the wilful nature they shared. Rani did not accept the same strictures as the Roman instructors, but advised Katya to learn all she could. In the short time they would spend together, Rani would talk of the power as if it were a living thing in itself. There was something special about her too, a weight to her presence which drew the eye. When Katya asked Hino about this, he smiled and explained how Rani had begun a change that only the most powerful of wizards ever experienced – a process that would end in her transcendence and becoming an 'eternal'.

"She will live forever then?"

"If she survives the process, yes."

At night, Katya wondered about that. She remembered the villagers and her family. At times she could still sense them, but the connection was weak now and grew weaker with each passing day. She thought about returning to the village and suggested this to Hino, but he shook his head.

"Your old life is gone. You must find a new purpose in what we do. In time, you will discover a place that enriches you just as your home once did. Perhaps it will come from here, or a land somewhere else. You should not be restricted by what you were."

She liked his words; they fired her imagination, but seemed at odds with the books and the quiet instructors. Occasionally she caught frowns of disapproval and saw them exchange looks that indicated their opinion. To them she remained a heretic, a Bogomil of the heathen past. It did not matter that they shared her belief in a heaven and a creator. She did not believe their way and perhaps she never would.

Her foot slipped on the rock, making her curse and focus on the here and now. It was difficult to breathe, the air tasted cloying and thick. The pulsing blue light that came from the earth invoked a matching throbbing sensation in her head. Behind her, the others managed the last few steps and spread out to examine their surroundings. There were wide fissures and seething azure liquid ran inside the cracks.

"What is that?" Katya asked, pointing at it.

Smogg walked cautiously towards a large tear and knelt down. "It's everywhere," he said, "as if everything beneath us is full of it."

Galina stumbled and fell to her knees. Katya went to her immediately. Her sister's eyes were unfocused and staring wildly. "Can't you see them?" she said, her voice cracking. "They're all around us."

"I see nothing," Hino replied, laying a hand on her shoulder. "What do you see?"

"Fragments, like before," Galina said, shaking off his hand, her eyes roaming the space. "Visions of pasts and futures, people who can't exist, mustn't exist!" She wiped drool from her mouth and tears from her eyes.

Cries from above distracted them all. Katya watched the tether line tumble from the rock wall. Then heard clattering echoes as the rest of their camp items were thrown down towards them. "They've found us," she said. "We can't go back."

153

"They must be terrified," Ibrox said. "Such change to their lands in only a few days. They must blame us."

"We must do something about this!" Magno urged, gesturing at the ground.

"What can we do?" Smogg asked, continuing to explore. "The girl is the most sensitive amongst us and warned me about using magic. The wardings in place when the other seals broke took years to construct. Here we have nothing and anything we start could trigger a further event."

"Understanding comes before solutions," Eleanor said. She knelt beside Galina. "We cannot sense what you can, so you must guide us and help us to understand."

Galina nodded, but her eyes roamed wildly.

Katya turned away, suppressing the flicker of jealousy. Smogg had almost reached the centre of the space and was poking things with his staff. "There's footprints," he said, pointing at the rock. "They start here and head towards the walls."

"What kind of footprints?"

"Many kinds," Smogg replied, "paw prints, claw marks, human feet, hooves, all sorts... I don't understand." He stared up at the walls again. "Where did they all go?"

"If this hole expanded as you say, they may be old," Katya said.

Smogg snorted and stood up. "I know my business. These are fresh tracks, made three days ago at most."

"The only place they could have gone would be that door," Ibrox said.

As he spoke, the ground underneath them shook. Smogg stumbled and fell over. Katya ran to the ledge. "We need to go back up!" she urged. "We can't stay here!"

"Indeed," Eleanor said. "Magno?"

The Genoese soldier nodded and retrieved the rope from where it lay. He wrapped it around his wrist, removed his boots and swarmed up the stone, finding invisible handholds. He reached narrow path, running up and along, making the climb to the door in seconds. He re-secured the rope by hammering a stake into the wall, tested it and called down. "Up quickly!" he urged.

Katya grabbed her sister, wound the line around her waist and pushed her to the thin lip of rock they'd come down. "Galina, you must climb," she whispered.

Galina's eyes refocused and she nodded. With Magno anchoring the other end she began to make her way up.

Hino moved to the edge and nimbly made his way passed her. A second tremor shook the walls and he slipped, but didn't fall and soon joined Magno at the door ledge, lending a hand. Together, they hauled Galina the last few feet to join them.

"Ibrox, you next," Eleanor ordered. "Hino, take Galina to the door and try to get it open."

With a grunt of effort, Ibrox started up the wall, his heavy frame making the ascent more difficult. Katya glanced back at the centre of the hole. The rock where Smogg had been standing crumbled and slipped away, disappearing into the widening fissures. "Hurry!" she cried.

Smogg nudged her elbow. "Is there really nothing we can do?"

"In the other place, my magic triggered the seal," Katya said, "if you tried a spell now..."

Smogg nodded and pushed past her to the thin ledge. After two steps, he made a grab for a hand hold, but slipped back and nearly fell. "If we stay here much longer—"

"We don't think about that," Eleanor said. "You are next."

"But you should—"

"You will go."

Ibrox reached the others and Smogg started his ascent. Together, Magno and Ibrox hauled him up then dropped the line back down. Another tremor rocked them all and more of the ground fell away. Eleanor handed the rope to Katya. "Now you."

Katya bit her lip and didn't argue. The line went taut and she grasped it, letting herself be dragged up the rock face. From above, she saw Eleanor's plight. The floor of the hole was rapidly turning blue as the unstable stones were absorbed by the restless mass. Soon she would be forced away from the wall and any chance of being rescued.

We can't lose her.

Katya was some distance up by now, the lip of rock had widened. "Eleanor!" she cried and let go of the rope, scrabbling for handholds and balance. Beside her the line went slack, then tight again. She didn't look down, but concentrated on her own circumstance, shuffling along the narrow ledge as it wound upwards towards the door way and the rest of her companions.

Another tremor – she froze – then another. Her hands began to cramp. The climb down had been easier with the security of people and rope, now it required complete focus. Her heart thumped in her chest as she tried to control her movements. Her foot slipped and she gasped, recovered and then glanced down.

The stone had disappeared entirely, engulfed by seething blue. A few feet above it, Lady Eleanor dangled on the line, climbing as best she could, but reliant on Ibrox and Magno pulling her up.

The churning mass captured Katya's gaze. She saw shapes within it, her mind making patterns perhaps? She thought there were people reaching out and felt eyes staring back, hungry eyes, eager to consume what she was, what they all were. This wasn't just about magic, whatever existed down there wanted everything, substance and soul. She was terrified, frozen.

"Katya!"

Her name called out from far away, but then a hand on her wrist. She blinked and looked around. Lady Eleanor was out of sight. Magno had climbed down with a rope around his waist and grabbed her. With impossible strength he dragged her from the wall and into the crook of his arm. "Hold on to me!" he said urgently and seized the line, coiling it around his hand. "Pull us in!"

They started to move. Katya clung to Magno and he got his feet under him so he could walk the rock. When they got to the ledge, other hands reached out and helped her to safety while he managed the last part alone, collapsing on the stone plateau.

"Thank you," Katya said.

"Thank everyone," said Magno, "when there's more time."

Galina and Hino were by the half-circle doors. Galina stood nearest. Katya followed the others towards them. She couldn't tell what the panels were made of, they looked smooth – unlike any wooden door she'd ever seen – and had no handle. As they got closer, Galina raised her hand and touched her palm to the symbol cut into the centre and the entrance opened.

"Caution my friends," Eleanor warned.

Galina didn't seem to hear, she stepped straight into the new passageway, Hino a step behind her.

"No, wait!"

Smogg was nearest to them both. Hearing Eleanor's call, he ran after them and stood in the entranceway just as another tremor started a cascade of rocks down on them all. Katya rushed towards him, her hands covering her head. She heard someone cry out, the doors were beginning to shut. "Smogg!" she cried.

The strange little man saw the danger and put his hands to the two half-circles, but he couldn't hold them back. He tried to wedge them with his staff, but couldn't brace it. "Hurry!" he yelled.

Abandoning caution, Katya ran at the narrowing space. As she approached, Smogg moved inside. The gap shrank as she reached it and she turned sideways, trying to fit through. It wasn't wide enough. She felt the two stones touch her arm and knew the danger. She stepped back.

"Galina!"

The doors slammed shut.

At night, Sredets was still a busy place. Wide streets and long lines of new merchant houses lined each side of the Vladaya River. By law, trade ceased at sundown, but few people respected this and there were many exceptions. The alehouses and whores kept their own hours, along with the cutpurses and murderers. The former might be helpful, the latter would be a hindrance at best.

On this night, Piers Gaveston stole out of the house, across the grounds and through the gates, heading into the centre of town.

He wasn't sure where he was going, but the business with the boy had awoken something within him. His previous drunken indolence and stupor meant no-one watched or guarded him.

He made his way quickly into the busier central district and selected a tavern at random. The common room was full and the low light belayed any questions of his dishevelled appearance. With a few small coins he'd scrounged from the discarded belongings of other house guests, he purchased a watered mug of the local brew and found a seat in a corner to gather his thoughts.

Rag's defiance and successful summoning of the gobelin had broken Piers' chains. As he'd walked away, the compulsion and numbness faded. He believed Rag – the daytime eyes and ears of his father. He'd become paranoid about a curse of retribution, trapped into the role of a slave, his knowledge of magic gradually sucked out just as the blood was drawn from his veins every night he met with the father. Even now, the fear remained, bubbling in his gut, promising a torturous revenge.

Piers glanced down at his twitching hands clasped around the chipped clay mug. He'd never felt as he did now, not even in the days when he'd been a prisoner of Warwick, or the night after Blacklow Hill. Somehow, he knew the taken blood meant he shared a bond with the father and the father was awake, calling for him in the house, he could sense it.

He wanted to get up and run, but he knew if he did, he would end up enslaved once more.

"All alone?"

A man sat down. Piers recognised him immediately, the Moor he'd seen near the fire that morning. The man's thin hands rested gently on the table as he regarded his new companion, the same stare from before, wide-eyed and powerful.

"You were at the house."

The man nodded and gave him a smile that didn't reach his eyes. "Indeed I was and fortunate to find you when I did."

Piers fingers dug into the mug and it cracked, the contents spilling onto his hands. "You were hunting me?"

The man shrugged. "Not exactly, but near enough."

"Are you here to kill me?"

"Not this time." He leaned forward. "The sanctorum taught you to let go of your mortal life, embrace the freedom your longevity brings. You abandoned your family and everything you once knew. With no community, many of our kind lose their direction. The Church tries to counter that by giving you a focus and a structure toward transcendence," he lowered his voice. "The only problem for you in that is you've seen the truth at the heart of things."

"There is no God."

"Exactly. When you learned that you ran and became a prisoner to a lesser wight. You are lucky I found you when I did."

"Seems strange hearing all this from a Muslim," Piers said.

"You judge my faith by the colour of my skin?" The man leaned back. "My name is Faim, I was born next to the Euphrates river, but I have not been back there in more than a century. By birth I am Assyrian, so yes you are partially right, but I lived in the western kingdoms for as long as I roamed Parthia and Assyria. Islam has no meaning to me, just as Christ has no meaning to you."

Piers frowned. "But you're of the old blood."

"Indeed, I have the gift, just as you do," Faim said. "Do you know much of the Muslims and the Hadith? The practice of magic is strictly forbidden and there is a fine line between soldier and sinner. The *malak* have no free will and exist only to carry the word of God. If they assert themselves, they quickly become outcast *sihr*. They find no good in this work. In their world, magic reduces freedom, for the benefit of all humankind." He laughed, a bitter laugh with no humour and wiped spittle from his mouth when he was done. He waved his arms, indicating the patrons of the tavern. "Regard these folk. Amongst them we are Gods, our kind worshipped by them for centuries. The religious orders created a framework to enable this worship, selling a promise of afterlife based on the dreams of the ascended. In turn these mortals work hard, obey the law and the commandments believing they will be rewarded in heaven. You are one of three survivors of Avignon. You saw their reward, didn't you?"

Piers flinched under the man's scrutiny. "The Temple was misguided, perhaps their actions were misdirected," he said. "Absence of proof in one instance doesn't not undermine all possibility."

"But that isn't what you believe," Faim said. "Otherwise, you would be in Rome, aiding your brothers and sisters extol the doctrine."

"What do you want from me?" Piers asked. "If you were part of helping me leave the house, you have my thanks, but so far I find nothing but torture for my soul in the words you spout."

"I want you to be free and make your own choices," Faim said. "But in this instance..." he glanced around once more and leaned in again. "I need your help."

"With what?"

"Returning to the house and freeing the child."

Piers frowned. "I've only just left, why would I go back?"

"Because you know what he is and you know what will happen now." Thin fingers seized his arm, drawing it across the table, their grip surprisingly strong. "The wounds are not visible on the skin, but I sense them. The creature has fed from you and if you leave, he will go back to feeding from the boy."

Piers felt the prickles on his conscience. "What are you suggesting?"

"We go to the house and burn it. We destroy everything, making it less than a memory, a shadow, to be forgotten." Faim let go of his hand. "I do not request without offering something in return."

"What would that be?"

"You know what it is to be alone. You understand the power available to those with faith and you wish you were able to believe as they do. Without faith, you are not what you were, easily exhausted by the magic. The half-breeds blinded you. There is an older source you can tap, a bottomless well of possibility. I will show you how to find it."

Piers stared into Faim's sunken eyes for a long time then nodded. The alternative was an aimless existence. "I'll help you," he said, "but when we're done, we talk and you pay up."

"Agreed."

Chapter 19: Tunnels

"We're trapped."

Galina reached out to the stone wall and leaned against it, steadying herself. The surreal sensations she'd experienced so close to the bottom of the hole were fading, replaced by an urgent need for her sister, stuck on the other side of the door.

"I am sure they will be all right," Hino said, his soft Japanese voice reassuring in the darkness. "The Lady Eleanor will think of a way to find us." He spoke arcane words and light welled from his hands. "We should decide whether to remain here or explore."

Elbo Smogg grunted and bustled past them both. "You can guess my preference," he said, heading into the unknown.

"Wait! We must stay together," Galina urged.

Smogg stopped. "Your touch opened the door. We don't know why. There is no symbol this side, but there is strong magic in this place. Perhaps it closed to protect us? We need to go further and ensure we are safe, your sister would want you to be safe. You cannot do anything to help by staying here," He pointed down the passageway. "They'll know where we've gone. If we come to a place where we may lose them, we'll leave marks so they will follow."

Galina turned to Hino, who nodded. "I too am curious," he said. "I can see no means of opening the doors from here. We might force it open, but I think this to be unwise and believe you will also."

Galina could still sense the unchecked vortex beyond the rock passage. Any expression of magic, including Hino's light spell drew its attention. She looked at Smogg. "Very well, but if we find nothing, we should come back."

"If we encounter the makers of this tunnel, we will ask them how this entrance works," he replied.

Smogg resumed walking. Galina followed with Hino behind, his light enveloping them both. The bearded explorer remained ahead, just beyond its reach, content to labour in the dark. Galina wondered how far she could trust him. He was a bumbling mass of contradictions, kept on a careful leash by Lady Eleanor, but without her there...

A cold breeze distracted her. She glanced to the left, seeing only darkness. "Hino?"

The Japanese man was at her shoulder. He extended a a glowing hand and the gloom retreated. "An intersection," he said and raised his voice. "Smogg?"

Galina turned back to the main passageway, but Smogg was nowhere to be found. She reached out with her senses, trying to harness the fleeting power of her gift, but it revealed nothing. "He's gone," she said.

Hino gestured and the light coalesced into a ball to float away down the passage. "We must follow him," he said. His hand took hers. "We cannot be separated."

They moved on. Galina glancing back. "They won't know which way we've gone."

"We will not abandon Smogg," Hino said, tugging at her hand. "Come."

Katya pressed her hand to the symbol. Something within it wriggled but remain out of reach. The doors did not move. She turned to Lady Eleanor. "It won't open."

"We should try the path," Magno said.

Ibrox scowled. "The people up there will kill us or worse. They blame us for this."

The ground shook again. The lambent blue glow began to creep up the rock wall towards them. "We should attempt magic," Lady Eleanor said.

"What spell would aid us?" Ibrox asked. "No creature could rescue us from this place and this rock is warded against any physical battering we might invoke."

"There must be something we can do!" Magno urged. "We can't give up!"

"And we will not," Lady Eleanor said. She placed her hands against the stone, exploring it carefully. Eventually, she found a section that satisfied her, next to the door. "The risk of doing this without knowing our destination is considerable," she said and turned to Katya. "You must do exactly as I do, repeat the words and gestures exactly as I perform them, understand?"

Katya nodded.

"Ibrox already knows this spell. He and I will assist Magno, but you need to help yourself if we are all to succeed," Eleanor nodded towards the wall. "When I invoke the magic, I will be able to pass through stone, but only a particular type. I will jump forwards in the hope that there is a gap on the other side."

"But that's madness," Katya said. "If you guess wrong and it's solid—"

"We die," Eleanor replied, her expression grim. "We have no other option. There are other dangers. If there is a vein of ore or something else in the rock, we cannot move through it. Similarly, if the material under our feet is the same, we will be unable to stand on it unless we act quickly to end the magic. This is why we make a leap and do not walk through."

"Very well."

"End the spell at exactly the right moment to give yourself the best possible chance, understand?"

"I think so."

"Good. Then we will begin."

Eleanor fell silent, staring intently in front of her and murmuring. Katya began to panic as she realised she wasn't catching the intonations. Like all magic, the phrases would not stay in her mind, but slipped away each time. She glanced at Ibrox. He leaned towards her. "Understand what she does and make it your own, rather than copy what she does or what I do. The gift comes from you, not from repetition."

Katya calmed and remembered her lessons at the sanctorum and with Faim a lifetime ago. She watched Eleanor's hands and the expression on her face. After a moment, her fingers sank into the wall. She nodded at Katya, her lips still murmuring words, then leaped into the stone.

And disappeared.

Katya stepped forward to the same spot and focused on the same portion of rock. She recalled Galina talking about resonance – how magic lingered, perhaps if she attempted the spell in precisely that place...

The ground shook again. "Hurry," Magno breathed. She gazed up at him. He'd seemed so assured and capable on the climb when he'd helped her, but now his courage wilted. She understood, he had no magic and needed their aid. His plight was clear, he'd always avoided these moments of powerlessness, but they defined him, made him real.

She turned to the stone and extended her hands, the words she spoke were a nonsensical string of syllables based on what she could remember, but when the magic awakened, they became a frame for its use; a guide to her will and intention.

She touched rock, felt it, but then didn't feel it. Burying the instinctive surprise, she concentrated, gathered herself and leapt.

Into darkness.

Less than an hour after they'd met, Piers found himself back on the streets of Sredets following Faim back towards the house.

They walked in silence. Only the click of the Assyrian's staff against the cobblestones of the wide street accompanied their steps. Little conversation had passed between them since the agreement was made and none at all after they left the tavern. Piers had started to ask questions but Faim had touched a finger to his lips. It made sense. Folk who cared to look stared at them both. An emaciated easterner and a man in clothes he'd worn for more than a decade were an odd pairing. Only when they reached deserted streets, did Faim speak again.

"As you know, the creature we seek lives in darkness beneath the house," he said. "Each of the disappeared guests is fed on like you, but also changed to become his servant and part of the brood. Over time, some are permitted to leave and begin their own broods in other places. Some cities can support more than one, but rarely does this occur."

"Why didn't this happen to me?" Piers asked.

"Because of your gift," Faim explained. "Like the boy, you were too valuable to be turned. Once this creature was a half-breed; a *Nephilim* in the old tongue. He was taught a ritual that allowed him to access the power of his weakened talent and enhance it with the blood of those like you and I," he stopped for a moment and gestured. "That is why he cannot bear the sun, a flaw brought about by the magic."

Piers frowned. "Are you saying the father is a wizard or *sihr*, like us?"

Faim shrugged. "The creature is capable of the same things, perhaps more capable. I mentioned before, there are other sources of power than faith? Here you will see some of them."

"Which ones?"

"Fear and blood."

The click of Faim's staff indicated the end of the conversation and they walked on, eventually reaching the marked district. The buildings on either side of the street bore the red cross of the plague and were abandoned. Piers was surprised to see so many doors broken and windows smashed. Faim read his expression and smiled. "The world turns my friend. People starve, sicken and die. Perhaps it is a portent of things to come? The world will outlast us or we will outlast the world."

They reached the house grounds. The gates were ajar, just as Piers had left them. Faim slipped through and he followed. "Be on your guard," the Assyrian said. "Whilst our prey might not venture into the twilight, he may send others. Their light sensitivity is proportional. They will be weak, but enough to trouble us."

Piers nodded and looked around. A thin mist hung over the unkempt grass. Nature had reclaimed this place long ago, creating an unchecked wilderness. He'd hardly given it a second thought when he'd left, but now...

Now the father was watching. Piers sensed his eyes all around them.

"They know we're here," he said.

Faim chuckled. "Then we best be prepared."

He planted his staff into a gap between two flagstones and began to chant. Piers felt the pull of the spell immediately; energy being drawn from every available source, including the beat of his heart and the breath from his lungs. The world around him grew cold and then he sensed they were not alone.

Three figures appeared, insubstantial, like the ghosts and spirits he'd heard of in fairy tales – a man, a woman and a child. Piers bit his lip. He knew of this magic, the rote was from a secret grimoire, forbidden to the sanctioned wizards of the Church. "You have raised the dead," he said, appalled.

Faim nodded. "The old dead of this house, we will need them."

A howling scream from the house silenced any further discussion. Through the mist, Piers could see figures running towards them, sprinting as fast as they could, he counted a dozen at least, their hunger like a wave. "What do we do?"

"Stand and fight," Faim said. He let go of the staff, leaving it standing vertical and drew a curve in the air with his hand. The rippling shape of a bow appeared. He pulled back its string and loosed an arrow of magical power into the darkness. One of the figures dropped at its touch. Faim loosed another arrow with the same result. "Only magic will release them," he said.

Piers nodded. He was no stranger to war, recalling his days as King Edward's lieutenant in Ireland. He stared at his right palm and traced a line from it with his left finger, finishing level with his head. A shimmering sword appeared. A second incantation hardened his ragged clothes.

Gaveston...

He glanced around, momentarily distracted. The sword wavered, the spell almost failing before it saw use, but he remembered himself and held on. The word came from the house and spoke only in his head – the voice of the father, connected to him by blood and magic.

A crazed man appeared out of the dark and sprang forwards. Piers swung his sword downwards, slicing through flesh and bone. The man gave a gargled gasp and collapsed on the stone, but another took his place then two more, their nails ripping at him, finding holes in his garments, tearing into his skin. He struggled and fought back, stabbing one, but stumbled with the effort and fell on his back. The air went from his lungs. They were on him, teeth against his throat, he screamed.

There was a flash of light and he was alone.

A hand appeared – Faim's. Piers took it and stood up. "What did you do?"

"A banishment spell, one of your church's better inventions," Faim said. The bow had disappeared. The click of the staff resumed as Faim strode towards the house. Around him walked the three silent figures he had summoned. "We must make haste, lest our prey turn loose more of his brood."

Piers stumbled after them, his breath a steaming gasp in the cold air. "They don't fight like men," he said.

"Were you expecting soldiers?" Faim chuckled. "There is no room left for humanity in these beasts, they are hungry and struggle to survive. Expect no quarter from them, prepare for claws and teeth. They will tear at skin and flesh to reach the prize inside your veins."

They reached the entrance. The door remained ajar, the hallway beyond dark and forbidding. Faim gestured to apparitions. The child spirit nodded and walked through the door, triggering more hungry screams. A further command and the others followed. Then Faim touched Piers on the shoulder and pointed to a window some distance to their left. "We'll leave the reception to take care of themselves," he said. "Come on."

Nervously, Piers went after him.

The stained glass had long since been broken. Faim made short work of the slivers that remained and clambered into the room beyond. Piers followed, making sure he kept a grip on his conjured sword.

They were back in the corridor leading to the old chapel. Shouts and running footsteps echoed in the distance. Faim stared at Piers expectantly.

"There is a cellar door in the kitchens, this way."

They walked quickly away from the entrance and turned right before reaching the chapel. A figure appeared at the end of the passage way. Faim didn't slow, but spoke a word and gestured with his hand. An incandescent burst of power flew through the air to immolate a woman as she ran towards them. She screamed as the magical energies burned her to ash.

Through the kitchens they went, reminding Piers of the abandoned inn outside Picardy where Pembroke had died. At the far end was a small staircase. He stopped on the first step and stared down into the darkness.

"Do you see something?" Faim asked.

"No I..." Piers swallowed. "I'm just remembering how many times I've been down here."

A reassuring hand squeezed his shoulder. "This will be the last time."

"I hope so."

He started downwards. The gloom seemed to swallow them both up, only the glow of his conjured sword kept it at bay. "We need a plan," Piers said.

"We have one," Faim said. He moved in front, putting his back to the small door at the bottom of the stairs. "When we enter the room, locate the boy and get him to safety. Leave the rest to me."

"What're you going to do?"

"Correct my mistake."

The dislocated sensation faded and Katya found herself in darkness. She felt stone under her feet. That meant the spell had worked, she'd passed through the rock to the other side.

Then, an explosion of light and the touch of a hand on her arm revealed her friends and made her smile instinctively. "We made it?"

"Yes, we made it," Ibrox said, but didn't return the smile. His hands glowed, illuminating them all in a cold glow. "Now we must find the others."

"They can't have gone far," Magno said, his voice trembling. He knelt down with a lantern and produced flint and steel. A spark and some patience rewarded his efforts and once it was lit, Ibrox let go of his spell. They turned in the direction of the doorway.

And found themselves facing another wall of rock.

"There must be a way around," Katya said. "We need to find it."

"That or a way out," Ibrox said.

"We can't leave my sister here."

"We won't," Lady Eleanor said. "We'll find her and return to the portal."

They walked down the passageway in the opposite direction, Magno led, lantern in one hand and curved sword in the other. The tunnel opened out into a cavern. Magno's light reflecting off a vast field of crystal all over the ground and ceiling. Katya gasped, she'd had never seen anything like it. "What is this place?"

"We are a long way into the earth," Ibrox said. "Very few eyes will have seen sights such as these." He turned all around gazing up. "There is magic in these stones, an old magic, older than anything I have known."

"Lost and waiting for us," Eleanor said. "Could this help?"

Ibrox frowned. "How?"

"To rebuild the seal; the first two are contained. We cannot prepare wards as we did in Isoloha and Avignon, but we can use this power against it."

Ibrox nodded slowly. "I don't know if such a thing is possible, but it has merit. We must inform the Cardinal."

"Indeed," Magno said. "But that means finding a way out of here."

Chapter 20: Lairs

As the day drew to a close, Hino Kunimitsu reined in his horse near the end of the hilltop path and caught sight of his destination.

The Kokubun-ji temple in Iga Province.

The fading sun flickered through the trees as he slipped from his saddle and led his mount through the temple gardens. An old man tended rows of plants with a rake and eyed him as he walked past.

"What are you seeking?" he asked.

Kunimitsu stopped and turned to him. "Your pardon, I am—"

"I know who you are, that wasn't the question I asked."

Kunimitsu stared. The man wore the robes of a monk, but didn't look familiar and carried himself like a much younger man. Kunimitsu bowed. "Your pardon again," he said.

The old man grunted and pointed up the hill. "You may enter the house," he said. "Perhaps after some time in contemplation, you will be able to answer questions more clearly."

Kunimitsu bowed again and resumed his walk. He soon reached the building and tethered his horse to the gate before climbing the steps and entering the open hall. He found no mat on the wooden boards and so chose a spot near the centre and dropped to his knees, to think as the old man suggested.

Why am I here?

Takuaji had been clear that he would not give up his pretend Emperor. Kunimitsu did not believe he was the source of division in Japan, but so long as he remained, the wound could not be closed.

After returning to give his report to the Emperor and responding faithfully and fully to all questions, Kunimitsu had left Yoshino and journeyed south. Once he was sure no-one pursued him, he turned back and made for Iga. The difficult roads and crossing of the Hattori river made the journey arduous, but he had high hopes for what he would find.

"Do you have an answer for me now?"

Kunimitsu glanced around. The old man stood on the steps. He stood up and faced him. "Yes, I am here seeking a legend."

The old man smiled. "You have a legend of your own, why do you need another one?"

"The story of my past is different from the truth."

"All legends are different from the truth," The old man's smile disappeared and his expression darkened. "Speak plainly, do not waste my time."

"I require knowledge," Kuminitsu said. He swallowed past the lump in his throat. "I must defeat an enemy who my legend could defeat but I cannot."

"You are here to learn then?"

"Yes."

"Then why are the words difficult?"

"Because... your ways are... dishonourable."

The old man nodded. "Where is your family sword?" he asked.

"I do not have one," Kunimitsu replied. "My father died and it was never returned."

"A house such as yours with no sword. Your honour is absent until it is found." The old man walked up the last of the steps and held out the rake. "I, also, have no sword, only this. You might say it is my sword, but unbound by the same rules."

Kunimitsu looked at the rake. All along its length he saw elaborate writing in a language he could not read. "You are the man I seek then?"

"I am a man and I will teach you things."

"To defeat my enemy?"

"In time, but first, to understand there are many forms of honour."

The underground lit up by moss and crystal; the half-light of dusk deep below the earth, where no human had lived, or would live.

Galina and Hino stared at this ancient world and the ancient world stared back.

The strangers were thin and tall, with long hair, angular faces, almond shaped eyes and strange pointed ears. The rocklight cast shadows on them, lighting them from below, making them severe and judgemental.

Ten people, dressed in loose fitting robes. They brandished bows and long hunting knives. Their leader wore a circlet of dark leaves, his open hand keeping the arrows at bay. Behind them, Galina saw a vast city on a midnight lake, curved towers and houses surrounded by an obsidian wall.

"Your kind is known," The leader said.

"Yet you are not familiar to us," Hino said, bowing his head. "We do not wish to intrude."

"Your world intrudes," the leader said. "In the eldest times your people drove us into this doom."

"We did not do this."

"No and that is why you live."

Hino bowed again. "My people honour the giving of names. I am Hino Suketomo, once *dainagon* of Emperor Go-Daigo of Japan."

"Hino," The leader said, tasting the sound as he spoke it. "You will come with us."

A flicker of movement drew Galina's attention, a horse walking across open ground, stark white in colour with a horn between its ears. On its back, a women, her hair long and raven dark across its back. She regarded Galina and Hino with a solemn expression, but did not speak.

The leader and his followers began to walk back towards the city. Galina glanced at Hino who nodded. They followed, side by side, the archers all around them. No further words were needed. They were prisoners.

The path wound through a field of moss covered rocks. Amongst them, small figures worked, crawling over stones, collecting things into shoulder slung baskets. "What are they doing?" Galina asked.

But no-one answered.

They walked on, the track twisting and turning. Ahead, the obsidian walls glimmered. As they passed through open gates, Galina reached out to touch the smooth glass, impossibly thick and strong. Above, she saw more strange figures staring down with unfamiliar eyes.

Hino's hand touched her shoulder. She gazed at him and he gave her an encouraging smile. She tried to return it but couldn't, too many people were watching.

Instead, she stared forward at their destination, a vast dome shaped building like nothing she'd ever seen. A spire rose out of its centre, as tall as the great houses of Rome and climbing away towards the cavern roof. The elegant curves and sweeps hid all sign of construction. Even the doors slid away in front of them with no hint of hinge or bracket. She noted the same symbol on them as she had seen in the tunnel.

Once inside the dome, they were taken to a circular hall. The chamber was mostly empty, but a few grey robed figures stared at them from raked benches around a stone floor. The leader of their captors indicated two chairs in the middle and walked to a place on the lowest tier of seats. The other guards departed.

Galina sat down under the expectant gaze of the people above. She eyed each strange angular face, trying to get an idea of them, a clue as to what they wanted, but they gave nothing away. She turned to Hino, but he too seemed elsewhere, his eyes on the ground.

Footsteps echoed towards them and the barefooted woman who'd followed them entered. The grey robed figures all got to their feet. Hino did likewise and nudged her. Galina copied him. The woman walked passed them to another place on the benches and sat. When she did, so did everyone else.

The silence and stares resumed. Eventually, Galina could bear it no more and stood up and faced the woman. "I am Galina. We came here through a door with the same symbol as these doors. My friends are still out there, can you help us rescue them?"

The woman smiled – an expression of sadness rather than joy. "That entrance has never opened for us. Its makers ensured we would not return to the world that way."

"Who made it then?" Galina asked.

"You did."

Hino stood. "Honourable lady, I have gifted you my name, we are guests in your hall. We know not who we address."

"Your kind never valued our names before," the woman said. "Why do you value them now?"

"Forgive me lady, but I believe much of this conversation occurred before we came here," Hino remarked.

"The memories of our people are long even if yours are not. Now we must judge your return to decide whether we gift you with knowledge you lack."

"Are you blaming us for the crimes of others?" Galina asked. "We've never been here before."

"That remains to be seen," the man who had brought them said. "Your people are known for all manner of trickeries."

A ripple of assent ran around the room and Galina began to recognise the mood. They weren't considered guests by these people, they were enemies.

Dangerous enemies.

"You will learn little without questions," Hino remarked. "Ask. Else we all remain ignorant."

The man leaned forward. "How did you get here?"

Hino shrugged. "We opened a door and it led to this place."

"Are there more of you?"

"Yes."

"How many?"

"Three of us passed through the door. Four more need rescue. Beyond them, many others await word." Hino's sparse words left no room for elaboration.

"My sister is trapped out there," Galina added. "We need to get back and help her."

"You ask us for our aid then?" the woman said. "What do you offer in return?"

"I..." Galina swallowed and glanced around. All eyes were on her now, including Hino's. "I don't know what I can do for you."

"You are the door opener are you not?" The woman smiled again. "I am."

"Then would you open more things?"

"I don't know how," Galina admitted. A slow flush spread across her face. "I touched the symbol and they opened," she turned to Hino. "The others couldn't get it to work, only me."

"Perhaps we should test your ability once more," The woman stood up and walked to the centre of the floor, beckoning Galina to her. She did as she was bidden and noticed another shape carved into the rock.

"Will you show us what you did?" the woman asked.

Galina knelt down and placed her palm against the stone. A tingling sensation ran along her arm and awoke, bathing the room in a soft blue glow. She glanced up at the woman.

"Now will you help us?"

The woman nodded. "In ways you cannot know."

Something shifted in the air and the ground underneath Katya's feet shook. "Are we not safe, even here?" she asked.

"It is not the same thing," Ibrox said and pointed. "Look."

The field of crystal they'd spotted had begun to move, rising up and undulating strangely. A clustered hill of boulders moved vertically upwards then rearranged themselves. Katya saw two lights appear amongst them and realised immediately what they were.

"They're eyes..." she murmured, then louder to warn the others. "The crystal fields aren't crystals and stones! They're alive!"

Magno scowled and stepped in front of Katya brandishing his sword, but Eleanor laid a gentle hand on his arm. "We must find out what they are before we make them hate us."

On cue, a lizard-like head turned towards them. It floated forwards as the creature's long neck extended, its eyes blinking as it stared at Magno's lantern, stopping a few feet away from them.

"What is it?" Katya asked.

"*Draco*," Magno replied tersely. She could see beads of sweat on his brow. "A demon of the ancient world."

172

"Such creatures no longer exist," Ibrox said. "Their bones litter the long sand."

"This one exists," Eleanor said, "and it does not seem so old."

A keening cry drew Katya's attention. A second creature emerged, similar to the first, but a little bigger. It waddled over on four powerful legs and she saw small furled wings on its scaled back. "What woke them?" she wondered out loud.

"We may never learn the answer," Eleanor replied. Cautiously she reached a hand out to the first creature. It moved towards her and let her stroke its head. "Hard, like glass or rock," she said. "A skin as strong as steel," she smiled at Magno. "You might have broken your sword."

Magno scowled in response, but lowered the weapon. "Our path leads us away from here if we want to find the others."

"True, but we are safe for now and can spare a moment."

Katya held out her hand to the first dragon, it turned to her, but then flinched, snorted and stepped backwards. She reached for it, but it cried out and retreated again.

"Strange," Lady Eleanor said. "Perhaps they sense nerves or something else." She touched Katya's shoulder. "Magno is right, we must keep moving, else we will not find your sister, come."

Reluctantly, Katya backed away from the creature, but it continued to watch her. Beyond, she saw more movement from several directions. She resumed walking, following Magno along the path they had been on before. The Genoese soldier still held his sword in one hand and the lantern in another and cursed in Italian as he prowled down the track.

They reached a sloped face of rock on the far side, slick with dark moss. "What do we do?" Katya asked.

"We climb," Ibrox said and pulled out the rope from before. He threw it up into the shadows. The hooked metal end clattered onto the stone and he drew it back slowly, making sure it held. Then, holding the line in one hand, he began walking up the slope. Eleanor followed and Katya after her with Magno last.

"They're following us," he said.

"So long as they remain curious and not hostile, we can allow that," Eleanor replied.

The incline flattened out twenty or thirty feet from the ground and a small path took them to a cave. As she got to the entrance, Katya glanced back. The land below seethed with young dragons, all walking towards the slope they had climbed. Those that reached it couldn't climb the moss and tumbled into their brethren causing all manner of confusion, but with their powerful legs, it was plain they would make it eventually.

"We need to hurry," Katya said.

Magno nodded and moved passed her into the cave. "Yes we do."

Shouts from below disturbed Tuia from his work.

He lowered his bloody knife and motioned for the mantled guard to find out what transpired inside the pyramid. The man bowed and disappeared back down the steps.

Tuia sat cross legged on the blood slick platform and waited.

He had wielded the knife every night for twenty years. He had tasted the last life of each victim and become a weapon forged for purpose; the executioner of humanity who brought power to the chosen warriors of his mistress.

In that time, the city had grown. The people made war in the name of their deities, roving the land and capturing the weak and the strong for sacrifice. Those who would not bow down became empty eyed stonebreakers and stumbling flesh for the staircase. These days, most bowed before the gods.

The pyramid had become tall and when Teotl was happy with it, she had ordered the slaves to dig down into the earth. The ground under their buildings was boggy and unstable, but still she pressed them to work and overcome the challenge. Now, the structure rested over a great pit, deeper than the height of their building. What Teotl sought in the earth, Tuia did not know.

Perhaps today he would find out.

He stood up and elbowed his way past the queueing slaves. He made his way to one of the lower entrances and pushed aside the door, running along the narrow walkway and down a thin ladder to the wide stone platform above the pit.

Far below he saw the supplicant warriors, their heads bloodied from anointment. They backed away from the centre of the excavation and stood around it in a circle.

Tuia climbed down, his hands finding hidden holds on the smooth stone. He felt young and strong, stronger perhaps than he'd ever felt. Only the sun weakened him. He avoided it whenever he could, sleeping fitfully in a dark cave and dreaming of the next night's blood.

He reached the supplicants and forced them aside, gazing into the space they had left. It lay immediately under the sacrifice platform on the top of the pyramid and blood still dripped from his last victim, down onto a large circular symbol carved into the rock.

As he stared, the earth groaned and the rock split in half, falling away into the depths of the world below.

From beneath it came a gout of flame, drawing shouts and screams from the gathered warriors, but Tuia did not react, he remained still.

A huge scaled head pressed itself against the new fissure. An eye as big as a small house gazed at the people above, it blinked, once, twice, thrice, then fell away into the void, to return a moment later, fixing its gaze on Tuia.

He did not move, his heart lurched in his chest, but he ignored it and did not flinch from the inexorable stare. The eye blinked and disappeared once more.

Tuia turned to the terrified warriors.

"The time for sacrifices has passed. Get the slaves down here and get them digging! Now!"

Faim opened the door into absolute darkness.

Immediately, Piers sensed several figures watching them. He didn't move for a minute, hoping his eyes would adjust, but they didn't. The gloom remained impenetrable. Even the conjured sword he carried only illuminated his hand and face.

"Welcome Gaveston," a voice purred. He recognised it – *the father.* "We've been expecting you and your friend."

Piers inched forward, trying to use any of his senses to get an impression of the room, but just like the times before, only father's voice gave him any idea. It seemed far away, but he knew in an instance it might whisper in his ear. *Enemy territory,* he thought. *Ground on which we cannot hope to—*

"Hello John."

"Faim, why are you here?" An abrupt change of tone, Piers thought he heard a trace of hesitation and... *fear?*

"You've broken the edict we placed upon you John. You know the punishment for transgression."

"You forget where you are, Faim."

"I forget nothing," Illumination bloomed in Faim's hands. For a moment, it struggled against the unnatural gloom, but then banished it, revealing the room, massive with figures standing along each of the walls. Piers counted a hundred or more.

At the end sat a man in a chair, flinching away from the light. His bald head seemed too large for his body, and his long fingernails were black, his eyes rheumy and surrounded by scars.

175

"Your power is borrowed John. You were given the gift of eternity and a place in our new society provided you performed your task correctly."

The seated creature gestured with a clawed hand. "Have I not done as you asked?"

"You have done that and more," Faim replied. "Where is the boy?"

John shrank into his chair. "You would begrudge a father his own son?"

"The boy is *not* your son."

"I'm the only family he's known, I've raised him and protected him."

Faim stepped forward, drawing hisses from the figures all around him, but no-one approached the light. "We can fence over this for as long as you like John. The boy is not yours and what you do breaks our agreement."

"You understand why I will not reveal him then?" A hacking sound came from the bulbous, hairless head, something approximating a laugh. "If you cannot find him, I can negotiate."

Faim smiled. "Name your terms then."

"I give you the boy, you leave everything else as it is."

"Including your petty kingdom?" Faim looked around. "These people are the sum of your achievements here I take it? Perhaps you should have remained in Bohemia as we suggested."

A woman screamed a challenge and lunged forward from the wall. Faim's left hand snapped out towards her and caught her by the throat as she reached for him. Long dirty nails flailed uselessly, grasping.

"I have no stomach for being another's lackey," John said.

Faim spoke a word and the light in his hands intensified. The woman cried out again then she began to burn, dissolving into ash.

He lowered his hand.

"You have no choice in this. You were given immortality and asked to create a family in the darkness, awaiting the world's change. Drinking the old blood is forbidden to you and forbidden to your followers."

"You mean to kill me then?"

"I do."

The room erupted. The people along the walls flung themselves forward, charging mindlessly. Piers grimaced and hacked, left and right into the shadows. This was the worst of warfare, the kind where you fought to live, knowing the press of bodies around you were all enemies who desired your end.

He felt fingernails and teeth on his shoulder. He turned and stabbed a wide-eyed man with straggled hair and a mouth full of fangs. Hands grabbed his ankle and he swept the conjured blade down in response, slicing them from the wrists of their owner.

The blade was an advantage. The people he fought evaporated at the touch of his sword. Being made of magic, it could not be snagged or notched, but the spell required constant maintenance. Without the faith he once had, the effort drained him with each moment.

Fingers dug into his back, raking down his spine, he screamed, and lashed out at a rabid child then twisted and thrust his sword into the gut of a woman intent on eating his face.

There are too many!

The world went dark. The press of bodies overwhelmed him. Something hit him on the head and disrupted his spell. The sword disappeared from his hands and he dropped to the ground, covering his face as best he could.

They were all over him, fanged teeth seeking the weaknesses in his spell hardened clothes. Killing was easy when it was the only way to survive. He remembered Ireland, a skirmish outside Malahide castle, being dragged from a horse amidst a rioting mob. He drew himself inwards like he had done that day, clenched his fists and fought to stand up.

A mouth clamped onto his neck. He felt pain at the bite and twisted, grabbing at the head fastened to him, tearing it loose and throwing the man over his shoulder into other enemies.

He traced a symbol in the air and spoke the words he'd been taught. Red flames erupted from the floor. Screams echoed all around as figures dissolved into ash. Others ran to the doorway and out to the stairs. He turned to follow them.

"No, wait!"

Piers looked around. Faim stood in front of the chair, his hand bloodied to the elbow. The lifeless form of the creature he had called John lay slumped in his seat, a hole in his chest where his heart would have been. "Let them go, we have what we wanted."

"Do we?" Pier asked. "Where's the boy?"

"Over here," said a voice. Rag sat in the corner of the room his head in his heads. Piers saw bite marks all along his naked arms. "I'm ready to leave," he said.

"Then let's go," Faim replied. "Quickly."

Chapter 21: The Act of the Oppressor

Blue light stole around the chamber and Hino eyed each of the people in attendance. As one they focused on Galina as she knelt with her palm pressed to the symbol in the centre of the floor. *They do not care about me,* he thought, *but they will not let her leave.*

His gaze went to the woman who stood beside Galina. "My name is Laurelatha," she said and gestured around her. "My people are the *aelfe* or *huldra* to some. I am the voice of this council. The warrior who brought you to me is Sethanas. I will introduce to the others gathered here when you wish."

Galina frowned and pointed at the glowing symbol. "What does this mean?"

"You have woken something that slept awaiting you," Laurelatha replied. "Beyond that, I truly do not know."

"Do you trust us now?"

"Trust is an acceptance of equals. We accept you Galina. We believe in your action because we must and it is part of a purpose."

Hino stepped up to Galina's side and took her hand, helping her to her feet. "We ask for aid to help and find our friends," he said. "One of them came this way and disappeared."

Laurelatha's expression stiffened. "We will not do this," she said.

"Our mission is urgent, the world—"

"Wakes up and changes, returning those banished to their rightful place," Laurelatha said. "All people fear change, but change comes and must be faced."

"We need to leave here," Hino pressed.

"The girl stays with us," Sethanas announced from his place on the steps.

Galina bit her lip. "I'm a prisoner?"

Laurelatha bowed and smiled sadly. "Try to understand. This world is not as it should be. We have lived beneath for so long our memories are preserved only in the oldest writing. We must keep you. There is much to awaken."

"What about Hino?"

"He may leave when he wishes."

They turned towards him. Hino inclined his head and bowed. "I cannot leave whilst you hold my companion against her will. Amongst my people, when paths incur conflict and cannot be resolved, a contest resolves them."

A murmur of whispers ran around the hall. "What do you suggest?" Sethanas asked.

"A duel of arms with no restriction," Hino replied. "Name your champion."

"Wizards are always tricksters in such trials," Sethanas said. "We have the advantage. Why should we permit such an opportunity?"

"With respect, you misunderstand your own position," Hino said. "We came to this place as explorers, we are expected to return. Our company will send word and when others learn of your city, they will come here to free us from your gaol."

Laurelatha held up her hand. "We do not seek conflict."

"Then you must release us both," Hino said.

"Our ancients foretold a time in which a wanderer would come amongst us and break the wards that contain us, but then, all imprisoned people require hope, do they not?" Laurelatha smiled sadly. "If deliverance came to you in the twilight of your life, would you not seize it?"

"You talk of the girl as if she were a prize," Hino said. "She is not, she is a girl."

Sethanas stood up and walked towards Hino, stopping two feet from him. "We accept your terms," he said.

Hino deliberately looked at Laurelatha who did not meet his gaze. He glanced back at Sethanas whose expression had darkened at the slight. "If you agree, we should move to a suitable place."

Sethanas nodded. "I will make the preparations," he said and strode from the room.

Galina's hand clutched Hino's elbow. "They said you can go. You don't need to do this for me."

Hino smiled at her. "I am not leaving you in the place. We do not know enough to trust these people and they certainly do not trust us. My life is little consequence in this, but yours... appears valuable to them. Whatever happens, learn everything you can and think carefully about the decisions you make."

"You could die..."

"All of us die eventually. My people already think me dead. My son believes this as does my Emperor. What life remains to me, I pledged to our cause. This is a worthy service."

Galina frowned. "I wish I could be that sure," she said.
Hino nodded. "I also wish that."

The new passageway grew dark and the cries of the dragons faded away. Magno's lantern went out. He tried to relight it without success, so Ibrox conjured new light in his hands. Lady Eleanor did the same. Katya considered making the attempt, but decided against it, particularly when she saw the look on Magno's face. His need to rely on others in these dark tunnels wore heavily on his shoulders.

They came to a wider space, almost like an alcove next to the path. In the distance, Katya thought she could hear running water.

"We will stop here," Eleanor said. "It was nearly dark when we started and must be far into the night by now."

Magno sat down and unshouldered his bag. "There's no sense of time here," he said. "Could be noon and it would still be the same."

Ibrox chuckled. "In my country there are mines where people dig for diamonds. In the darkest places, people learn ways to tell day and night. There are rhythms in the body which respond to the sun and take many years to fade away."

"I wonder who built this place?" Katya said. "It cannot be natural for such a network of tunnels and passages to be here."

"No indeed," Eleanor said. "Someone created the ward your sister defeated." She perched on a small rock and released her light, leaving Ibrox's spell to illuminate their little circle. "Many creatures exist in this world, some known only by legend and song. I never believed I would live to see a dragon in my life time."

"Nor I," Magno said, his tense lips finally breaking into a smile. "Sailors talk of dragons at the edge of the world, none ever spoken of them beneath the earth."

Ibrox shuffled forwards. "Lady, when you touched the skin of the beast, you spoke of it as stone?"

Eleanor nodded. "Yes, like smooth marble, but strangely alive, warm like a living thing."

"I would be concerned if we had to fight such creatures," Ibrox said. "We do not know their weakness, we must be cautious." He glanced around. "I will watch first."

Eleanor looked at Katya. "Wake me next," she said. "I will try to teach you the light spell."

Katya sighed. "I might not be able to control myself," she said.

Eleanor smiled. "Nevertheless, we make the attempt."

"I want to be helpful," Katya said. "So far I don't appear to be much use."

"You will find you place and time," Eleanor said. "When it comes, you will be invaluable, do not worry."

Katya nodded. She turned to Magno. "Can I ask you a question?"

"Of course."

"How does your gift work? You cannot cast spells and such – like my sister, but what can you do?"

Magno smiled, but there was a tightness in the expression, betraying his feelings. "What makes me useful you mean? You noticed something of it earlier perhaps? Balance and agility for the most part, although I can sense the magic in things a little, like many mixed blood folk, though not like your sister, she's different."

"In what way?"

"She sees things," he said, "like down there in the hole, when she was babbling. I couldn't see what she meant."

"Of any of us, you would be most attuned," Ibrox said.

"Perhaps," Magno replied and frowned. "There's something there, a potency or latent power, but I didn't sense anything when it erupted."

"I wonder if it will reach us..." Katya mused.

"We are some distance from the seal," Eleanor said, "but I share your concerns."

Katya turned to her. "We're trapped here, aren't we?"

Eleanor smiled. "We are four keen minds and remain whole in body and spirit. Do not give up on us yet."

Accompanied by two guards, Laurelatha led Galina from the chamber into a corridor. At the end, there were another set of doors with a symbol spread across them. "No-one has been beyond this entrance since the first days of my people in this place," Laurelatha said. "Will you open them?"

Galina stepped forward but hesitated then stepped back. "Will you answer my questions if I do?"

Laurelatha nodded. "To the best of my ability, yes."

Galina held her eye for a moment then turned to the doors. She placed both hands on the symbol. Once more she felt the tingle and glimpsed the flash of blue and they swung back at her touch; she walked inside.

She entered a long hall with tall stone columns in two rows. Around each, a coiling mass of crystal and etched writing, the first she had seen in the caverns. The crystals glowed gently, brightening as she approached and illuminating the etchings. She recognised them immediately; they were the same as those in the ritual chamber of Isoloha, the city she'd been rescued from by Hino and Lady Eleanor.

At that moment her stomach grumbled. "No doubt I could spend forever in here learning," she said. "But without sleep and food I will not last long."

Laurelatha bowed. "My apologies, a meal will be brought. Your requirements are unknown to us, but we cannot be too dissimilar."

"No indeed," Galina said. "But you also promised to answer my questions."

"Yes I did, perhaps I can remain here as you eat?"

"I would like that."

Laurelatha bowed again and went to the door. A few minutes later, a man entered carrying a bowl of dark leaves and two stone cups. He knelt and placed them on the floor then left. Laurelatha seated herself and beckoned Galina to join her, which she did, making herself comfortable on the stone.

"They are maple," Laurelatha said. "The deep maple is a tree that grows in the darkest caverns and is harvested by my people." She lifted a leaf into her mouth and chewed slowly. "It has a bitter flavour, but it will sustain you."

Galina picked up a leaf and copied the action. The sharp taste wasn't pleasant, but she was hungry enough that it didn't matter. She took one of the stone cups and sipped its contents. Cool and clean water diluted the leaf's tang.

They ate in silence for a while. In between mouthfuls of leaves and sips of water, Galina studied Laurelatha, noting the differences between them. Pointed ears peeking out from beneath her long black hair, the angular lines of her face and the strange shape of her eyes were all evidence of her different ancestry. Galina thought about Ibrox's dark skin and Hino's slanted features. Both were unusual, but when she spoke with them they responded in familiar ways and found common ground. With this woman though...

"We are not alike," Laurelatha remarked as if reading her thoughts. "To my people you are the scion of a dangerous enemy, one who defeated, mastered and imprisoned us, but these are stories of long ago, before those left alive in these halls was born."

"I can't use magic," Galina said.

"You opened the door. That required magic and means you are of the blood."

"But how can I be blamed for the actions of those I know nothing about?"

"How can anyone judge?" Laurelatha replied. "Only by what we experience. We know the maple leaf may be eaten, but perhaps one day I will sicken and die because I eat one that is not the same. I drink water as others drank water. I know your kind is the enemy because my elders experienced it."

"It's not the same," Galina said. "People are different."

"People are *not* different," Laurelatha replied. "All things that live respond according to their nature. When that nature is understood, we form judgements."

"Where did your ancestors live, before they came here?"

Laurelatha smiled and her eyes grew distant. "On the surface amidst the trees and the birds, we sing songs of the sun and the moon; we remember the stars."

"This place is not the world above," Galina said. "Yet your ancestors survived and you live here. You changed."

"The twilight is no true life; we grow less with each generation," Laurelatha said, her smile fading. "We are resourceful and your kind devised this cage to sustain us. Others were not so fortunate."

"What do you mean?"

"Do you think we are the only creatures banished from the surface of the world?"

Galina thought about the *juje* and what he'd said to her years before. *Many! But not here, away. Gone.* "There are more creatures? Living with your people?"

Laurelatha shrugged. "The tunnels are vast, who knows where they go? Only those wizards who came here in the earliest times would remember all the different prisons they made."

Galina nodded. "This is why you hate us then?"

"It is one reason." Laurelatha stood up and walked over to the nearest of the columns. "Your kind made this place and wrote upon this stone then sealed the doors with the ward you touched. I cannot read these words, can you?"

"No."

Laurelatha traced her fingers over the writing. "Eventually my people will learn their meaning, perhaps they tell a different story to the one we hear all our lives, but I sense there is not enough time left." She faced Galina again. "The people who wrote this, devised a way for the door to open. It is possible you learned that way, or it is instinctive to you?"

"I told you before I don't know how I did it," Galina said. "I touch the symbols and they respond."

"Have any not awoken?"

"Only one, a door in a chamber long ago, it wouldn't let me out."

"Then perhaps you were supposed to stay there," Laurelatha mused. "Either way, you are a key. The world changes around us and your power affects it. That makes you important."

"I'm not important," Galina said. "I can't change anything."

"You say you cannot use magic like your peers," Laurelatha said. "Do you not see? This is your gift. To my people you are significant. You may be our salvation."

Galina frowned. "You said your imprisoning was one reason to hate us. What other reasons are there?"

If it were possible, Laurelatha's expression became more cautious. "There is magic used to summon and compel. The wizards cast these spells to bring us here. Your friend Hino is capable of such magic, which is why we must be on our guard."

Again, Galina was reminded of the night she met the *juje* annd what he'd said about her sister after she'd caught him lurking around the fire. "If you are summoned, you must obey the wizard?"

"So the old stories say."

"You can't just walk away?"

"No," Laurelatha sighed. "Two things are prized amongst my kind – life and free will. Wizards threaten both of these rights."

Galina frowned. "But is your answer to deprive me of freedom and Hino of his life?"

"Your friend made his own choice. I see the contradiction in your fate, but better this than our end. Perhaps you understand how heavily this decision weighs upon us."

Galina chewed her lip. Moments before her mind had teemed with questions, but now there was nothing to be said. "I think I will sleep now."

"As you wish, blankets will be brought to you." Laurelatha bowed and walked towards the doors.

"I am to stay here then?" Galina asked.

"There is no better place," Laurelatha replied and slipped out of the door.

Kunimitsu sat in the dark.

184

After some rudimentary questions, the old man had left him and told him to remain in the hall until he returned. Kunimitsu accepted this restriction, but explored what he could, examining the room to exhaust his curiosity.

The place was scrupulously clean, but there were few clues to the identity of his host. He did find nicks and cracks in the wood of the walls and floor around waist and head height. Evidence of weapon practice, perhaps?

His mind wandered over the stories that had brought him here. Legends of shadowy *Obake* demons, summoned to murder men, women and children in their sleep. Iga was a place of old Japanese myth and tradition, its people hardy and close knit, unlikely to listen to the whispered words of dissent that concerned the Conclave. If strangers promised reward and stirred trouble they would do so in the towns and cities where they could hide amongst the foreign traders. Here, an outsider would be known.

I too am an outsider to these people, he thought.

He walked to the steps and stared out into the night. His horse nickered a greeting He yearned to go to it to retrieve his staff, to unpack blankets and food, but the old man's instructions had been clear. Beyond the gate, a mist gripped the woodland, shrouding everything, as if it were being devoured by another world. In some ways it was. This was the land of the *Oni*, according to superstition. Kunimitsu knew the truth lay somewhere else, but the blood of his gift burned as he sensed magic amidst the fog. A presence stared back, vast and powerful, curious and tempting.

"You were wise to obey my instruction."

Kunimitsu started in surprise. The old man had returned without a sound. He was dressed in grey garments that blended with the mist. "The wards are set and the lords of this valley appeased. You are allowed to remain and may unpack your things."

"Thank you," Kunimitsu said. "Where am I to stay?"

"Here of course," the old man said. "You may roam further in the daytime as you wish, but at night, only when permitted."

"I understand. Are you to teach me?"

The old man shrugged. "At first, yes. After that, others will come, demons who will offer instruction in exchange for payment. You may accept or refuse. If you refuse there will also be payment. If you do not pay, you bring dishonour to your presence and the wards will fail. What happens then…"

"Of course. You need not elaborate."

The old man grunted. "I have spoken for you, remember that. Any punishment you bear will also come to me."

"Why would you do such a—"

"My reasons are my own, you have no right to ask of them."

"Very well."

"One more thing," the old man said. "Worthy people survive on what they forage for themselves. Eat and drink nothing you are given, lest it curse you."

Kunimitsu bowed. "My thanks for all you have done," he said.

The old man stared at him for a moment. Then returned the gesture. "I met your father once. Others sacrificed a great deal to help him. Be worthy of that. Be worthy of them." He gestured out into the darkness. "See to your horse."

Kunimitsu turned away to do just that.

Chapter 22: Freedom of Choice

"This way."

A gloomy wet tunnel on the outskirts of Sredets, a wide expanse of foul water leading out of the city, moving slowly in the dark. The smell reminded Piers of the well outside Picardy, the battlefields of Ireland, or the aftermath of the ritual in Avignon. The rot and rubbish of humanity was a world forgotten to those who could afford it. Only the desperate would follow them here.

It had been a long walk from the abandoned house, but they needed to get out immediately. The sewers were the best way to leave unseen. Rag led the way as if he knew where he was going, the glow of his lantern casting huge shadows all around the tunnel roof. Piers came after him and Faim brought up the rear, leaning heavily on his staff, plainly exhausted by his efforts to free the boy, but he kept the pace and followed without complaint.

The path narrowed, forcing Piers closer to the edge. He'd heard stories of people dying having fallen in such filth. He stopped breathing through his nose so he wouldn't retch, but he could still taste the stench in the air. He focused on the light in front and kept moving, each step taking them further from danger, unless more danger lay ahead.

Rag halted. Piers caught up to him, Faim a few steps behind. The lantern illuminated a spiral staircase set into the brick wall. "That'll take you up and out of the town," he said. "I'm not coming with you."

"Wait a minute," Piers said. "The reason we did this was for you."

"And I'm grateful," Rag replied. "But I'll not trade one prison for another."

Piers opened his mouth to answer, but he felt Faim's hand on his shoulder. "The boy is right. Freedom is the right to choose, not to live as slave to a different master. He must make his own way."

"After everything we've—"

"You are also free my friend, another reason for what we did. You know you will not be followed."

Piers sighed. "What will you do?" he asked Rag.

The boy smiled. "Practise what I learned from you, There's a whole world to explore. I plan to see all that I can."

Piers realised they weren't alone. Eyes glittered in the gloom behind Faim and in front further down the tunnel. "Friends of yours?" he asked Faim.

"Friends of mine," Rag said, "in case you didn't agree to let me go."

Faim laughed, but the effort turned into a tired cough. "You do not know me, child. My purpose was never to control you." His gaze strayed into the darkness. "I am pleased with the path you have taken already."

Rag scowled. "I don't need your approval."

"No indeed, you don't." Faim's staff tapped a rhythm as he moved to the stairs. "Nevertheless you have it," he said and walked up the steps.

Cautiously, Piers followed.

Galina slept. As her body rested, she left it behind, wandering the vast hall and exploring its pillars and walls.

She reached beyond the stone. The writing was enchanted and resisted her, but she slipped between the flaws in the ward. Outside the chamber, outside the building, outside the city, through stone and flying down darkened passageways, until she found a glimmer of ghostly light.

Ibrox sat awake, guarding the others as they slept. She stole past him then froze as he glanced around, his gift disturbed by her passing. There was a shadow about him and his magic, something she didn't understand. But he didn't do anything else and soon turned away, leaving her free to reach her destination.

Katya.

Galina stared down at her sleeping sister. They'd never been this far apart before and she'd never journeyed such a distance from her own body, but finding her twin was an instinct she could never switch off, nor would she want to.

Since childhood they'd shared thoughts, finishing each other's sentences like other twins, but for Galina there was something more, something she'd always been able to do, but withheld for many years, allowing Katya her privacy.

She made her way into her sister's mind, gently probing so as not to wake her. She swam amidst a chaotic whirl of fitful sleep. Turbulent emotions always ruled Katya, held in check only by force of will and redirection. Anger would fuel her work or sadness or some other passion, depending on her mood. Now she was gripped by fear and worry at their separation. Galina sailed these storms until they became quiet and calm then set about her task.

She called up memories; all that she had seen since they parted, sharing them as gifts to a mind the twin of her own. They were different in many ways, but the same in others, enabling the old blood to empower their connection.

When she was done, she stole away, evading Ibrox's gaze, to return to her body. She returned to gaze at the pillars. She looked down at the twisted crystal creepers peering into them. Something moved in their depths, something alive.

She felt things around her, three minds, prowling the cages of sleep, trapped in the crystal, whilst she roamed free. She watched them, peered into their delusions. Some were dreams of aspiration: invented lives, loves and ambition carved from the memories of their time awake. They had transcended mortality, becoming masters of their fate; powerful beyond measure to the worshippers they attracted and so in accepting reverence they become drunk on adulation. Faith cast an image of them, told a story of their past that wove truth with embellishment. Later the truth disappeared leaving only legend and myth; upon this they built dreams, making castles from the lies and ignorance of their followers.

These were the wizards who constructed the chamber and the prison for Laurelatha's people. They never left, but lived in the hall until their lives ended. They found a means of preservation in the magic and the memory of their charges. The stories of the old ones invoked fear and fear preserved them within the crystal.

They became aware of her and stared out of their translucent tomb. At first she feared what they might do, but they could not touch her unless she joined them. They commanded her to do so, but she refused. After that they threatened, promising retribution, but still she held back, recognising the purpose behind their words. They wanted her – to feast upon her memories and knowledge.

She stared at them, ignoring their demands until they began to beg. Eventually they offered to show her what she wanted. She waited a little longer and then moved towards them, accepting their offer and joining with them for a time.

The world turned backwards...

Her name was Ether and she asked to remain. With her were Tepeu and Enlil, two male wizards chosen to share her fate.

The spells woven into the door wards would mean years of work for anyone attempting to gain entry. A breach of the outer door might give them access to the reservations and the beings contained within them, but it would trigger alerts throughout the network.

Each of the three had reasons to accept isolation. For Ether, the task suited her purpose. Her mortal life would end soon and the role of guardian would permit her time to transcend. The node chamber gave her time and space without interference. She could explore the nature of her gift, the old blood of the first strangers who brought life and knowledge to this world.

Tepeu and Enlil would not disturb her. In the first times were all close. The last vestiges of mortality and the responsibilities of guardianship gave them common cause. Day and night had no meaning below ground, so they shared learning and lore in the timeless twilight, but then they retreated to their own research, each etching their life's work into different sections of the walls.

When Tepeu died, she held his hand and pressed it to the crystal as he passed. She found Enlil's body wrapped around the pillar a few days later.

Being alone had been harder, it was one thing to be solitary, another to know you would never touch another living being. The creatures in the reservations were prevented from entering the chamber. All that remained were the preserved souls of her two companions.

From the node chamber, she would summon creatures to perform tasks as she wished. Sometimes she did that just to see a different face.

In those last days she questioned the purpose. She recalled the words as she'd been taught.

The world lies at the centre of all things, bound together by a coincidence of magic. In all existence, there is no place like it. Over time these bonds loosen. Our work maintains them and preserves it. Without our effort, the seams break and the world shatters.

Our power is fuelled by the people who accept us. Faith, fear, love, loyalty, these are the ways we are tied to one another. Those without gift, give of what they are, these gifts empower us. Those who cannot or will not give must be contained. Only through fear can they be forced to assist our grand design.

Imprisonment and subjugation were necessary shackles. Without them, the world would fly apart. To maintain the land, magical seals were constructed deep below ground. These were empowered by all who pledged to the Earth's keeping.

The guardians were the apex of that pledge. The most feared and worshipped sent into exile to ensure the magic would hold. Each would survive into eternity as they passed into the crystal and eventually, another would come to replace them.

Now Ether sensed this other. *Have you come to rescue us?* she asked, but the other did not reply. She was strange, lore blind, but instinctive and powerful. She did not speak to any of them, but examined their memories.*Perhaps she is here to judge?* Ether hoped after all this time she would be found worthy. She stayed silent, leaving the threats and begging to Tepeu and Enlil, waiting until she was called.

But the other withdrew and hope faded.

Small red flames lit up a circle around three sleeping figures and Katya who sat awake concentrating. Eleanor had been unable to teach her the light spell, but they'd worked out a way she could help. Katya took the third shift, after Rani and now an impossible fire burned out of the rock, illuminating the group.

For others, the magic might have been strenuous to cast, but for Katya it was an effort to keep in check. Her mind raced with fantasies of the whole cavern ablaze, the red flames consuming everything in its way. Without her sister's reassuring presence she doubted her restraint and fought to stay focused, staring at the conjuring, looking for any hint it might slip from her control.

She'd woken fresh from a dream of being in the tunnels and meeting strange people. It felt real, but was jumbled somehow, a mix of perspectives overlaid with her own memories. She struggled to reconcile what she saw with what had happened and questioned both versions of events, like the nightmares she'd had as a child. Back then she'd woken from falling in physical pain, to find it was her own gift making real what she believed. Those dreams scared her even now. The thought made the flames flare. She cursed under her breath.

The sound of quiet laughter from one of the sleepers distracted her. She looked around to see Magno awake and gazing at her. "This is difficult," she warned. "I don't want to hurt you."

"Indeed," he replied and sat up. "Maybe nerves and over thinking are hindering you."

"You've seen this in others then?" she asked.

Magno shook his head. "No, truth be told I've never met anyone like you or your sister. What she sees is beyond anything I can sense. Perhaps the *sibylline* would understand her, but I doubt it."

"And me?"

"You? You're plainly full-blood gifted and more than capable of doing anything, but none of the rotes and spell frames work for you." He shrugged. "Strange in many ways, since the most powerful wizards usually become so by joining the Church or some other order and cultivating their worshippers, but you... there's nothing of that."

"I don't know what I am," Katya mumbled. She searched inwardly. Faintly she could still feel the people of her village and remembered the lessons of the elders. The flames wavered and she turned her thoughts away from those unanswerable questions. "Do you think the dragons will come for us?"

"Hard to say," Magno replied. "The slope kept them back for now, but if they're smart, they'll find a way up."

"Are they dangerous?"

"Everything's dangerous. The question is whether they'll be dangerous to us." He picked up his scabbarded sword and drew the weapon, examining the blade in the flickering red light. "Likely this place holds other strange things. We've yet to meet them, could be those encounters that end our quest."

"You think we're doomed then."

Magno smiled at her, but the expression held no humour. "Not doomed while we breathe, but a way out would settle my heart."

"We need to find my sister first," Katya said.

His expression tightened into a grimace. "Indeed, I wish for that as well, though these tunnels are vast..."

The fire flared again and Katya cursed her lack of self control. "We'll find her," she said.

Magno held up a hand. "Do not mistake me; I will do all I can for this end. If we are to escape, you and your sister are those I would see saved first. It is plain there is something to your gift that will aid us, though I know not what."

Katya sighed. "I'm being selfish, but her not being here is like losing my arm."

"Then we must seek her out," Magno said. He reached out and touched her hand. Katya gasped in surprise and snatched her hand away. The flames around them wavered. In response he looked hurt and turned away, staring into the dark and waving her quiet when she started to speak. Katya frowned, but then heard something scrape against rock. Could it be the dragons, or—

"Ho the camp!" said a familiar voice. "Do I find friends?"

Magno stood. "You do indeed Master Smogg, we wondered where you'd got to."

The little bearded explorer appeared on the edge of the firelight, his eyes glittering in the gloom. "You found your way in then," he said and smiled. "Well done."

"Where's my sister?" Katya asked.

"With Hino," Smogg replied. "We were separated, but I managed to track them. We should be able to pick them up on the way to where we're going."

"And where is that?"

"To a portal I found," Smogg said, his smiled widening into a broad grin. "And, our chance to leave."

Chapter 23: Pathway

The grey pre-dawn stole across the hilltops some miles from Sredets. The sun was still a good hour from rising and mist clung to the fields and woodland, but it was already light enough to see.

In the shadow of an oak tree, Piers sat against a log, staring at the town in the distance, watching a line of merchant carts on the north road. In front of him, the remains of a campfire glowed and smoked, the last of the wood now brittle ash. He'd stared into the dying flames asking himself the same question ever since they'd arrived.

What do I do now?

Faim lay behind an old fallen tree, his staff still clutched in his hands. His breath rattled in his chest and his painfully thin frame shivered as he slept. Piers wasn't sure what to make of him. Whilst they'd been allies against the blood drinker he'd called John, it was clear Faim had some prior relationship with the creature. Now as he stared at the sleeping Assyrian, Piers wondered what other secrets he kept. *But then I have secrets too,* he thought and sighed.

He walked from the little camp to another tree some distance away, undid his drawers and pissed in the dirt. Pursuit was unlikely now and every bone in his body ached with effort. He wanted nothing more than to close his eyes and rest, but bite marks and scratches he'd acquired needed treating; a little boiled water and a wet rag would do the trick, but had to be done before he rested. The old blood might protect him from common infections, but there was no way of knowing what curse John's brood carried.

He cleaned up and walked back to the pile of ash. Faim was awake and sat on the tree he'd been sleeping against, and now leaned on his staff. He glanced up at Piers and gave him a tired smile. "My thanks for your assistance in all we have done," he said.

"I don't understand all of what happened," Piers said. "But I'm grateful to you for ensuring my freedom."

"My purpose is to grant that for anyone of the blood," Faim said. "The boy needed to find his own path."

"Let's hope he does."

"Indeed."

Piers hesitated for a moment, but then decided to speak his mind. "I heard what you said to John. What was he?"

"A half-blood," Faim said. "A true wizard's blood with the right ritual unlocked his gift. The side effects are severe, but worth it to some."

Piers frowned. "Such magic cannot be right."

"What is right?" Faim asked. "Who is to judge? Who lies behind the doorway to heaven? You know far better than I."

Piers flinched and stared at the ashes. "No-one," he muttered.

"Indeed."

Piers scratched his chin in the thought then raised his head again. "What is your purpose in all this? You say you seek to free wizards, but John was not one of us."

Faim smiled. "I want to free anyone. When John used powers against you and the boy, he lost my favour."

"Such freedom will not sit well with the Church."

"It may, it may not. At times my methods are welcomed, but not always."

"Where will you go now?"

"Somewhere to rest and recover, then to liberate the minds of others who would remain trapped otherwise." Faim stood up, but still leaned heavily on his staff. "There is an old portal in a pagan circle near here, I will go there and return to a safer place."

"But you're not going to tell me where, are you?"

"No." Faim shuffled a few steps toward him and clasped his shoulder. "This is where we part. You need time also, so you can find your own path, but do not take too long. Change is in the air."

"I need to work out what I believe in," Piers said.

Faim nodded. "Yes, you do. It will help you find answers to your questions. You think you lack purpose, but really you stand on the threshold of many paths. You must choose which you take up."

Piers glanced at Sredets in the distance. "I'll not go back there," he said.

"Then the road is your next friend," Faim said. "May she be good to you as she has been to me."

And with that he turned and walked away.

The scraping sound of a metal bolt being drawn back made Hino glance up. The door to his small chamber opened and Sethanas stood in the arch. "It is time," he said.

Hino nodded and rose. He hadn't slept. The featureless room offered no comfort and the sullen cautious stares of his escorts suggested they would be waiting should he try to escape. He remembered the monks of Sado Island. Confinement there had included torture and interrogation, but at least he understood their motives and character. Here, the faces were alien and impossible to read.

Both his staff and family sword had been confiscated by the guards. They provided no food, so he sat in darkness and turned his mind to the forthcoming trial. How would Sethanas interpret his challenge? It was plain that these strange people feared wizards and had little stomach for letting Galina leave after she awoke magic in their cavernous kingdom.

Outside, he found a gathering of soldiers who fell into step around him as before. Sethanas led the way, his walk a rolling flow of movement. In his role as *dainagon*, Hino had witnessed the training of warrior monks and *shinobi* who sought to move with relaxed precision, but the efforts paled in comparison to the unconscious ease of Sethanas and his cohort. A swish of Sethana's cloak revealed Hino's curved *tachi* blade strapped to his belt. Hino smiled.

They walked further into the city, passing more of its strange arced buildings. Here and there, Hino spotted more warding symbols. People stepped aside as they passed, watching them with sullen stares. There were more of the horses with horns that he'd seen before and groves of dark leafed trees, all illuminated by the glowing moss that ran in veins along each building and over the cut stone of the road.

The entire place fascinated Hino. He wanted to ask a hundred questions, but knew he would get no answers as they might give him an advantage. Sethanas' escorts stared straight ahead, ignoring him completely as he walked in their midst. One of them carried his staff, but stayed some distance away, lest he should try to take it back. The pace was brisk but not taxing and the activity warmed him for what was to come.

On the outskirts of the city they ascended a set of steps leading to a promontory thirty or forty feet from the streets. Ahead lay a narrow span of stone and below a vast chasm that dropped away into the centre of the world. On the other side, was a ledge and a large cave entrance.

"We have arrived," Sethanas announced.

Following some prior instruction, three of the escorts walked across the span, taking up positions in front of the cave mouth.

"You are next," Sethanas said.

Hino nodded, guessing the intended game. A duel on the narrow stone would favour the more dextrous competitor, perhaps balancing his gift of magic. He pointed at the three soldiers ahead. "Why are they there?"

"To prevent your escape," Sethanas replied.

"You have my word I will partake in your challenge," Hino said. "Is this not enough?"

"No."

The insult was short and blunt. Hino shrugged, undid the clasp of his travelling cloak and dropped it to the stone. He bowed to Sethanas, turned and stepped onto the span.

She awoke in the node chamber.

For a moment, she was confused. The room was both incredibly familiar and new at the same time, as if she'd lived here for years, but also as if it were the first time she'd awoken in this place.

I am Galina.

She sat up as the memories and thoughts of another person settled into the back of her mind. The three souls she'd encountered remained in the crystal, but not for want of trying to break free. The two men had fought her, attempting to possess her, but they'd been there too long and become weak by being forgotten.

The woman had waited quietly and shown her memories of her mortal life. It was these recollections Galina struggled to reconcile with her own.

She stood and went to the door. It opened at her touch. Two guards loitered outside in the half-light – a man and a woman. Their expressions were cautious. She stepped forward and they glanced at each other. The man nodded and ran off, the woman stayed in front of her.

"You are to remain," she said.

"I want Hino," Galina announced and took another step. The woman backed away.

"The voice decides what is to be done."

Galina stared at her. "You cannot compel me to stay," she said. "If you hurt me, your voice will be angry."

The *aelfe* woman hesitated and didn't reply. Galina looked around. The streets and buildings were familiar to her now, as if she'd helped with their construction. She saw no-one else around, but felt drawn to a particular road. She began heading in that direction. The guard fell into step behind her. "You should stay in the hall," she said.

Galina ignored her and kept going. She sensed Hino somewhere ahead in a different part of the city. She made her way towards him, walking quickly. The memories she'd obtained from Ether meant she knew the quickest route and selected streets accordingly.

"Stop!"

She turned. Laurelatha was running down the road, flanked by a group of soldiers. She waited until they got close and let them surround her.

"Will you try to prevent me finding Hino?" she asked.

"You should return to your chamber until the matter is concluded," Laurelatha replied.

Galina shook her head. "I need Hino. You will take me to him."

"Apologies but that will not—"

"If you do not, I swear no more doors will be opened in this place." Galina clasped her hands together and lowered her tone. "I have heard your plight. I have learned more in the chamber and I believe I can help you, but you must let me speak with Hino."

Laurethala expression became pained. "I have said, it is difficult to trust your kind when so much blood has been shed."

"But you are trusting me," Galina replied. "You already chose your path. To treat me as you were treated makes a lie of your intention and means you are as bad as those who caged you."

Galina waited for a response, but Laurelatha stared at her and said nothing.

Eventually, Galina turned away and stepped up to one of the male guards she'd seen outside the node chamber. She gazed up into his strange eyes. "Out of my way," she said.

Silently, he moved aside.

"We must hurry," Smogg urged. "The portal will disappear soon!"

They ran through moss-lit tunnels, along a cliff and down further toward the centre of the world. Katya followed Ibrox, with Magno a reassuring presence behind her. Her cloak caught her ankle and she stumbled, but righted herself on the edge of a long drop, watching stones and dust disappear into the void below.

"Quickly!"

She ran on, focusing on Ibrox ahead. Time had no meaning here. Tunnel, passage, intersection, lake, pathway; each time they descended, taking them further away from the way they'd come. Only Smogg's memory of the route could bring them out now. She turned a corner and almost ran into Ibrox who'd stopped and crouched behind a rock. He pulled her down next to him and raised a finger to his lips. She nodded.

"Three guards," he whispered. "Eleanor and Smogg are concealed ahead."

Katya peeked out from their hiding place and noticed the silhouette of a man facing away from them in the entrance at the other end. The dream of before came back to her, the two were connected. "Who are they?" she asked.

"An intriguing question," Ibrox said. "Perhaps we will learn the answer."

"Where is the portal?"

"Over there."

Flickering shadows betrayed the presence of something on the far left of the cave. It looked like the light playing off water. To get to it, they would have to climb over rocks and gravel, alerting the watchers.

"What do we do?" she asked.

"We wait," Ibrox said.

Hino reached the centre of the stone span, stopped and turned around.

Sethanas stood on the promontory with his soldiers around him. He made no move towards the thin bridge.

Hino frowned. He peered down. The sides of the chasm converged in the distance below. He wondered how far he would fall if he slipped? Probably long enough to consider the impact awaiting him at the end. *If there is a bottom,* he thought.

A keening scream echoed out from the depths. There was movement, huge wings riding an updraft towards him. Instinctively he named what he saw.

Nihon no ryū.

Dragons. The oldest stories he remembered being told as a child. The great *Ryūjin,* father of the first Emperor Jimmu and *Yamata no Orochi* the eight-headed serpent. The creature he saw was neither of these, nor a *Nāga* of the Buddhists, but he recognised it for being kin of those ancient legends.

A shout went up from Sethanas' followers. The captain ventured onto the span, making his way to the centre. When he was three steps from Hino he stopped. "A straight contest between a wizard and a mortal would never be fair," he said.

Hino frowned. "You leave a matter like this to chance?"

Sethanas shrugged. "Chance and skill. I know my worth. Honour is satisfied. The survivor will be the victor."

The dragon screamed again, landing on the far side rock face, it began to climb up, using its claws to gouge out grip. Then it leapt into the air once more, beat its wings once, twice, and returned to stone, climbing again. *It doesn't have enough room to fly freely*, Hino realised. *Such a creature was never made to live underground.*

The scrape of metal on leather alerted him. He ducked under Sethanas' sword swing, barely keeping his balance on the thin bridge. "We are still to fight then?"

Sethanas nodded. "I gain nothing if I do not defeat you."

Hino backed away a few steps and turned around. The three guards remained alert. One held a bow with an arrow notched on the string. They would interfere if he gave them reason. He glanced back at Sethanas. "Where is the girl?" he demanded.

"Safe for now. The voice is with her."

"How will you deliver her?" Hino asked.

Sethanas shrugged and stepped forwards. "If you win, she will be yours to claim and I will be dead, so she will mean nothing to me."

The *tachi* flashed out again, a straight thrust, forcing Hino back or sideways. He chose the latter and lost his footing, a leg left dangling in the void for a moment before he regained his balance. "Your possession of my sword makes this contest uneven," he remarked.

Sethanas smiled. "The ancients tell us a wizard is never without a weapon."

Hino retreated another two steps and muttered the words he'd been taught. Immediately the air tightened and the stretch between him and Sethanas discoloured. A dark ooze dripped from the stone, spreading rapidly all around it, reaching towards them both. "Let the girl go free and this ends," Hino urged.

Sethanas' smile was gone. He knelt in front of the slime, touching it carefully with the tip of his sword. The weapon stuck and he could not remove it. He cursed and drew a knife, flinging it at Hino who ducked and heard it clatter against the cliff.

"I will not yield!" Sethanas snarled, gathered himself and leapt, over the dripping slime and straight at Hino.

He could not dodge. Sethanas' weight bore him backwards. Pain lanced through him as his knee twisted and he fell back. He flailed, grabbing for something and managed to hook his arm around the stone as his legs slid away, leaving him hanging.

Sethanas knelt on the bridge, breathing hard. He stood up and pulled out another knife. "You have a choice," he said. "Die by the blade or the fall."

Hino closed his eyes and chose.

Creepers sprouted from the underside of the span, grabbing his arms and legs. He relaxed into their embrace, flowing and moving with them until he could grab the rock again, the other side of the slime. He let go of the spell, the plant shrivelled and he clambered up, to stand in front of the trapped *tachi*. He grasped the hilt as the ooze retreated. The weapon was his once more.

Sethanas scowled and turned to the guards on the far side. One threw him a straight blade. He caught it with an easy flowing motion and faced Hino, his eyes glittered with cold intent.

Hino remembered the first day he'd been allowed to hold the family sword, the sense of pride he'd felt had been palpable. When the *tachi* had been placed in his hands, he'd hardly dared breathe. They'd let him keep the weapon all night, whilst his father and grandfather had told him the tale of its making and the legend of its use. Theirs was a young family, not steeped in the old ways like the Minamoto or the Fujiwara, but a code of quiet wisdom and loyalty bound each generation to the Emperor's service as they took pains to preserve their heritage and the gift of magic.

In later years they'd trained him with wooden weapons, then blunt sword and lesser blades, all to make him worthy of the artefact. The day he'd fled Japan he'd remembered his son, left alone without the weapon or the knowledge of his father's fate. It was a dishonour he still wished to rectify.

But while he lived, the *tachi* remained his.

Sethanas lunged forwards, handling his sword with polished ease. Hino stepped back and checked himself from sidestepping into nothing. He held his curved blade above his head, timing his opponent's moves and waiting for his chance.

A second lunge and an over extension. The *tachi* came down like a hammer on the thicker blade, its razor edge notching the straight steel. Sethanas retreated, swung again. Hino parried to his right and let the magic flow. The sword responded like an old friend and began to shine with power. He stepped towards Sethanas, slapped away his notched weapon and aimed a cut at the strange man's throat, stopping inches from his flesh.

"It is over," Hino said.

There was a scream from the far end of the cave. He glanced around.

A huge clawed hand grabbed the first of the guards, dragging him from the ledge and into oblivion. Katya's heart lurched as she saw the beast that it belonged to emerge, plainly an elder to the dragons they'd seen in the cavern. This one fully grown and deadly.

The two figures sprang to the attack, a fight for survival as they scampered away from the creature. As one retreated towards them, Magno stepped out and smoothly stabbed him through the chest from behind. He gestured to Ibrox, who also stood and ran forward. Katya followed.

Smogg appeared and pushed her to the left, "The portal!" he urged.

She shook her head. "Not without my sister!"

He scowled and turned away. Lady Eleanor moved passed them both to Magno's side, Ibrox was already there. Katya joined them to see what was going on.

The dragon was too big to fit into the cave or to stand on the ledge. It scrabbled awkwardly against the cliff face, trying to maintain its position whilst the last guard loosed arrow after arrow at it. Six fletchings lay buried in its side.

Beyond the fighting, there was a narrow stone bridge. On the bridge, Hino stood with a glowing sword in his hands, facing another soldier whose own weapon tumbled into the chasm below.

On seeing Hino, Katya couldn't help but run forwards, oblivious to the danger. The dragon's head snapped around and its eyes met hers.

She saw anger and fear in those eyes, the beast knew what it faced and could sense its young in the chambers beyond. It wanted them, as any mother would. Katya and the others were in the way, the rock face was in the way. The dragon would tear them all down to reach her kin.

Another arrow caught the creature along the jaw and it turned away. Ibrox knelt over the dead soldier and shouted strange words. The corpse stiffened and unnatural light sprang from its eyes. It stood up, its movements jerky and awkward then made for the dragon, charging straight at it. The impact dislodged it from the ledge and sent the soldier tumbling into the abyss below.

For a moment, the dragon too seemed like it would fall, but then its wings came to its rescue, it caught an updraft and righted itself, screaming at Katya and her companions as they charged forwards.

"Hino!"

The shout came from across the bridge. Katya recognised the voice and her heart missed another beat.

"Galina!"

She reached the promontory in time to witness the dragon regain its balance in mid-air and watch the soldier drop to his doom.

"Please! Do not go to them!" Laurelatha begged. "You abandon us to oblivion!"

Galina ignored her and shouldered her way through the ring of *aelfe* soldiers. None of them made a move to stop her. She stepped to the edge and out onto the span. "Hino, release him," she called.

The Japanese *dainagon* turned towards her. "Honour must be satisfied," he said.

"It is," Galina replied. "You won. I have the right to choose."

Hino bowed and lowered his sword, allowing Sethanas to get to his feet. He eyed the dragon hovering above them. It stared down, drew back, inhaled, and spewed fire, immolating the *aelfe* who screamed as he burned to ash.

Hino ran towards Galina, reached the promontory and grabbed her wrist. "We must hasten!"

"I'm not coming with you," Galina said.

His face tightened, the schooled expression of his upbringing cracked into shock and surprise. "But..."

"You gave me the chance to choose," Galina said. "I have. I know what my gift is for now. I need to stay with these people."

Hino let go and glanced back at the dragon. "Will you doom me as well?" he asked.

"No," Galina said. "You can still make it." She snatched his staff from the *aelfe* beside her and handed it to him. Hino took it and nodded. He sheathed his sword, turned and made his way back onto the span.

Katya saw Hino turn and run towards them. "They won't make it!" she cried.

"They will," Eleanor said and signalled to Magno who ran forwards. Ibrox and Smogg followed him to the ledge. Ibrox pointed his staff at the creature and released a ball of energy from its tip that streaked upwards. The dragon twisted and dropped, dodging the magic, but also losing altitude, giving Hino precious time.

But Galina wasn't moving.

Katya screamed, but her sister remained where she was. None of the people around her moved or stood in the way, but she still didn't move.

Then Hino slipped.

Magno had reached the middle, past the scorched rock where the soldier had burned. He leapt forward and caught Hino's hand as he fell, dragging him back onto the bridge with impossible strength.

The dragon screamed and soared upwards, shattering the span as it powered into the air above them. Magno shouted as he jumped from the stone, flinging himself at the wall. Somehow he twisted in mid-air. Got his hands and feet in the right position and grabbed the rock as he smashed into it. He cried out in pain, but held on.

Katya looked for Hino, but couldn't find him. "Where is..."

"He's gone," Smogg said.

"As must we be," Eleanor announced. "There is nothing more for us here."

"But my sister—"

"I will not lose anyone else."

"I can't leave her!" Katya cried. She moved for the shattered bridge, but Ibrox grabbed her arm just as the dragon lunged at them all. Claws snapped at where she would have been and fire followed, scorching the ledge.

"Move!" shouted Ibrox, pushing her back into the cave. She fought him, but he was too strong and wrestled her towards the portal. As she passed through, she caught sight of Magno behind them all, covered in his own blood.

Five skandas have formed this transient shape
Whose four elements return now to true being;
I hold my neck against the naked blade—
The cutting is like a gust of wind.

Chapter 24: Plight

"I couldn't save him. I had to let go."

The story told, Magno fell silent.

Katya stared at the wooden table in front of her. The empty chairs stared back like scars; Hino, Smogg and Galina. None of them had returned. She remembered the burning house and the huddled woman. She'd withdrawn into herself that time, become senseless to the outside, perceiving the world as if through a fog or dark tunnel. She felt dislocated again, like she were watching herself and powerless to do anything but the most basic things.

A tapping sound brought her back and made her raise her head. Lady Eleanor's fingers drummed against the table. She glared at each of them, but didn't speak. It wasn't her place to. She looked at Cardinal Giovanni Colonna last, waiting for his response.

"There is much in this tale that is hard to accept," Colonna said at last. "If what you found is a city beneath the island protected by seals of magic, how many places may exist elsewhere?"

"Everything we have told you is the truth," Katya said.

Colonna nodded. "I understand child, but you must let an old man absorb these revelations, give him time to ponder for meaning." He glanced at Rani. "Could such a history be hidden from us?"

"We need to go back, find my sister and save her," Katya said.

"If she wishes to be saved?" Colonna's smile was full of sympathy, making her seethe. "As you say, Hino went back for her, but she did not accompany him."

"She wouldn't abandon me."

"Indeed, I think much of our hope rests upon this conclusion."

They all fell silent for a time. Katya's eyes went back to the wooden table. Galina would sense something in its texture, its whorls and grooves, but to her it was just wood, cut, scrubbed, painted and polished. In her mind she saw it ablaze, her friends leaping for the windows as the fire spread after them, higher and higher reaching out, reaching—

"You cannot go back," Colonna announced. "The portal is closed to us. The way you came here was lost soon after you arrived and the route to the island no longer works. A ship might be commissioned, but the journey would take weeks and even then—"

"I'm not leaving her." Katya felt the wood give a little under her fingers as they dug into it. "Find a ship."

Colonna glanced at Eleanor who met his gaze, nodded once and rose from her seat. "I must attend to something," she said. "I will return shortly."

After she had gone. Collona spoke again. "We will not go back now. I think our business is concluded for the night, you should all get some rest."

"I won't rest," Katya growled. "I can't I'm—"

"You will rest," the Cardinal's tone was quiet but firm and helped her remember herself. "We are your friends. We *will* aid you."

"I'm sorry I just—"

"I understand."

One by one they left the table, leaving for their prepared rooms. Katya didn't move, but rode the whirl of emotion, seeking calm. When only Rani remained, she raised her head again. "How do you control it?" she asked.

Rani smiled. "Age helps. Experience tempers what you are, although I cannot claim to have had your power when I was young."

"I want to burn everything to find her."

"I lost everything. My husband sacrificed himself for me. I too wanted to burn the world, but settled for burning my own physical form. As it was consumed, so I was set free."

"Are you suggesting I do the same?"

Rani shook her head. "Your time has not yet come. Your sister still lives."

The woodlands around the Iwashimizu Hachiman-gū temple were thick and lush with few trodden paths. The man who was once called Hino Kunimitsu avoided these anyway and set about his work by living alone in the deepest brush and avoiding prying eyes.

It had been days since he'd visited Iga and faced the nine trials of the *Oni*. To a mortal, one such pact would be more than a soul could bear, but a gifted wizard might endure more and the demons were intoxicated by the opportunity They had come to him each hour, bonding with his magic and granting him the shadow lore of their kind.

But each demanded a different price.

206

Overnight, his hair became silver and scars decorated his face. He gave up the little finger of his left hand, the little toe of his right foot as well. He'd given blood, bile, seed and saliva, but all of these paled to the last sacrifice.

You must give up your name.

He was Kumawaka now, the name given to him first as a child, the price for his abilities, to become the creature spoken of in stories. The demon bargains would hold until he could restore the honour of his house. *When I find the family sword.* He knew it would never happen.

He could not return to his life. Counsellors, nobles and attendants of Emperor Go-Murakami's court would worry at his absence, his family would worry more.

But I cannot go back.

Kumawaka came to the woodland near the temple in the dead of night and began his work. He cast the *Oni* seed into the dirt, cut his wrist and whispered words over it. A tree ripped its way out of the ground in moments, its leaves a strange tint of blue. He stepped forward and its trunk opened. He could stand inside without effort and the strange tree shared its strength with him.

All through the day he remained there, watching and waiting. Servants from the temple came and went. If they noticed the new tree, they gave no sign. Inside, he carried out his preparations, changing clothes and mixing liquids as he'd been taught. He became a part of the tree, feeling how it drew from the earth, the sun and the rain, using the natural alchemical processes of its own body to sustain itself. If other matters had not been pressing he might have stayed there for weeks, learning all he could.

It grew dark and he emerged, dressed now in shadow grey, the same colour the old man from Iga had worn. The shoes and gloves were soft and supple; the shirt and breeches, light and close-fitting. Over them he wore belts, pouches and a carry sack. An assortment of knives adorned two cross bandoliers, his wrists and the side of his boots. Across his back was a short black stave, a wizard tool he'd traded for his ornate staff. His other weapons were concealed.

Kumawaka moved through the woodland slowly at first and then with increasing speed as he became confident in how quiet he could be. When he reached the walls of the temple complex, he dropped to a crouch and waited.

Gradually, the sounds from within came to him.

The *ashigaru* soldier taking a piss over the battlement twenty yards away, the horses whimpering to one another in the stable on the other side of the wall and the low murmur of conversation around a warming fire in the courtyard.

Kumawaka touched the wall with his fingertips. The rough planks held an echo of their former life as a tree. He called to this memory with the magic and his acquired knowledge of forests, pushing his fingers into its mass. The sensation was strange, as his body became intangible and occupied the same space as the wood.

Two gifts used...

Moments later he was through and on the other side. He could see figures loitering around three wagons across the courtyard, clustered around a small fire. He recognised the red sashes and flags of the Ashikaga shogunate. The attendance of Takauji's soldiers and travelling entourage confirmed the presence of their master in the temple.

Nearby, he saw an open cart, its haul covered by dark canvas. Strangely, a horse remained yoked to the front. It raised its head, eyes gleaming in the dark as it stared straight at him. For a moment, he held his breath, but the beast made no sound and looked away.

Kumwaka kept low, moving along the wall in the shadow of the battlement. He'd been here before, as an eight year old child accompanying his father on a visit to Osaka. The private shrines were in the main building. On normal days, the temple priests and servants would retire at sundown, gathering only for the evening prayer. But the shogun's presence meant a change to protocol. The entrance was guarded by two samurai and more would be at each door.

To attempt entry by such a route would invite discovery.

Kumawaka pulled his cowl over his face and tucked his hands into his sleeves then whispered the words the fourth *Oni* had taught him. He moved out of the shadows and crossed the courtyard, heading straight for the guarded doors, repeating the same words over and over. When he neared them, the whisper became barely audible.

"You hear something?"

"No."

Kumawaka slipped through the open door and kept walking. He continued whispering the words, passing two other guards, until he reached an intersection. He turned to the left and found himself by a staircase. He crouched beneath it and let the chant end.

He was tired, as if he'd been running for a mile or more. It took several minutes to calm his breathing and steady his thumping heart.

He moved from the staircase back into the passageway. Time was of the essence now, so he walked quickly, almost at a run, reaching another door and slipping through into a wide lantern-lit hall.

I remember this place.

Twenty-five years ago he had been brought into this room and told to sit on a bench while his father went to an adjoining chamber. Now he found himself in here alone again for very different reasons.

Which one will he be in?

Kumawaka reached into a pouch and pulled forth a pinch of dust. He threw it into the air and watched where it went – towards a closed door on his left. *That one.*

He turned and walked in the direction the dust indicated.

"I can't let you do that."

Kumawaka froze. *I've failed,* he thought. The voice was a man's, the words, roughly spoken in English, a language he'd learned at his father's insistence. He turned around and found himself staring at the old shrunken face of a white man. He wore a hooded cloak and carried a long staff with a thin curved blade on one end – a scythe – the tool a farmer used for threshing crops.

"Who are you?" he asked.

"My name is Obidyah and you'll not be disturbing the lord, my friend," the man said.

A twitch of Kumawaka's wrist brought a knife into his hand and in one fluid motion it spun across the room towards Obidyah to lodge in his shoulder. He gasped and staggered. Kumawaka charged forwards, another knife flashed through the air and another after that, catching ribs and thigh. A fourth blade in Kumawaka's hand punched into Obidyah's chest, right where the heart should be. The man coughed, stumbled and fell backwards. His scythe clattering to the floor. Kumawaka was already turning away, towards Takauji's prayer shrine.

A second, identical Obidyah figure stood in front of the door, scythe in hand and a wide rictus grin on his face. "We are alike you and I," he said. "Both gifted, both finding power in the stories others tell of us. To those whispering in the dark, I am the harvester of souls, who steals the breath of the strong and the weak alike. I come for them as they sleep, work and pray. Young or old, I do not discriminate. To them, I am the last light and face before oblivion. In that moment, I feast and they die."

Kumawaka glanced over his shoulder. The body was gone and his knives lay discarded on the floor. "If death is what you want, why do you protect Lord Ashikaga?" he asked.

Obidyah stepped forwards, gripping his weapon with both hands, the blade of the staff gleaming in the lantern light. "Because, like you, I swore oaths for my power," he said. "The shogun will not be harmed, but you... you are another matter."

The scythe blade flashed as it moved in a horizontal arc. Kumawaka leapt backwards to avoid it, but Obidyah kept coming towards him, reversing the weapon impossibly fast and swinging it again and again. Kumawaka wondered why no soldiers or priests came to investigate the noise, but learned the answer when he reached the far wall and tried a door handle.

Locked.

"You are mine," Obidyah said. "There is no escape!"

Kumawaka ducked under another swing. He could sense the magic of the blade and the man. Obidyah emanated power, more tangible than anything he'd felt in the years being schooled by his father and other gifted tutors. "What are you?" he gasped.

"The product of myth, belief and story made flesh," Obydiah said. "What you might have been, if you'd lived."

The sixth talisman of the *Oni* was in Kumawaka's hand. He cast it upon the floor and there was a flash of light and fire and Obydiah stepped back. Kumawaka spoke the word he'd been taught and everything swirled away into a dark empty void.

The last of the rocks fell away into darkness.

On his knees, Tuia peered into the void below the pyramid. No amount of torchlight would illuminate the space, any they sent into the gloom disappeared with no sound of reaching bottom.

He couldn't see the monster from before, but he knew it was waiting and appraising his efforts. The warriors who he'd pressed into service murmured to each other *Quetzalcoatl* – the feathered dragon god. As the hours of labour wore on, more and more of them disappeared, no doubt believing themselves cursed or worse.

Tuia knew different. If the creature was a god, he would be setting it free, if not, his mistress would covet its power.

Something stirred in the dark, a lambent red glow seething up from below. Tuia stood and backed away from the hole. The remaining people with him needed no prompting to do the same. One man screamed and ran from the blood stained chamber. Part of Tuia wanted to follow him, but another part yearned for the sight of what he had liberated in all its glory.

A noise of surging wind came from the depths then a huge claw reached out and clutched at the crumbling flagstones where Tuia had been crouched moments before. A scaly head emerged, bigger than the rafts loaded with stone and red eyes speared him to the wall. He gripped the knife in his hands and tried to hold that gaze, to muster his magic, but this mind would not be mastered by him. He sensed the fury and relief of a prisoner kept in slumber and chains, far from dreams of open sky and mountain tops. Countless time spent in numb darkness, now at last, free.

The head rose into the chamber, its mouth opened, sucking in air then gaped and exhaled. Flames immolated the walls, splashing downwards.

Tuia ran, the heat scorching the hair from his arms and scouring his skin. People cried and fled in front of him. He reached the entrance and the cool night outside the temple, slowed and looked back.

Fire soared into the black sky. Stones cracked and tumbled from the highest tiers of the pyramid, crushing those unfortunate enough to be beneath. A fragment struck Tuia on the shoulder, numbing his arm and knocking him flat. There he remained, to witness the redemption of his subterranean prisoner.

A massive hole appeared in the side of the building. Powerful scaled claws grasped the fractured walls and the creature emerged, its keen of triumph drowning out the panic of the fleeing crowds. Its wings unfurled to their full extent and it leaped into the air, climbing toward the stars, until it disappeared amongst them.

All the while, Tuia lay on the ground, watching in awe.

AD 1345

Night time along the river outside Auberoche. The land seethed and undulated. Hundreds of men marching through the shallow water; the English army under the command of the Earl of Derby had come to relieve the besieged town.

Piers Gaveston marched with them, his unkempt appearance, rusted armour and sword concealed in the darkness. He kept his head down and matched their pace. His boots were wet through, but it felt good to be in a familiar place, amidst Plantagenet and Gascon soldiers on their way to fight the French.

They began moving uphill. Ahead, Piers could see rank upon rank of men struggling up the incline in the twilight, carrying packs and polearms. It wasn't hard to stay hidden. There were no torches and few conversations. Occasionally, the people around him whispered to each other, avoiding the angry glare of their sergeant.

About halfway up the slope, the men ahead of him stopped. Word got around and gradually people unslung their packs and sprawled in the dewy grass. Piers sat with them, but kept his eyes on the ground and his thoughts to himself.

Fifteen hundred men mustered to fight a French army of several thousand; a simmering war that had been building for years, ever since the time before his exile and execution in England. It had been decades since he was a part of the military councils and royal courts, but Piers still remembered the arrogance and the fervour of eager nobles keen to gain the favour of kings. *They will be talking together now,* he thought. *Planning their surprise attack and claiming God is on their side.* He could hear people around him murmuring their own prayers and smiled bitterly to himself. *Your angels fight amongst you and bicker over who has rights to this land.* He remembered the stories in the *Summa Magiolaie,* how the first wizard kings had commanded vast armies and brought ruin to the world. He thought they were fairy tales when he first read them, but now…

"Ain't seen you before." An old man was speaking to him. Broken teeth shaped the words with a thick Cornish accent. He was thin, with a loose fitting helm, filthy tabard and pack that looked larger than him. "When'd you join up?"

"Gascony," Piers replied.

"Then you'll be thankin' us, returning your lands to the rightful king."

"Farmers sow the same crops, no matter the colour of the pennant," Piers said.

"Sounds like you ain't too keen to fight," the old man said and turned away.

It began to rain, big heavy droplets pattering on armour, drawing groans from those around Piers. This wouldn't be the usual battle of archers against cavalry. If reinforcements didn't arrive, it would be a surprise attack in the darkness, a chaotic massacre where friend and foe would blur together in a struggle to survive.

Piers glanced at the old man again, and felt the sense of belonging evaporate. *You're right. What am I doing here?*

He stared out into the mist. Shadows and shapes looked like soldiers in the half-light. He remembered battlefields in Ireland and England and their bloody aftermath. Always, lives lost and little change to show for it. He was a man out of time, this war, no longer his business or part of his life.

He waited another hour, until exhausted soldiers began to fall asleep where they lay. Then he got up, murmuring the words he'd been taught. Wisps of magic that would help him disappear from their minds, to help him fade away, back into his life of aimlessness and nothing.

Except it wasn't nothing anymore; seeing purpose in others, sharing it if only for a moment, helped. Piers remembered that awful void he'd seen inside the arch made by the Templars. *In their arrogant search, they found no God and were cursed for building Migdal Bavel.*

For forty years and more he'd believed the absence of God on that day meant no god existed. He'd seen the Church as a self-serving parasite, milking the faith of mortals to serve the gifted in their quest for power, but the crude loyalty expressed by the old man was touching. He missed the sense of comradeship he'd felt for a while amongst those ramshackle soldiers, united by words and a cause. There was a power to being a part of that; a different kind of power from that expressed by people who set themselves apart.

After a time, he stopped walking and found a small copse where he hunkered down to rest. The hard tack biscuit he'd been given the previous morning was unappetising fare, but took his mind from the chill.

The night hours waned and the sun rose. Piers gathered up sticks and used slivers of magic to light a fire. He ventured a little way and discovered a brook and filled his helm, returning to boil water with herbs.

He saw Auberoche in the distance, a stone tower of the castle peaking over hilltops. Outside it, the dark stain of the French camp oozed smoke into the morning air.

Piers stared at both for a long while. He had no reason to remain, but he had nowhere else to go either, so he waited a while to ponder the devotion of mortals with their short lives. What did a day matter to a man who was dead inside?

He sat down and turned away from the sight, but remained for the inevitable. The first shouts and screams started at mid-afternoon. After that the distant sound of horses and the clash of steel confirmed the fate of his companions.

It grew dark and he lay down to sleep, but the noise continued. He couldn't see what happened, but his imagination painted a gruesome enough picture.

The morning after was quiet. He rose and walked towards Auberoche, diverting toward the rubbish and refuse of battle. He strode amongst the corpses and scavengers with his head low, ignoring stares, threats or hails. Eventually, he found what he sought – the old man, lying face down in a pool of his own blood and shit. That uneven mouth would speak no more Cornish words.

Piers dragged him from the carnage to an undisturbed field. With helm, sword and hands he dug a shallow grave, his heart warming to the honest labour. When he judged it deep enough, he placed the old man within and buried him. Above the head he affixed a spear and a broken sword, bound with twine in the shape of a cross. Then he knelt and stared at his work.

A hand touched his shoulder. "Friend of yours?" said a man's voice.

Piers didn't look around, but shook his head. "I hardly knew him," he said.

"Then why—"

"Because the dead deserve a memorial for what they did, whether it was right or wrong. He gave his life as did all of them. As do all those who die in battle for causes they barely understand. They are slaves to kings, queens, princes and priests, told lies to serve those who think they know better. I cannot do them all. The unknown man is for all of them who'll never be found and never be known."

The hand disappeared. The stranger grunted and moved away, leaving Piers alone.

After a while, he got up again and started walking.

AD 1348

The noise from the kitchens awoke Gurda. It took a moment or two for her to identify where she was, but then she remembered.

The underground kitchens of the Palais des Papes.

She sat up. Gradually the details came back. The wine cellar of Clement VI newly constructed residence – the *palais neuf* – an extension to the older buildings of Benedict XII which were built on the Rock of Doms. The new chambers were complete and every care had been taken to blend the architecture with the old, but the differences were noticeable, particularly where artisans could not contain their exuberance.

The shadowy alcove she huddled in, surrounded by barrels and bottles held very little of that exuberance, built for function rather than form, it would not be toured or seen by the persons whose wines and ales it stored.

Which suited Gurda perfectly.

She stood up slowly, brushing the dust from her thin cassock and giving her legs a chance to rediscover their strength. Her walking stick lay propped against the wall. The feel of it in her hand reassured and restored her.

She peered out from her hiding place. Candlelight revealed three figures dragging out a selection of caskets, their throaty French conversation indecipherable to her at first, but gradually as her strength and magic returned, so too did her understanding.

"...there is no point in arguin', vittles for forty-three, we were told."

"Aye, no arguin'."

"Then bend your back and still your tongue."

Gurda slipped around the wooden shelves, staying to the shadows, out of sight of the three men. A whispered word brought forth the magic and kept her hidden as she slipped from the room into the tunnel beyond. At the far end was a closed door. She opened it.

Into the main kitchen.

"Who're you?"

Gurda opened her mouth to reply, but a wave of heat stole the words from her lips. A red-faced woman glared at her as more folk bustled around tables, stone sides and several stoked ovens. One or two stopped to stare.

Gurda coughed and acclimatised. "Sent from Gascony with the Cardinal," she said.

"An' you're here to help no doubt?" the woman scowled. She was old, bent almost double as she leaned over a stone table. "We've plenty of special folks from all the red guests; one more'll make no difference. I suppose you're to taste the soup an' check my work for belladonna and hemlock?"

"No, just asked to help."

The woman's scowl became a frown. "In that case, what are you good for?"

"Washer work mostly," Gurda said and held out her calloused hands.

"Strange to send someone extra for that," the woman said. She pointed to the far end of the kitchen where Gurda could see a small knot of people attacking the fresh baked loaves. "Help them," the woman said. "Work fast and steal nothing, else you'll feel my wrath, cardinal's bitch or not."

Gurda nodded and hurried quickly toward the group, taking her place at the far end. She'd planned to be awake earlier, before the breakfast service began, but somehow she'd overslept – the frailties of her continued mortality. She picked up a round loaf of bread and a knife and cut two pieces from it. When the woman looked away, Gurda whispered another phrase, pocked the bread slices and slipped away from the table, through another door at the far end. No-one saw her leave. The magic took care of that.

A thin winding stairwell took her up to another floor and past a thin stain-glassed window. The fragmented light of the early morning sun illuminated the turn of the steps and the figure coming down the other way. Gurda bowed her head and let the manservant pass without catching his eye, then carried on.

Alone on the next landing, Gurda paused to catch her breath, leaning heavily on her stick. She drew back her sleeve and unwound the stained bandage from her wrist. Weeping sores and scabs began to itch in the open air. She pinched one and let the pus ooze onto her fingers then walked on down the corridor and to the next staircase.

Three floors above, she found the bedchamber she was looking for. A soldier stood outside the door. As he turned towards her she spoke a word and made a hooking gesture with her walking stick. His eyes lost focus and he fell senseless to the ground. Gurda winced at the noise. The blatant use of magic might have drawn attention to those sensitive to it somewhere else, but in Avignon, close to the contained rift, such perceptions were truncated. She could feel the distortions of the tear affecting her own gift, calling to her from its prison deep below the oldest part of the palace. She'd made some attempt to investigate it the previous night, but the number of wizard guards discouraged any thought of gaining access to the warded room in which it was contained.

Matters at hand.

She stepped over the soldier and opened the door.

The room remained dark, the drapes drawn and the air dusty. A figure lay sleeping in the large bed, grey hair spread across the pillow. A quill, ink and parchment discarded at a writing desk.

Gurda approached the bed and the small table beside it. From within her robe she drew out two hunks of bread she'd taken from the pile in the kitchen and placed them next to an empty wine goblet. She wiped the pus from her fingers across them both and whispered more words of magic. The sweat from her hands would help it spread and take root.

The sleeping man stirred, mumbled something in his sleep and turned over. Gurda shrank back and held her breath, but he made no further sign. She could see his old face in the half-light – a proud Roman nose softened by Italianate cheekbones and worry lines. It wasn't someone she had known, but it was the face of an enemy.

Cardinal Giovanni Colonna.

She moved quietly to the door, opened it and hurried away.

A fiery pre-dawn greeted Piers Gaveston as he walked the last half mile to Fontevraud.

He watched the sun as it climbed into the Loire valley, painting the fields in rich hues of orange and red. The old legend came to mind – *and in the morning, it will be foul weather, for the sky is red and louring.*

What warning do you bring? Piers thought. *How can my fate become worse?*

He made his way through quiet streets and buildings towards the abbey. After leaving Faim, he'd elected to try to find the only other gifted person he knew who wouldn't kill or capture him on site.

Eleanor of Aquitaine.

He walked around the low walls until he was sure no-one was watching then climbed over, jumping down onto tilled earth and rows of sowed crop. A side door stood ajar and he hastened towards it. A hunched woman appeared in front of him, carrying a basket and mumbling; he elbowed her aside and went in, moving quickly along a narrow passage, his magically attuned senses seeking out anything that might lead to his quarry – a portal, a doorway, anything that would—

"Gaveston."

He recognised the voice immediately and turned back. The woman he'd passed raised her head, drew back her hood and stood up straight.

"How did you know it was me?" Piers asked.

"I always know where you are, I came here as soon as I sensed you," Eleanor replied. "What do you want?"

"To find you, I assumed since this was the place you lived in your last days..."

"A place I return to occasionally when needed," Eleanor crossed the distance between them and laid a hand on his shoulder. "They told me you died."

"The same was said of you."

Eleanor smiled sadly and stared at him. "Did you let it all pass though, like I never could?"

"I was executed on the road. No choice."

"And you held our secret, all this time?"

"I did, I still do."

"So why are you here?"

"I have... nothing else."

She sighed then. "I followed your path from afar. Truly, that night in Avignon blighted your soul. It made you doubt all things, just as it would anyone. Only you and I remain who saw through that door into the nothing beyond."

"I can't live with it." Piers sank to his knees. "I can't carry the burden any longer, knowing what we are, that all faith and all is a lie... I can't..." The words wouldn't come out. Instead he buried his face in her habit and let the grief have its way, his body convulsing with each utterance.

Eleanor held him there, her hand moving to the back of his head, gently stroking his filthy matted hair. "Not all hope is lost," she said softly.

Timeline of Significance

1348: Cardinal Giovanni Colonna dies in Avignon. The Black Death reaches France, Denmark, Norway and England, striking at populations weakened by nearly two generations of malnutrition. Around one-third of the people in affected areas are to die.

1349: Plague reaches the city of Basel. The Jewish communities are cast out.

1350: Belief in witchcraft is revitalised. Convinced that the end of the world is at hand, some engage in frenzied bacchanals and orgies. Those called flagellants believe that the plague is the judgment of God on sinful mankind. Walking across the countryside, men and women flog one another. They preach that anyone doing this for thirty-three days will be cleansed of all sin – one day for every year that Christ lived. The Church is on guard against creative, heretical theology and Pope Clement VI condemns the movement. In Tenochtitlan the Aztecs build causeways with canals.

1351: The towns of Florence and Milan go to war as Milan tries to extend its power south-east into Tuscany. Plague reaches Russia.

1352: Rebellion by Chinese against Mongol rule erupts near the city of Guangzhou.

1355: The Scots ally with the French and declare war on the English.

To be continued in _The War of Orders_. Book 2 of the Death of Gods Trilogy.

ABOUT THE AUTHOR

Allen Stroud is a University Lecturer at Buckinghamshire New University in High Wycombe, England. He runs the BA (Hons) Creative Writing for Publication course. He is also the editor of the British Fantasy Society Journal (http://www.britishfantasysociety.co.uk). His website is here – http://www.allenstroud.com/

Other Works By Allen Stroud:

A Bag of Bedtime Tales
ToryTimes: A Collection of Tragic Poems
The Sword of Wisimir
The Dragon of Wisimir
The Lord of Wisimir
The Magic of Wisimir (Forthcoming in 2016)
Elite: Lave Revolution
Chaos Reborn: The Loremaster's Guide

Allen also contributed the short story *The Last Tank Commander* to Newcon Press' *Crisis and Conflicts* 10th anniversary science fiction anthology.

You can find more information about the world of Chaos Reborn, here – http://www.chaos-reborn.com

www.ingramcontent.com/pod-product-compliance
Lightning Source LLC
Chambersburg PA
CBHW070818120626
46556CB00002B/567